I0588394

Kozy Krampus

COSMIC HORROR HOLIDAY STORIES

EDITED BY
FRANCES LU-PAI IPPOLITO & MARK TEPPO

Underland Press

Underland Press
www.underlandpress.com

Kozy Krampus

TABLE OF CONTENTS

THIS ONE IS FOR TRUE BELIEVERS

'Tis the Season

~ *Sara Wilson*

No silver trumpets ever herald the arrival,
it just rolls slow and heavy from the horizon,
we have the time to watch the grey drag over us.
Let's get cozy for it.
Fireplaces, steamy tea and sweet biscuits
a soft blanket tucked around your feet
a good book, poetry or a spooky short story, or
the fumbled translations of an ancient and angry god.
Something soft hitting the glass, like snow or rain,
not locusts, not birds.

The fire stays in the fireplace
this time.

❄

He's Coming

~ *Martha Hipley*

Alina already knows that this Christmas will be bullshit even before they wake up earlier than she ever has, before they pack their clothes into their little plastic suitcases, before they pour the cookies from the second-best bakery in the neighborhood into tupperware to make believe they baked them, before they all slouch down the six flights of stairs in their building and slink down into the subway, before the train doors clunk open and they scramble out into the Midtown haze of buskers screaming holiday songs to tourists, before they lose David for a minute in the Duane Reade and she sees that their mother looks too tired and gray to be scared about anything anymore, before they meet him, this old man who Alina barely remembers, standing dumbstruck right in front of the sign that David stumbles to read aloud as PORT AU-THO-RI-TY BUS STATION. They go inside, and their mother hands their grandfather a packet of print-outs from the Jackson Heights branch of the Queens Public Library with their ticket codes. Alina, David, and the strange old man walk through the door to their gate, and Alina sees her mother staring through the milky glass window like she is already dead and haunting them.

The bus ride is long, longer than Alina has ever sat still for a movie or even a video game, and the motion—nothing like the stop and go of the subway trains or even a city bus—makes David sick. He throws up all over himself, and no one seems to notice or care except Alina, who wipes him off with the sleeve of her coat and David's stuffed dog Freddy. The vomit bakes into the dog's fur in the heat of the bus, and Alina feels her guts squirming from the smell of it. She felt too angry to eat anything before they left the apartment, and now there's nothing to flip back up her throat and into her mouth but bile and phlegm. The bus finally pulls into a cement smear along the side of the road. Then they walk, and the little plastic wheels of David's Paw Patrol suitcase skitter along until they lock in place with the gravel and mud. He cries.

Every house in town is strung with lights and tinsel, and inflatable Santas and Grinches wobble and wave at the two children and the old man as they walk by. Alina is old enough to see the grid of her neighborhood in her mind's eye, with little pins of light for their apartment building, their school, their subway stop, her friends' buildings, the park; but here the roads weave and wind amidst the trees without any sense. After two turns off the main road, she knows she is lost. When they reach the little house at the end of a dirt path—the only house she's seen that isn't covered in decorations—she feels trapped before they even cross the threshold.

The house is cold and dark when they enter, even though their grandmother has been inside all day. The old woman takes the tupperware tub of cookies and scolds David for making a mess of his clothes. In an instant, Alina understands something that had puzzled her the whole bus ride. She could understand why her mother might not want to see her father, much as she never wants to think of the man who yelled all the time and left when David was a baby. But she couldn't understand why anyone would choose to travel so far from their mother. Standing here, in front of this old woman, she feels nothing of the warmth she left in Queens.

The children carry their suitcases up a creaky staircase and through a small wooden door to an attic room filled with the detritus of their own mother's youth—books that have long been pulled from circulation at the public library for this reason or that, posters for bands they have never heard of, and molding cardboard full of decades of domestic sludge. Alina finds one that says "XMAS" on one side and asks if she can decorate.

The old woman says, "I don't care."

Amidst the yellowing paper Santas and tin foil chains, Alina finds a near-complete nativity set. She tries to clean the pieces and even asks for a rag and soap, but the grime seems as painted-on as their expressions. As she labors over their ceramic faces, she notices that none of them seem quite right. Mary's gaze is a little too blank and distant for the Mother of God, and her eyes are ringed with daubs of red pain as though she has been crying. Joseph's eyes are wide, white blobs with pinprick black pupils. He holds up a lantern and seems to peer into some great darkness. The array of animals – just one lamb, one donkey, and one odd little turkey – all look thin and rangy as though they have barely survived a famine. A lone shepherd reminds Alina of an actor she has seen on TV, always a bad guy, but the kind who smiles when he is doing something wrong. Worst of all, the little manger is made of real, half-rotted wood that leaves a splinter in her thumb.

"I don't like them. They're ugly," says David as he watches Alina work.

"You're just as impatient as your mother," says the old woman when Alina asks why there is no baby Jesus in the box. "He's coming, he's coming."

She stands on tiptoe to arrange the little figures on the mantle in the dingy living room. No matter how she places them, they seem to stare down at her in disdain, a look she has only seen before on the faces of her teachers when their mother has arrived late to pick them up at school once again. And every time Alina ducks down to the box and then pops back up to the mantle, she wonders if the lamb has moved a little to this side or that. She tucks the shepherd as far back as she can reach, halfway behind an old brass clock, to better hide his gaze.

After the trip and this desperate merry-making, Alina feels soul-tired, cold and sore in her bones, but the old man makes the children bundle up again and walk back into town.

"Your grandmother needs space to cook dinner," he says.

David looks like he might cry again.

The decorations in the little town square have nothing on the extravagant displays back in the city. Alina misses all of it at once like she has been slapped by a wave—the giant tree right in the center of Manhattan, the lights in every color that stretch down every avenue in every borough, the department store windows full of toys and games, the neighborhood parties with punch and piñatas. Here the town square is ringed with little stalls selling food and crafts, and it all feels too shabby and real to be a holiday. Alina is surprised when the old man hands them each a paper bag of little donuts doused in sugar, but even the sticky sweet warmth can't wash away the strange feeling in her gut.

They walk past piles of lumpy wool mittens and ceramic mugs made by old women with flushed pink cheeks and fat smiles. Alina thinks of the gaunt old woman back at the house cooking dinner, and wonders if these women have grandchildren who they love. She wants to scream and run back to the bus station, back to the city, back to their mother who everyone says is looking better these days even though Alina knows it is a lie. As they walk back to the house, she sucks a coat of powdered sugar off her thumb and rediscovers the red, sore pinpoint of the splinter.

When they arrive the second time, the house feels more inviting thanks to the warmth radiating out from the kitchen, but Alina notices that the shepherd seems to have moved out from behind the clock. His beady eyes seem to be looking right at her, following her as she crosses the room.

"Did you change the decorations?" she asks as the old woman enters from the kitchen.

"What are you talking about?" she replies. "I've been cooking all evening so you two can have a nice dinner. When would I have time? If you want more decorations, take care of it yourself."

They eat a meal that is adequate but empty, all silence and salt. As soon as they have their last bites of dry meat and cold potatoes, the children head upstairs to share the musty attic mattress.

Alina feels like she will never fall asleep thanks to the draft from the attic window and the noise of the old man watching TV downstairs, but she somehow drifts off just enough to snap up with fear at the sound of something scratching at the attic door. Everything is now heavy and silent aside from the scratching. She lays still, holding her breath. She notices that David is also awake and as rigid as a fresh corpse.

"Did you see that they moved?" he asks. "I don't like them." He rubs his face against her shoulder, and she can feel the wet smear of tears and snot through her pajamas.

In the thin sliver of electric light that passes under the attic door, Alina can see little flickering shadows. The scratching continues. Something wants to get in.

"I want Mama," whispers David. Alina covers his mouth with her hand. She can now hear a strange, warbling sound in the distance, first like dogs howling in unison before taking shape as a horrible choir.

"He's coming, he's coming," they sing.

Alina takes a breath and holds it like she does before she jumps into the deep end at the YMCA pool at the Sunday swim school. She runs to the lone window facing out from the front of the house, opens the curtains, and looks out into the dark street for any sign of movement. There are no street lights on this dirt road, no people, not even a stray cat—just the dark facades of other houses in the distance as the invisible, chanting voices grow ever closer. She runs back to David and finally releases her lungs with a gasp. They huddle in the bed and press against the cold wall, willing themselves as far as they can be from the door to the tiny room and the moonlit window.

The scratching grows more violent like the sound of the near-mutant rats that live in their apartment building's basement. Alina remembers the horrible painted smirk of the shepherd as she sees his little crook fish under the gap below the door and then wiggle up along the side of it. The crook climbs impossibly high, much higher than the height of all the figurines stacked together, until it comes parallel with the doorknob and begins to fight with the latch.

The singing grows louder and clearer: "HE'S COMING, HE'S COMING."

Alina slaps herself, hoping all of it is a dream—the sad little town, their loveless grandparents, even their mother's sickness. She wishes as hard as any child does at Christmas that she will wake up at home in the city with their mother just a thin plaster wall away. David cries and wraps himself around her so tightly that she feels the air squeeze out of her lungs.

"HE'S COMING, HE'S COMING, HE'S COMING."

The latch on the door finally clicks and gives way. The door swings open with a flood of light. David screams.

Mary glides across the floor first, cold and resigned. The shepherd follows, slapping the animals along with his crook. Joseph enters last, holding out his lantern in one tiny porcelain hand and dragging the manger behind him with the other.

Alina can barely hear herself scream over the chanting as she sees the new little figure now pressed up against the window, casting a shadow across the room in the moonlight: its glowing red eyes, its needle-sharp horns, the bloody smear it leaves as it claws against the glass.

❄

Dead Wood

~ Em Starr

Pa killed our lemon tree today. He hacked at its trunk with a rusty saw and down the little sapling went, dirt spilling, roots ripping. It had just started flowering with blossoms that would have birthed Lisbons, but now it's lying sideways on the linoleum, so there'll be no fruit for remedies, no citrus for antibacterials. Dead wood is dead wood, though, and the Guest must be placated.

"We'll have the best offering in the street," Pa says.

"The very best," says Ma, dental pliers clicking. "Now hush and open wide."

When my father yawns for extraction, Ma sends me away to salvage the fallen blooms. We hum holiday hymns as she pulls and I gather—hum them loud and joyful, in case Pa says fuck or shit from pain, and Olin Mosely knocks on our door, all fish-eyed and righteous through the peephole (*I heard what I heard, and what I heard was unmerry!*). I didn't cuss once when Ma took my teeth, but they came away easier than Pa's. It's a shame my new ones hold so fast to the bone. I miss the game we used to play—string to the doorknob and count to three—the angel wings Ma made that were so pearly. So pleasing to the Guest.

The kitchen countertop was last year's deadwood offering, so I scatter my harvest on the stovetop to dry. When Ma asks me to bring her the jar of lemon tincture, my fingers smell like zesty perfume and I feel almost blessed-grateful-good 'til I see Pa in the bathroom, holding his tooth. It's yellow and cracked, and he looks disappointed, but Ma never loses her festive mirth.

"I'll make a golden angel this year," she says. "It will shimmer and shine, and our gift in return will be wonderful."

She grinds the tooth to dust under her bootheel. Cuts tin lids into angel wings and bejewels them with enamel glitter, because nothing screams *merry* like shattered incisors.

Before the Guest arrives, we sip blossom tisane and admire our sad little sapling, dressed and propped by the empty woodstove. If it wasn't frowned upon, we might whisper truths about our visitor—where it comes from, the awful gifts it sometimes brings—but most of our talk is of dead wood and where to find it.

"Remember when we used the bed frames to make a tree as tall as the ceiling?" says Ma. "The gift we received that year?"

"Yesh," replies Pa, mouth swollen.

"Let's hope we get something wonderful like that again," she says.

I sip my tisane and pray for something less dangerous. I wonder why she doesn't recall the days before we were gifted the aqua filter—before the collective envy of our neighbors made Pa barricade our front door with Besser blocks, Olin Mosely at the spyhole, saying it's unmerry not to share all that good, clean water.

"Of course," Ma continues, "we must always consider those less fortunate."

She whispers of the families with no dead wood offering, careful not to speak of the gifts they might receive—of gifts I do not want. Not hives filled with bee corpses, the honeycomb burnt out and bitter. Not rotting gourds or poisonous mushrooms or fish with half-sucked spines. Or, worse, no gift at all . . . nothing new for the next twelve months. A lump of coal would, at least, be something; we could use it to draw happy faces on each other, scrawl season's greetings on the wall, the Guest Rules on the ceiling—never to be seen, never to be spoken to.

Later, when Ma pulls my blanket tight around me, we recite the rules three times, lest I wake in the night and forget.

"Promise you'll keep those peepers shut tonight," she says.

"I promise," I reply.

Still, when something scritch-scratches in the nothing hours, I open my eyes and adjust my vision to the pixelated grey. My parents are asleep on the floor, beside me. Pa snoring, jaw swollen. Moonlight catching silver threads in Ma's hair, so she looks like an angel.

Scritch-scratch. There it is again . . . like claws inside the wood-stove. Like the budgerigar I rescued from the flu last summer and liberated through the kitchen window. Pa said it was probably somebody's pet—that it would die with no trees for shelter. Ma said we could have enjoyed a real banquet and used the feathers for decorating.

Neither of them stirs, when I tiptoe between their coiled limbs, praying the bird hasn't returned. The hallway is lined with tapestry, the Guest rules stitched in red on each one—never to be seen, never to be spoken to—words barely legible in the pre-dawn murk, still they play on mental loop as the shapes of the living room take shape.

The dead wood offering is gone—no. Not gone. Suspended mid-air, roots-up. Held by something unseeable, until the moonlight catches gelatinous folds of arm skin, grey flesh bulging at the waistline. The Guest stares with black goop where its eyes should be. It doesn't use its manners when it eats the lemon tree whole; swallows with a throat that opens and constricts, opens and constricts. It belches. Considers the offering. Heaves, and shudders, and vomits the sapling back up.

The remedy jar is empty, eleven months of infected jawbone turning Pa's good blood septic. Ma hums seasonal tunes as she tends to his sores with saltwater, stopping only to speak of this year's offering.

"It will be our best yet," she says. ""And our gift in return will be wonderful. Something healing, something medicinal . . ."

Except there's not a scrap of wood in the house, only beams that support our walls and ceiling, the yellow-tongue particleboards beneath the vinyl floor. Nothing to offer the Guest when it comes, not even a regurgitated lemon tree. Not that we didn't attempt to replant the rejected offering, Ma sobbing as I teased out the roots.

The sapling crumbled to pulp, days later, leaving an empty pot and a biting guilt in my belly.

Ma doesn't know I broke the rules (never to be seen, never to be spoken to). She says dead wood is scarcer than ever, our neighbors singing songs of cheer, even as they tear their households apart for a single splinter. When news of Olin Mosely's death buzzes in the street, it's a bonafide holiday miracle. Olin, a collector of oddities and antiques, mostly collected in lieu of unpaid debts, has more wood than he can account for, his offering always the biggest, the grandest, the worthiest of gifts in return. But now that he is face down in his driveway, open season has been declared on his belongings, and there are walnut buffets and mahogany trunks being ferried across the bitumen at rapid pace.

Ma and I hum a medley of merry tunes as we tear down the breezeblock barricade—merrily, merrily, even as the neighbors loot, dragging Jarrah tables and blackwood stands, and pushing wheelbarrows of pine bric-a-brac. Even when we find Olin's house cleared of its furniture, nothing left but load-bearing girders and his unclaimed corpse.

The body is in the early stages of rigor mortis. Ma says it won't be malleable for long. We haul it home and prop it up by the woodstove, twisting arms into branches, his torso thick like a tree trunk. When it turns hard, like wood, Ma fashions a tin-lid angel to sit atop the dome.

"We'll have the best offering in the street," I say.

"The very best," says Ma, dental pliers clicking. "Now hush, and open wide."

Of Wilbur, Trains, and Snails

~ *Michael Huyck*

He sat on his bum, his hands on his knees
Sniffing his sniffles while staring at trees
His vision was blurry and a tear warmed one cheek
What to do? thought Wilbur, because things looked quite bleak

The glued toothpick firs were smashed and bent over
The legs were broke off the plastic dog Rover
The Lincoln Log houses lay a-tumble and scattered
And shards of Lake Mirror were splintered and battered

The river was ripped up and the town just a jumble
The post office, the market, Mrs. Bear's Brac-A-Bumble
Ruins and rumble took the train station to pieces
Plastic cows lay silent beside plastic geeses

There'd be nary a train out on the rail
No travel nor glory because this day did fail
At stopping the evil in Wilbur's new world
Surly, a snail, and brain waves all swirled

Back up, just a moment, there's story more early
About a boy and a mom and a bloke – that was Surly
About love and compassion and toys for the heart
And terrestrial mollusks with eye-pods that dart

The boy Wilbur, the subject of this dire tale
Had mum, his dear mother, who loved without fail
Until last year she'd been Wilbur's alone
But now Surly, that bastard, had entered their home

One December, the first one with Surly in household
With Wilbur asleep, or so then his mum told
They prattled, then argued, about Christmas for kiddies
And Surly told mum that she suffered from giddies

They hardly had change for tobacco or wine now
Or horses or numbers or betting on bow-wows
And Christmas is only to make money for churches
For the needy, the wanty, and those dirty street urchins

Wilbur cried in his room, he begged and he plead
He kneeled on his knees and he prayed by his bed
Still, Surly sneered and dear mother, she pouted
They talked on in private and in private they shouted

"It's a gift" said his mother, "A nice train for the boy"
"I'll work for each cent and we'll all know the joy"
Surly took out his wallet, freed a moth from inside
"You buy him that damn train and I'll tan your hide!"

Mom toiled at the café and the library, too
At the drugstore she sold their blue dandruff shampoo
All the labor near killed her and left her too sore
So one night, after whiskey, she decided to whore

Her friend Annabelle said just one night in a teddy
Would provide enough cash to make any girl heady
And, as her proof, she pulled out a big wad
Of C-notes she said came from one fellow nicknamed "Odd"

Mom started *her* career with one fellow named Rick
He may not have been large, but man was he quick
Customer two had a belly like jelly
He left a big tip—that was good, he was smelly
Then came the mechanic and a blues saxophonist
And a twill-vested smoker who buried his bone-ist
Mom made the money, but she saved it for Wilbur
If only she'd known Wilbur's dearest friend Gilbert

Gilbert the snail had big plans in store
Ideas for controlling the world and more
He'd start with the boy and then go after mom
But then, after them, every fellow named Tom!

Then Surly, the mailman, the city, the earth!
The thought of that power left him full of mirth!
Gilbert laughed—he could do it! For he was THE SNAIL!
With his mind control waves he knew he'd never fail!

But, for the moment, he had only the boy
And, so far, the boy had been hard to destroy
The best Gilbert did was make Wilbur real sad
And sad boys were not much for a snail so bad

So he made friends with the boy in the garden at first
Oozed on his palm till his oozers near burst
With snail mind control waves he bent Wilbur's thinking
Left the boy sitting and gawking and blinking

Gilbert lived in a box, tall walls with no ceiling
The boy fed Gilbert leaves and spoke to him with feeling
They were friends, said the boy, and they'd be friends forever
And stay in their bedroom till the fifth Thursday of Never

But back to the mom now, enough with the snail
She made wads of money, and her other jobs paled
Surly was kicked out with no more than his top hat
And Christmas was coming; you know you can't top that!
She bought Wilbur a train set and a broad slab of lumber
Bottles of paint and brushes by number
Toys to make houses and mirrors to make lakes
If it all wasn't real it was the very best of the fakes

On Christmas Eve mom couldn't wait anymore
She trundled the last bag back up from the store
Gathered up Wilbur and took him to the attic
Gave him his train very early and without any static

He cried out when he opened it then cried out again
At the city he'd build and the landscapes he'd bend
At the animals, schoolyards, the fences, the signs
He'd make bushes and trees, Junipers . . . Pines

They painted and glued till their fingers were numb
Outside the dawn broke and the fat elves were done
Before sleeping they both sat, watched the train go around
And Wilbur hugged mom before to bed he did bound

Regardless the train, regardless the morning
Gilbert was unhappy, displeased without warning
Up from the leaves, at the lip of his carton,
Sat Gilbert the snail, and his humor was smartin'
The boy was too happy, his mind wasn't warping!
He smiled, he laughed, he giggled till burping!
It was time to act fast and it was time to act mean
And Gilbert the snail was the meanest you've seen

He grimaced his snail lips and curled one eyestalk
Shook off his shell and shunned off his foot sock
Leaning into his work, Gilbert thought only of rudeness
As can only a snail chockfull of bad tudeness
A snail's brain waves are the most worsestest kind
They attack you with nightmares that fill up your mind
Wet tentacles slapping and shadows all gibbering,
Dismembered limbs all crawling and flippering

A clubbed baby seal or a tired, frozen beggar
They'll soundtrack your dreams with old Suzanne Vega
I've digressed a bit, so let's get back to the point
Snails are the nastiest gastropods in the joint

Then, barely then, there arose such a clatter
Downstairs someone stumbled and dishes did shatter
A string of drunk curses arose from the house,
Surly came back, though not quiet as a mouse

Wilbur peered from one eye, then the other came next
He rolled to the floor and underbed he did rest
With fingers in ears he barely peered from his place
And wished for a pitchfork or at least for some mace

Above, on the box, Gilbert flipped around, u-turning
He aimed at the door with his brain waves all churning
There, at the threshold, met a Surly and mother
Both were so pissed that they flapped till they hovered

"Slut" he screamed at her, and "Prick" she replied
"Certainly", thought Wilbur, "One of them lied."
"Oh I heard what you did to get trains and all that"
Surly pointed at the attic—"Is that where it's at?"

She fought him with punches and fought him with nails
But Surly was big from throwing hay bales
He pushed her aside and stomped up to the attic
And that's when young Wilbur decided to panic
"Take me," he heard then, as he crawled from the floor
"If that's the snail," thought Wilbur, "I need to sleep more"
But it was just the snail, only a snail, at that
And so Wilbur grabbed Gilbert and ran off lickity flat

The three of them met there at the top of the stairs
There was gnashing of teeth and the pulling of hairs
There was kicking and biting and spanking and beating
But the squabble about trains was short-lived and fleeting

When first in the attic Wilbur set Gilbert free
On the train set, no less, because Wilbur didn't see
How now Gilbert could take them with brain waves in force
The snail did just that, as a matter of course

As in to perfection as a snail can be
Gilbert formed brain waves you wouldn't believe
He aimed them at people, the three in the room
And when he triangulated he let them go BOOM

Just then, with the fighting all moving around
Wilbur dropped down to get close to the ground
He flipped the power on to move the train over there
Because Surly might kick it and that wasn't fair

The train came around from the back forty with zest
Mom bashed Surly with an old jewelry chest
They stood close together, growling their growls
When snail brain waves forced empty their bowels

They fell to the floor, then, suddenly, they shrank!
Dear mum and mean Surly, to be very frank
Their clothing, their shoes, all for folks really small!
They stared in dismay, for they'd been fairly tall
In awe, Wilbur stared, unsure of this thing
As if all he believed had suddenly took wing
And the snail stood up (if a snail, in fact, can)
And yelled out to Wilbur that he had a plan

But Wilbur was angry, yes, Wilbur was pissed!
That was his mother the damn snail had dissed!
Wilbur pushed to his feet and then jumped in the air
He'd smash that snail flat to teach it what's fair

Seeing his plan going awfully awry
Gilbert decided to let his big weapon fly
A snailish sort of nuclear explosiony thing
It'd level this attic and make that boy's ears ring
So he thought, but then Gilbert had thought wrong before
Thinking in grand scales of dominion and gore
But his nuclear thingy was just a small blast
It leveled the train world but the attic stood fast

And Gilbert, he'd taken the worse side of the shoe
Wilbur had smashed him into snailular goo
His shell was all crinkled and his green guts a smear
As a slow snail he should have known more about fear

The train world was wrecked and the grown-ups, it's bad
They flopped in the carnage of the train world gone mad
And that's where we found Wilbur at the start of this text
Staring at his train world that the snail just wrecked

Staring at his dead mum and the lackluster Surly
At two inches tall, Surly hardly looked burly
Wilbur picked both up and petted them like birds
Then flopped them on train station benches like turds
He picked up the trees and he straightened their boughs
He righted the sows and he righted the does
Like a puzzle all the lake shards he matched to the shore
And he rebuilt the log houses right up from the floor

When everything was almost as good as beginning
He ran the train round and started to grinning
With a paper towel Gilbert was wiped in the trash
Soon after the small Surly became just as mashed

And mum, she just stayed there, all right in the station
Awaiting some train to take her on vacation
Her face is all bloated so it's hard to see
Her tiny corpse eyes beneath her toothpick fir tree

Wilbur will sit there and run his train in that loop
His eyes are all blank, like his brain's flown the coop
His train world is rumpled and his repairs have all failed
He's not the same boy since his brain waves were snailed

And that, my friend, is the story to end
And nary a fact did I twiddle or bend
So next time, after rains, see you snails needing mucked
Think of poor Wilbur and how his brain is all fucked

Alive as He Could Be

~ *Ryan Van Ells*

It was not right. Julius gently held the top hat on his fingertips as if it might crumble under his touch. He'd retrieved it from behind a glass case in dad's study and, like everything else in there, was covered in a thick layer of dust. The hat was more archaic relic that could have belonged to a demonic circus ringleader in the late 19th century than top hat to put the finishing touch on a snowman but, it was the best thing that Julius had on hand. He blew the dust off, again half-expecting it to blow to dust itself, and placed it on top of the snowman's head.

"Merry Christmas," Julius whispered to himself. He wasn't expecting any presents. Mom had been snoring at the kitchen table when he'd gone inside to get the hat. She slept a lot nowadays.

The snowman was good though. He stepped back and admired his handiwork. The last time he'd built a snowman was when he was eight-years-old. Maybe he wanted to feel that way again. Or maybe he was struck by an artistic muse. It was impressive.

The shiver down Julius' spine caught him off guard. It was cold, but not that cold. It was like the temperature had dropped ten degrees in half-a-second.

The sky darkened. A violent wind whipped and whistled in rage. It stung at Julius' eyes. The chill pierced into his bone marrow. Julius's teeth chattered relentlessly.

Then, it was over. The wind dampened to nothing. The snow stopped falling. Yet Julius felt the weight of the storm around him, pressing downward, like he had fallen into the eye of a hurricane that was moments from passing overhead. His chest tightened.

He took a step back. He should be inside. At least until this, whatever this was, was over.

Wait. A voice murmured like a parent calling from another room. Julius heard it though. He scanned the backyard but he was the only one outside. There wasn't another person in the streets. The tightness spread to his belly. He turned to leave.

Wait. The voice said again, still dampened and Julius understood why he could hear it—the voice was inside his own head.

Please. Julius didn't want to believe it, didn't want to consider it, didn't want to hear it, let alone turn and face it. *I need your help.* But turn he did, to the snowman who, despite being frozen solid and immobile as a department store mannequin, was speaking to him.

Julius waited until it was dark to bring the snowman what it wanted. Even at ten-years-old, there was a little voice inside that told him it was better to wait until a time when the neighbors couldn't look over and ask what the strange little boy next door was doing in the backyard. He knew they watched because Ms. Johnson yelled at him when he crossed into her yard after she'd sprayed it with pesticide. Ever since that first incident, he'd been watched like a hawk—the troubled child dangerously roaming into neighbors' yards and god knows what else. She'd even put up a fence and tried to bill his mother for it.

He lay the frozen chicken breasts in a circle around the snowman, as close to the base as he could manage. Then, he threw a few handfuls of snow over the top of them. No reason for it to look any weirder than it had to. Was this what the snowman wanted? He hoped so.

The next morning the chicken was gone. Julius's first thought was that his mother discovered the wasted food and thrown it away. His stomach dropped.

Then he saw the snowman. It looked more real. That was the only way to describe it. The coat button eyes hadn't sprung pupils and there weren't any nostrils on the carrot nose, but still the snow-man appeared more solid and put together then it had yesterday. As if it's snowy body had taken on a more skin-like sheen. And Julius understood where the chicken had gone.

Flesh and blood. Its voice said in Julius' head. The voice was clearer today, no longer muffled. It was starting to sound familiar.

It wanted more? Where was he going to find more meat? He had taken a big risk just by taking the chicken from mom's freezer.

Flesh and blood. It repeated in a firm voice as if in answer to Julius' thoughts.

"I can't."

The snowman screamed in Julius' head. Julius' wouldn't have his first migraine for another decade, but when he did he would think of this moment. A piercing screech that reverberated off the inside of his skull emanated from deep in his cerebellum like a primal scream of his animal forebears. Each high-pitched *whump* sent an agonizing throb throughout Julius' head. It lasted just as long as it took for him to remember that there was more meat in the refrig-erator he could take.

After the headache dissipated, Julius returned to the kitchen. Inside the fridge was an unopened pack of moldy deli-sliced ham. One of many questionable items. Julius took it out to the snow-man and dropped the unwrapped deli meat at the snowman's base. Then he waited.

He didn't know for what. He waited long enough to think he was crazy. Then the ham digested. In open air, the ham slices, blue-grey mold and all, digested into incomprehensible slop at the snowman's feet before absorbing into the snow.

Julius ran back inside.

If he had stayed, he may have seen carrot nose of his snowman lighten and shorten and his button eyes shift in his head like eye-balls.

"I'm sorry!" Julius blinked back stinging tears afraid that if he let them fall too far out of his eyes, they would freeze his eyelashes together. He took in choppy, sobbing breaths that iced the back of his throat. He didn't know the back of your throat could get cold. It could. And it hurt.

Scattered around his feet and the snowman's base, were scraps: grains of rice, chunks of old bread, and vegetable peels. Days had passed and he'd run out of meat. Mom hadn't noticed and hadn't gone shopping.

The snowman, whose eyes were now a beady black like a sparrows, regarded Julius silently. An aura of disappointment emanated outward. It was worse than the cold, worse than the stinging in Julius' eyes. He wilted, wanted to fold in on himself, so total was his failure.

Out of his teary periphery, a small snowbird flitted down to the pile of kitchen waste at Julius' feet. It regarded Julius shortly, decided he wasn't a threat, and began pecking at a chunk of stale bread. What happened next happened quickly. Julius was not sure if he saw it correctly.

The bird, having misjudged the threats he landed among, hopped once, twice, in the direction of the snowman. Then, it crumpled. Like a sheet of paper with the wrong idea, it folded in on itself. Cracks of bone and a cheep cut off halfway echoed through the crisp winter air. The bird, if it could still be called a bird, was a heap of disconnected muscle and feather bent into unnatural and impossible shapes until what remained was something like the molder's clay of a bird. The pieces of a bird you would get before putting it all together.

Acid rushed to Julius' throat. He swallowed it down and covered his mouth.

The bird leftovers dissolved. As though someone had poured a vial of acid over the remains, they melted away and disappeared into the snow below until all that remained were a few light sparrow footprints.

Julius could have sworn the snowman burped. He ran back inside, the echos of the snowman's laughter in his head the entire way.

❄

The orange tabby belonged to Ms. Johnson. Like everything belonging to Ms. Johnson, she swore up and down that it was an angel walking the earth and would never hurt a fly. Never mind that Julius had seen the fat beast ravage a vole, three sparrows, and Chucky, his own pet rabbit who he let play outside in a pen. Julius did not like the cat. Every time it pranced through his mother's backyard it stopped and stared at him as if challenging Julius to say something, do something about this. His mother wouldn't let him get a dog.

Despite all this, when Julius saw the tabby prowling in his backyard, he ran out screaming after it, howling like a feral child raised by wolves. The cat froze, raised it's hackles, took a moment to seemingly assess the situation, and darted back under the hole in Ms. Johnson's fence. When it was gone, Julius panted. He'd never yelled like that in his life. His throat hurt.

The glowering of the snowman burned at Julius' skin like a heat rash he couldn't reach. It was a maleficent energy. Julius wondered how the snowman hadn't melted away with all this hot hatred in its heart—he could only assume it had a heart. It had eyes, beady and rat-like as they were, and it had a voice, albeit one that only Julius could hear inside his head; why wouldn't it have a heart?

There was a dead sparrow that lay, undigested, on the snow a few feet outside the circle Julius had drawn to mark where the snowman's circle of death was. That must have been what the cat was after. It did not appear to have decayed. Before Julius could inspect it further, it vanished underneath the snow. Julius jumped back. How far could his snowman reach? How long until it could reach outside his backyard? Inside his house? Could it reach inside? Julius didn't want to find out.

Before he could run back inside the house, he stopped. There was a tug in the back of his mind, tethering him in place like a fish hook snagged in weeds.

Wait, Julius.

Julius wanted to run. Some part of him knew that if he did, his brain, stem and all, would be uprooted from his skull. The image of his favorite fighting game flashed in his mind: fatality.

I need more.

"No," Julius said through streaming tears. "No more!" As if the piles of dead birds and neighborhood pets wasn't enough. This thing wanted more.

I need you to help me, Julius.

He shook his head no.

Why don't we help each other? I've seen the way you look at her. Don't pretend you haven't thought about it.

"Ms. Johnson?" Julius considered this. He considered it more than he ever imagined he would have. He considered Ms. Johnson's hateful one-eyed cat, the neighborhood pet murderer. He considered how every spring, Ms. Johnson would glare at him from inside her porch door just in case he stepped a toe over the line on her property so she could yell at them. He considered her crone-like hands and spiteful gaze. Did he want her dead? He certainly wouldn't mind if she wasn't alive. But was that the same thing?

No, he wasn't doing this. He wasn't considering feeding his neighbor to a bloodthirsty magic snowman no matter how much of a bitch she was. He wasn't fucking doing that.

"No, I won't help you."

That's too bad. Your dad will be disappointed.

The air went still. A breath caught in Julius' throat. "Wha—whaat?"

And he was looking forward to seeing you too.

"What are you saying?"

Where do you think I came from, Julius? I wasn't always a snow-man. I used to be something more substantial, something more alive, before I wasn't. Then you helped bring me back. I could help you bring back good ole pappy pap too. You just have to make me whole first.

"What do you need?" Julius asked before he could think about what he was saying. Was he really doing this? It felt like he was watching himself from a mile away, unable to change anything that was happening.

I need more. I'm almost there, I can feel it, but I need more. And not fucking sparrow either. Something more substantial.

"Like Ms. Johnson's cat?"

Something more human.

Julius remembered his father. He had been a bumbling man; a gray-haired, cardigan sporting, spectacled reader of a man. Julius' earliest memories of his father were playing on the thick rug of the study while his father poured over ancient, leather bound manuscripts of indeterminate origin. It never seemed that he wanted children. Just had the misfortune of making one right before he crossed the line into too old to have kids territory, and then he was stuck with it. But Julius loved him.

His heart yearned to hear the sound of a heavy book closing and a pair of glasses being set on the desktop signaling an end to studies for the day and the beginning of father-son time. Sometimes when he cried, he sat on the end of the bed and bounced because dad used to bounce him on his knee and read The Hobbit and the motion always made him feel better even if dad wasn't there. He never finished The Hobbit. It didn't seem right to read it without him—to experience the adventures outside of dad's gravelly voice. They could finish it together.

No. He shouldn't do this. Killing people was wrong, even to save someone you love. But a nervous twinge of pain in his stomach told him that it was too late; he'd made his choice.

It didn't take long for Mrs. Johnson to come out from behind her sliding back porch door. She rarely did when Julius was, in her words, acting up in a way that would have gotten the belt in her day. Normally it was something as innocent as laughing too loudly or walking on her grass, or menacing the neighborhood with his imaginary voices. This time, it was because he'd thrown snowballs at her window.

When she opened the sliding door on her back porch, he launched another at her face. She dodged it with surprising speed for a woman her age. Her mouth fell open to a shocked fish gaze.

"How dare you," she sputtered. Julius threw another snowball. The anger must have made her slower because this one hit, not in the face where Julius had been aiming, but her neck.

She gasped and heaved in air like a linebacker who just had the air knocked out of them. Her face went red. Big teardrops fell from her eyes.

Julius held his breath. He wondered what would happen next.

He didn't have to wait long. Ms. Johnson, in only her slippers and a robe, caught her breath and charged out her backdoor.

Julius had a moment before she unlatched the fence. He positioned himself on what he hoped was the edge of the snowman's new limit, throwing a glance behind him to make sure his heels were outside the freshly drawn circle.

The fence blasted open. Ms. Johnson, robe flapping against her frail old body, marched deliberately forward to Julius, one arm raised like it was poised for a slap. Julius waited until she was just in front of him.

"You may not have a father to do this for you . . ." She never got to finish her sentence.

As she stepped forward, Julius jumped nimbly to the side. While he stayed outside the line, she, thrown off balance, took one step into it.

One step was enough.

When her foot touched the snow, it sunk in to the ankle. And it held. Before Ms. Johnson could utter a sound of surprise, she crumpled inward like an emptying Capri-sun on a hot day. All of her juices ran out of her. Her gaunt face sucked inward. Her body drained to skin draped over bone and then crumpled into a paper towel wad of a human body before disappearing entirely beneath the snow.

The next day, Julius stayed in his room. He did not go out to the backyard. He did not even go downstairs. It took all of his willpower and a shaky hand to move his curtain aside from the window and look out. The snowman looked at him. Its lips, which Julius had not given it, were snow-white flesh curled into a contemptuous grin. Julius ducked back down from the window and hid under the blankets the rest of the day. He played videos on his phone to distract him.

He stayed that way the next day.

And the next.

And the next.

Until days had become weeks. Until winter break had passed and he had not left his room save to find old cans of food to eat for dinner and scurrying back to the safety of his bed. Until the cops showed up, banging on the front door.

Julius did not want to see them. He did not want them there. He threw the blanket over his head and played his video louder.

The banging on the front door got louder. Someone yelled. Louder banging. The sound of the front door caving in.

Someone said "oh my god."

Julius imagined what happened next. He saw in his mind two cops hurry through the busted front door into the living room. He saw them rush to his mother's body on the couch and recoil. The two cops put a hand over their mouths in shock. Maybe one wretched. They both saw her, his mother, drained over everything but bone and skin just like Ms. Johnson, as thought someone had hung flesh-colored drapes over a scarecrow. There weren't even any flies because there was nothing for them to eat.

Downstairs, one of them clomped to the kitchen with heavy boot steps and wretched. When he finished, he heard him walking the wrong way.

Julius jumped out of bed and ran to the stairs. But it was too late. The cop had already opened the back door and taken a step outside. He didn't even scream. His partner, perhaps startled by the sudden silence, ran out back to. Julius yelled for him to stop, but he must not have heard. Or he heard too late. But he was gone too.

They were good, Julius.

Julius could hear the voice from anywhere now. He stayed at the bottom of the stairs.

I need some more.

"And then you'll bring dad back?"

Of course.

Julius hesitated, but only for a moment. Who else was going to take care of him? He went back upstairs, found his phone, and called 911.

"Hello? There's some men in my backyard."

※

Aged to Perfection

~ Margo Pecha

The fruitcake arrives in a battered brown box with no return address. The cardboard is leaking, emitting a yeasty, fermented odor. We open it on the kitchen counter, peeling the damp flaps back and unwinding its wrapping of soggy waxed paper.

It is spongy and dense, studded with raisins and flecks of jeweled candied peel peeking through. We search for a card, but the box yields nothing more than this most unholy of baked goods. I wrinkle my nose, the smell tickling my sinuses unpleasantly.

"Disgusting," you say, wiping your sticky hands on your jeans.

"Is this yours?" I ask Nanna as she shuffles into the kitchen.

Nanna peers into the box and her face lights up, soft wrinkles creasing into a smile.

"A fruitcake," she says. "What a treat! Who sent it?"

"We don't know," I say. "There's no card."

"Probably from someone who knew your grandfather," she says. "Such a nice gesture."

She stares at the loaf for some time, her watery eyes focused on something beyond the rectangular cake. Her features have slackened, and she's cocked her head to the side as if tuning in to an imperceptible sound.

I pull a knife from a drawer and lower it into the box, preparing to slice Nanna a piece, but snaps out of her daze and slaps at the back of my hand.

"Not yet! It needs to age; put it away."

And so it's tucked into the back of the walk-in pantry, relegated to the shadowy company of canned food and bins of flour and bags of dried beans. If we'd had half a mind, we would have stashed it somewhere else, somewhere it would have promptly been forgotten, but we did no such thing.

Nanna begins communing with the fruitcake before December is well and truly underway. A dusting of snow powders the ground like confectioner's sugar, and we've only strung a few colorful strands of lights around the farmhouse to mark the start of the season.

First we hear her whispering. We think she's looking for something—a strange spice, perhaps, or a long-forgotten tin of tea—but she's been in the pantry for half an hour. A frown wrinkles your brow and you linger beside the door, ear pressed to the wood, straining to hear.

"Come on, I want make paper snowflakes," I say, but you shake your head.

"Nanna's losing it," you say. "She's singing to the fruitcake."

I stifle a giggle, and your fingers tighten on my elbow, pulling me close.

"Listen," you insist, and your tone is so serious that the laugh lodges in my throat.

We nudge the door open a crack. Nanna's small body is hunched over the cake, her back to us, a thin bathrobe draped over her frail form. The tune is hushed, a low melody that rises and falls rhythmically, hypnotically. She pauses her song and pinches the cake between her knobbled fingers.

"So dry," she murmurs, shaking her head. She picks up the song again, swaying slightly on her feet.

We retreat to the den and snip snowflakes from white paper, Nanna's eerie crooning floating through the house as she tends to the cake. I hum along, feeling the notes vibrate deep in my throat, and you scowl at me, your scissors flashing.

"Stop that," you say. "It's creepy."

I shrug. I can't place the song, but I think I've heard it somewhere before.

We snip more snowflakes. Your brow remains furrowed—whether in concentration or consternation, I can't say. The pile of cut paper grows as the light fades, and Nanna still hasn't left the pantry.

Early Sunday morning Nanna hovers in the kitchen drowning in her robe. She simmers a pot of something foul on the stove, stirring as she hums under her breath, that same lilting song that neither of us can place. The steam billowing from the pot is sour and fruited, the substance bubbling within jammy and congealed. She reaches for a bottle of cinnamon and the sleeve of her robe slips. We catch a glimpse of her skinny arm, wound with bandages from wrist to elbow.

"Girls," she says, straightening herself and smiling. "Would you like to help me feed the fruitcake?"

We shake our heads and exchange a quick glance, and I know you've seen it too. We back away, and I follow you up to our shared bedroom.

"What do you think happened to Nanna?" I whisper.

"Nothing good," you say.

Nanna remains enamored with the fruitcake. Most afternoons we find her in the gloom of the pantry, humming that same strange song and basting the loaf with the warmed liquid, of which she brews a fresh batch every day. We are never sure exactly what goes into it, but something about it makes our nostrils twitch and stomachs turn.

The chickens begin to go unfed, their few eggs left cold and frozen in the nesting boxes. We pick up the slack on the farm, ferrying fresh water to the animals and laying down clean bedding. We stomp through the snow and lug buckets of feed, withholding our speculations about what exactly is amiss with Nanna. Even after our parents passed and she took us in, Nanna never neglected her chores. The unease balloons between us, widening uncomfortably like the expectant cow in her stall who watches us with wary eyes.

The holidays creep closer. Snow drifts and swirls around the house, burying us in a deep layer of solitude. The school bus can't make it through the treacherous hills with their twisting roads, so our winter break begins early. We watch cartoons and scribble in the stack of holiday cards that have sat forgotten and wanting on the dining table for days, sending cheerful tidings on Nanna's behalf.

Everything is fine, we write, *Nanna has been busy baking!*

We stuff them into envelopes and carry them down the long, winding driveway to the mailbox, the wind buffeting our backs. Neither of us can drive the tractor, so the road remains unplowed, the snow now up to our knees.

"Has she been in there all day?" you ask, stomping and huffing, lifting your feet high above the crust.

"I don't know," I say. But I do know. She has, crooning that unusual song.

We fix our own supper when we return; Nanna is too preoccupied with the fruitcake. She's still in there when the light fades and we eventually head up to bed, and we're not sure when or if she does the same.

"It's almost ready," she announces each morning as she emerges from the pantry and places her saucepan on the stove. "Just another week or so."

By mid-month the pantry reeks of sour wine and old pennies, the stench unbearable. It wafts beneath the door and into the kitchen, surrounding us in its foul aroma. You gag and crack the windows, a freezing current of air flowing in. It does nothing to diminish the odor.

We sit near the window, shivering, unspeaking, while we spoon soggy cereal into our mouths. The paper snowflakes taped to the glass flutter in the incoming breeze. The twinkle lights have gone out, and I fiddle with the plug, unsuccessful, before giving up. There will be no merry cheer today.

"We need to move it," you finally say, and I don't need to ask what you mean.

"Yes," I agree, sipping the sugared milk from my bowl. "The cellar?"

You nod, and Nanna waltzes into the room. She seems to move easier these days—spritely, almost gliding into the kitchen to prepare another saucepan of fodder with which to soak the cake. Her skin seems more vibrant—luminous, even—but perhaps that's just the winter light reflected into the house.

You lean toward me. "Tonight," you murmur, and a chill skitters down my spine.

You wake me when the moon has risen high over the surrounding fields, shedding its silver light across the landscape and splashing haphazardly across our bedroom walls. We carefully traipse downstairs, our bare feet soundless on the wooden floorboards.

The pantry gapes at the back of the kitchen, too deep for the moonlight to penetrate its depths. We step into its darkness, our eyes slow to adjust to the gloom. But it is there on the far shelf, a doughy brick nested within a mass of waxed paper.

It is spongy, saturated in liquid, and surprisingly warm, reminding me of the offal we helped Granddad clean from a deer last year. I gag, not wanting to touch it, but I'm the oldest, so the burden belongs to me. I swaddle it in the limp papers and lift it from the shelf, holding it away from my body.

We hurry it down into the hungry belly of the root cellar, dripping a trail of juices behind us. I imagine it contracting and expanding in my hands, shuddering with breath, squirming beneath the tension of my fingers.

"It's just a cake," I whisper to myself, gripping it tighter, and you, two steps ahead, shoot me an annoyed glance.

"It's not, and you know it."

And then we are in the cold underworld of the house, braids of onions and garlic swaying from the rafters and scattering crazy shadows across the earthen room. Moonlight leaks in through the egress windows, spilling silver against the stores. You clear a spot on a sagging shelf, scooting aside dusty jars of pickled plums.

"Nobody eats these," you say. "She won't notice it here."

I shove the fruitcake to the back of the shelf and we rearrange the jars. I wipe my hands on my pants, smearing the sticky red sauce down my pajamas.

It takes three wash cycles until the stain and its accompanying smell come out, but it doesn't take Nanna long to discover the cake is gone.

"Girls, did you eat the fruitcake?" she asks the next day, a tense smile fracturing her face as she pokes her head out of the pantry.

You grimace in disgust. "Gross, no."

"It's ok if you did, I won't be mad." There's a stiffness to her smile that doesn't feel natural.

I shake my head, perhaps too quickly, and she narrows her eyes but says nothing. She slinks about the house, poking through the cupboards and rifling through the kitchen drawers. She's distracted, her mind preoccupied with visions of her dense, sticky cake, so we flee upstairs.

From our bedroom we hear her rummaging around downstairs, the steady tread of her feet on the floorboards like a metronome as she paces and mutters and searches long into the night.

The days inch toward the solstice, each one darker than the last. Nanna has become distraught, tramping through the house in a frenzy and scouring every nook and cranny for the missing fruitcake.

"Just admit that you ate it," she hisses, flinging open cabinets and digging through closets with surprising agility. Our coats and scarves are tossed in haphazard heaps, and dishes are piled on the countertops. She's even torn apart the carefully wrapped gifts nestled beneath the tree, strewing colorful paper and tangled ribbons across the floor.

We cower on the couch, watching Nanna's rage unfold around us. She stomps from room to room, slams doors and rattles the framed photographs on the walls. The twinkle lights flicker, then go out entirely.

"It was almost ready," she wails. She tugs at her disheveled hair and utters a crazed laugh that ends in a bloated sob.

"I thought she'd get better," I whisper to you, "but she's only gotten worse."

You squeeze my hand. "We did the right thing." But a frown tugs at the corners of your mouth, and I know you're just as troubled as I am.

In the morning all is quiet; the only sound is the soft spattering of large, white flakes against the window panes. The house is cold; no fire has been lit in the hearth. We shiver and take in our surroundings, now tidied with everything in its proper place. Even the gifts have been rewrapped, tucked once again beneath the boughs of the tree.

Nanna is nowhere to be seen. The absence of her continual rummaging is jarring, and my ears strain to pick up her presence. Is she upstairs? Down in the cellar? The prospect makes my stomach clench.

"Do you think she found it?" I ask, stacking logs in the fireplace.

You chew on your lip and stare out the window at the swirling vortex. I arrange kindling and crumpled paper beneath the firewood and light the match, its flame flaring into brightness that dances and catches.

"Maybe we should check," I say, and we leave the blooming warmth for the damp chill of the cellar.

"Nanna? Are you down there?" you call down the steep staircase, but there is no answer.

We slip down the stairs, a musty smell rising to meet us the deeper we descend into its tomb-like embrace. I half worry we'll find Granddad's mummified remains propped in a forgotten corner; with Nanna's strange behavior, it doesn't seem too far-fetched.

But the cellar is as it was before—cluttered, dirty, and packed to the gills with the spoils of summers' past. No sign that anyone has been down here except for a clear trail we've disturbed in the dust.

We push aside the purpled quarts of pickled plums, their murky contents sloshing, but the space behind is empty save for the cake's crumpled wrapping. We scour the shelving, shift crates and boxes, scoot bloated squash aside and peer behind bushels of apples, but one fact remains: the waxed paper is licked clean; not a crumb is left.

"She couldn't have eaten the whole thing," you say, but there's an element of uncertainty in your voice. "She probably hid it somewhere else."

"Then where is it?" I whisper, shuffling clouded jars. Panic blooms hot under my skin, and I shove more preserves aside, searching, searching.

"We'll find it," you insist, pawing through a crate of soft apples.

The floorboards groan above us, vocalizing beneath the tread of silent footsteps. You reach for my hand, clutching it tight, and we duck behind a barrel of potatoes, holding our breath.

The door creaks open, and Nanna steps lithely down the stairs, her eyes gleaming yellow-bright as candied citron. Her arms are wound to the shoulder with crusted bandages. A horrible smell wafts off her—yeasted, sour—as she slinks toward us, and I press my face into the crook of my elbow to keep from gagging. Her pale visage looms above the potatoes, smooth and ageless.

"Good morning, girls," she says, and she smiles a terrible smile, her mouth ringed in jammy red. "It's time for cake!"

❄

My Hanukkah Kraken

~ *Devan Barlow*

When maliciousness made other places
too pain-mired to bear
I escaped to this cottage, perched amid
sand and shell-wrack
It belonged to a relative I never got to know,
a woman linked to me by an alchemy of greats and removes

On the first night of what I thought was Hanukkah
—days and nights had become impossible, with all the world
cloud-anger and storm-chaos and indiscernibly-distant shrieks
the sun a thing of only memory—
I removed my relative's mildly-cobwebbed menorah
from the cupboard, placed it on the windowsill facing the shore

I lit the shamash, then one candle more
watched, as water heaved upward
revealing a kraken
five time bigger than the cottage
her mantle the blue of lapis-lazuli

Her tentacles propelled her oh-so-close to the coast
as candleflames reflected in her elegant, enormous, emerald eyes
My kraken stayed until the candles went out
then sunk beneath the sea
as clouds flared and flashed above

I slept when the screams of cloud-victims allowed it
When awake, I sought connection, comprehension

the few ways I could
my relative's journals were within the cottage
written in two languages
the second of which slowly, steadily
began to make sense to me

Second night, third night, fourth night
my kraken joined me for candle-lighting
and my best attempts at prayers

I stared at my relative's photographs
struggled to connect faces to those mentioned in her journal
while distant rumbles and roilings
told me of more places devoured, destroyed
I read of times, places, rituals
I yearned to know more about

Fifth night, sixth night, seventh night
my kraken swam close enough her tentacles extended
to just outside the cottage window
where they swayed, flame-like

There's always been a gulf
between what I know now
and what I fear I should have learned earlier
An ocean of tradition and phrases I
fear I might drown in
so dearly wish to swim

Finally my best attempt at keeping this holiday
reached its eighth and final night
my kraken's eyes encompassed the world
her beak glinted in fireglow
as I contemplated
the sea and its advantages

❄

Krampus Air

~ *L. E. Daniels*

It feels like you've been traveling forever. You're freezing and your hair smells like airplane fuel and canned farts and you no longer have ankles.

Buckled into the aisle seat beside your teenagers, you're on the third of four airplanes from Sydney to Boston, trying to get to New England in time for Christmas Eve with your parents.

Once upon a time, this trip included two planes, a short layover in Vancouver, and a tidy twenty-two-hour flight path, but things went sideways early. After a delay and missed connection, here you are, rerouted to the frozen far-north; someplace in the Yukon called Blood Knife. Max and Gretchen thought it was hilarious at first, but now they're sour as they stare out the windows into the abyss of Christmas Eve, your stained, disheveled reflections staring back at you.

Some thirty-odd hours ago, you entered a holiday hedge maze where Mariah Carey gaslit you through an accordion of terminals and freezing cabins all the way to Blood Knife, an airport so far off your flightpath, you had to find it on Google Maps to believe it was real.

"Yeah . . . apologies, folks," the captain's voice streams overhead. "We're uh . . . holding the flight for one last passenger boarding momentarily . . . we'll uh . . . push off soon."

"Merry Christmas." From her window seat, Gretchen puts her hand out to Max. "Want a Mentos?"

Miserable in the middle seat, he opens his palm and Gretchen drops a crumpled, snotty tissue.

"Filth!" He jerks away as the tissue tumbles. "You're pure filth!"

"Pick it up," you tell Gretchen, who makes a show of unfastening her seatbelt and worming toward the floor in the cramped conditions.

Max shoves his size-elevens toward her.

"Knock it off!" Your breath hangs in the chill and you know you're out of consequences so you pawn off a distraction. "Have some sanitizing wipes. They smell like coconuts and burning. Do your screens, tray tables, armrests."

There's jostling at the front of the airplane and a broad figure enters coach in a long, dark coat, his hair dusky and windblown. A rucksack is perched on his shoulder. He looks like a lumberjack. As he turns down the aisle, the bag obscures his face, but a salt and pepper beard hangs jagged to his chest. Footfalls thrum and his coat brushes your arm as he passes, dragging colder air behind him. The scent of woodsmoke trails him toward the tail section. Cedar.

"Krampus is onboard," you whisper to your kids, "so you'd better behave." Oma, your maternal grandmother, told you all about him when you were a child and you loved the stories, but Max and Gretchen just roll their eyes.

Cabin doors are sealed and the change in air pressure pinches your eardrums. The plane jerks, then stops.

The kids sit back and the pre-flight safety video shudders in the head rests. It plays kaleidoscopic across the screens of the near-empty plane, reflecting infinitely along the rows of the windows. Instructions crackle through the cabin. Your eyes blur and really, you don't care anymore about losing oxygen. Suicidal ideation is your secret superpower when you're sleep deprived and emotionally plundered by teens in Blood Knife.

You glance into the rows behind you through empty seats and see the big man stowing his bag overhead. Closing the compartment, he looks at you sharply and you shrink back into your seat and face forward.

At last count, there were only about thirty passengers, sad souls like yourself, nowhere near their destinations and probably wondering where their luggage went. According to the app, your bags (and all your wrapped gifts) are still in Sydney. As you shift in your seat, your spine crawls with a spasm that grips your rump. Your knees ache but you're already out of ibuprofen and need something stronger.

You shiver and fantasize about the plane exploding right there on the tarmac. You see the flash and feel the heat. And it feels good, for a second. Then you shame-spiral for such thoughts, especially on Christmas.

You close your eyes. The engines flare and relax and flare again.

Long ago, back in Sydney, you were drunk with optimism. You finished up your teaching job for the year on double-time, then shopped and cooked and wrapped the gifts and put on a Christmas feast for your husband and kids a day early. You didn't even kick up a stink when you decorated the tree by yourself, after asking everyone to join you three times. You put on Mariah Carey and did it yourself because you were excited to take your kids home for a white Christmas with their grandparents.

At the airport, you kissed your Australian husband goodbye and cleared security.

In the terminal and over a hot and hearty breakfast, you said, "As we fly across the world, we get Christmas Eve twice!" With a finger, you traced the flight path over the international date line, past the Midway Atoll in the Pacific, to Vancouver then all the way to Boston.

But—there was a technical problem with the plane and your husband was home by the time the alert pinged. Three more hours were added to the wait, and you knew you'd missed your connection to Boston before you'd even left Australia.

"It's in the lap of the gods now, kids," you told them. "I'm just grateful they're being safe."

After the emergency tutorial, you open your eyes to an advertisement for the airline swirling from a snow globe. Santa is cozy in first class sipping champagne. Plum pudding is served steaming. Sleigh bells jingle.

Christmas is a special time to fly, the voiceover fills the cabin. *We're so glad you're here with us.*

But you're in coach and there's no food unless a Biscoff is the holiday winner.

A headache blooms before Santa bites into a forkful of turkey dripping with gravy so you paw through your bag for some NSAIDs. You find gum, your daughter's Laneige lip balm, tissues, antihistamines, and the kids' Vicks eucalyptus nasal inhalers, and think you must have packed the medication into a checked bag.

You reel back in time, but memory is shaky now, addled by packing fleece in one-hundred-degree heat. Suitcases were gutted on beds. You wrote sticky notes for the kids with bite-size bits of information:

5x underwear, 5x socks, no aerosols
toothbrush, travel-size toothpaste, liquids <50 ml in clear Ziploc
old undies to throw away after big flight

You sorted pills while your son prattled about wanting to shoot guns in New Hampshire while your daughter couldn't "possibly take *this* neck pillow." Unzipping packing cubes, you said, "Please don't talk to me right now."

Now the pain in your head tightens and a swell of nausea breaks. You shiver and press frozen fingers to your forehead and burp up the poutine you shared in Vancouver.

The ad ends. Santa is gone. The screen blinks to the home menu just as Mariah's voice fills the cabin for one more hit. Not again. By now, you know Mariah doesn't really want you for Christmas, but she won't rest until she eats your heart like an apple.

Your dark thoughts are getting darker as you fish into your pocket for your headphones and your children do the same. The kids scroll for movies as you find the oceanic documentary you started on the flight that landed you in the Yukon.

Fish, to lower your blood pressure. Fish, such lovely colors. Fish, so dreamy they might cast you off into a ten-minute nap.

You fast-forward until you find where you left off: the giant Pacific octopus streams blood-red through a towering kelp forest off California. She unravels and curls against stone, camouflaged by chromatophores that change her color and the papillae that change her shape. And you wonder how handy it would be to take on the shape of the couch when the kids come at you with problems they can solve themselves.

Then the documentary gets emotional. Fast.

The octopus, who's been galivanting about the shoals feeding on crabs and mimicking rocky cobble, is about to become a mother. She sequesters herself into a bedrock gullet and lays a field of eggs to a somber cello score that plucks you to pieces. Teeny octopus eyes form in the field of eggs as she ceaselessly circulates the water around her brood.

A sharp swat on your arm startles you.

"Ew. Mom." Your daughter's voice bleeds through orchestral crescendo. You hit pause. "Why are you even crying over that gross octopus?"

Gretchen leans over Max, her fake French tips like daggers.

You put up a hand before the demented weight of her pasty Edwardian stare.

She snaps her gum and continues, "Never cry on airplanes. You told me that. You get sick. You get me sick. I don't wanna to be sick for the holidays. It's been shitty enough."

"Shut the hell up." Max clenches his fists on his knees. "When is this stupid plane going to get off the ground? This sucks ass. I wish I stayed home with Dad."

Dad said he was working. Your husband had a grin and a large cappuccino when he waved goodbye and went home to watch the cricket.

Max folds into a crash position.

"You wanted to come." You hold one earphone, the mother octopus frozen on the screen.

"Yeah, because Uncle Steve is taking me shooting."

"You're not old enough."

"I'm old enough in New Hampshire."

"No."

"I can get a training certificate in a day!"

"No."

"You're insufferable."

"Suffer me more," you hiss.

The lights dim. Gretchen growls. "This is the worst Christmas ever. These seats are so small. How is this even legal?" She kicks out sharply at Max's leg which has again strayed into her zone.

"OW!" He roars, "I hate this and I hate you! I hate your stupid face! Why are you even wearing makeup at a time like this?"

"I wear makeup especially at times like this." She aims duck-billed lips at him.

"I hate that you're my sister. Mom, you should have stopped at one."

"Oh my God, shut your mouths. Both of you." Your headache anchors now.

"I hope the plane crashes," she says, "and you're the only one who dies."

"I hope the emergency exit blows open," he says, "and sucks your stupid ass right off the plane."

"Yeah, well I hope the automatic toilet flushes and rips your guts right out your fat butthole."

"*Stopitrightnow!*" You hiss like a bog witch and spring, your hands blue chilblained claws. The children sink into their seats.

"As soon as the seatbelt signs are off, you can move seats." You grip your son's arm, "Max, you'll cross the aisle and sleep flat in the empty row beside me."

"I can't wait."

Gretchen puts her hands up. "I'm staying right here next to you, Mom."

"Fine."

You lean back. Think of the fish. Think of the octopus who got one shot to be a mom and she's acing it.

The plane moves with a jerk and the children return to their screens. They droop toward sleep as the plane taxis and you hit play.

The plane accelerates for takeoff as the narrator tells you that the octopus will die. Your eyes fill again, brimming and becoming octopus eyes themselves as you look up at the halo of dim cabin lights through water, as if you yourself are in a tank. At lift off, you sink into your seat. The plane leans. You gently roll your eyes up and down to massage the salt water back into the well that you have become. Your nose burns.

And you let the documentary take you.

The mother octopus fans her clutch of eggs with each pulse of respiration, starving herself to death for her offspring. She loses her vibrant red and grows paler, slower, more limp, and you learn that when her babies hatch, they will eat her.

The kids are fast asleep and plane stays dark. Your daughter wears an eye mask that reads *I should be in first class* while your son scowls, even in his sleep.

Chains rattle from the back of the plane, suggesting an incoming beverage cart. You pull in your elbows but there's nothing there.

You need to stretch so you slip out of your seat and head toward the back of the plane.

The big man stands alone in the kitchenette, unlaced work boots rooted to the floor, despite a spot of turbulence that rocks you sideways. His long, shaggy hair has been smoothed into a manbun and your instinct is not to engage. You reach for the lavatory door.

"Those children," he grunts. "Yours?" His voice so baritone, it cuts through the drone of the engines and penetrates your body. Your cheeks flush and a surge of blood rushes to your pelvis. You don't want to answer him. You don't want look at his mountainous landscape again.

He continues, "They are too big to fit into my sack but I can beat them. If you like." His accent is Germanic and that last bit feels added for a measure of manners. He leans back onto the kitchenette counter, usually off-limits for passengers. His biceps contour the sleeves of his coat. The muscles of his thighs define his woolen trousers. There are miles of him and there's no waxing or manscaping here. His self-care is to become as monstrous as possible. And it works.

To gather your thoughts, you look down at yourself—the grubby yoga pants you've been wearing for days and the poutine gravy stain on your sweatshirt. "What did you say?"

"Your children. I'd be delighted to beat them for you."

You hold it together before this sexy beast who's as insulting as he is total daddy energy.

You say, "They're rude and entitled but they're mine. I'm sorry they disturbed you." You cross your arms, the smell of woodsmoke pluming into your nostrils. Cedar. Just like Oma told you.

"They do not disturb me. No." He frowns and pours himself a coffee—another forbidden act on behalf of a passenger. "I love teenagers."

"So do I," you say, "for the workhouse."

When he belly-laughs, you know. As he doubles over, you see the horns sprouting from the thick locks pulled into his manbun. He gathers himself up and tugs at his beard. With his thick fingertips, he brushes his horns to their full extension into knobby scythes that nearly touch the ceiling. He straightens his coat and leans his elbows on the counter. "Das is gut. Forget the children. I have another proposition for you. Be my new bride."

"I'm already someone's bride and I'm hardly new." You imagine your husband in his underpants on the couch watching the Australia versus India cricket match, a plate of baked beans on toast balanced on one knee.

He yawns like a lion then says, "If you are my bride, you will spout horns and grow stronger and our lovemaking will be extravagant as we shake needles from spruce trees and pound valleys between mountains." He stares at you, expectant, his eyes orange, smoldering coals.

"Oh, that does sound nice. Especially the horns."

"They are . . . " he says, tipping his head, "wunderbar."

"What else?"

"You will never make another Christmas for your family. Never put up another Christmas tree. Never get headaches or carry hand sanitizer or endure obscenity or dismal selfishness."

"I'll never have to Christmas shop again?"

"You will never Christmas shop again."

"Or wrap presents?"

"You will never—"

"I'll never have to listen to the endless stuff my kids want because the internet tells them to buy it from sweatshops and tech giants who enslave five-year-olds to mine cobalt?"

"That's Santa's job."

"And I'll never have to deal with airlines?"

"Ah, you have got me there." His shoulders slump. "That's the stinker."

"It's a deal breaker, ja." Oma told you that Krampus loves a chat and a flirt and once, he came onto her in upstate New York when your mother was still a screeching toddler. And she said, *Should you meet him, make him laugh, endure his propositions, and take his goddamn coat.*

"Well, the answer is no." You soften your tone and say tenderly, "Nein, mien Schatz. Nein."

"Seriously? How do you say no to such treasure then?"

"I say no to treasure every day. That's what mothers do." You reach for his great lapels, stand on your tiptoes and lean into him.

You touch your forehead to his. "Danke," you say. "I mean it. Danke schön for asking me. And for the balance you bring to this madness."

You kiss the surprise in his smile until he grips you by the hips and pulls you into his vastness where you find a cosmos of everything old and haunted and craggy and it feels like shingled cabins and roast beef and dark beer while his beard scratches over your cheeks with a scattering of sparks.

You slip your fingers over his shoulders, roll the fabric back, and tug the coat from his arms. It drops away. By the time he starts to fight for it, you're slipping on the coat and he's hornless and shrinking into the tiny old man he truly is.

Gently, you lead him away from the light of the kitchenette back into the dark cabin, right into his seat where he's grown sleepy and placid. You get him a pillow, buckle him in, and cover him with a blanket.

When you step back, you open his overhead compartment and search his rucksack—just in case. But there's only another coat. You click the compartment closed.

When you return to your seat, you're not freezing anymore. Your son is sprawled across three seats in the row across from you. Your daughter is awake and accusatory. "Ew, Mom. Where'd you get that coat?"

"It's mine," you say. "Get some sleep. We'll be there soon enough."

Luminarias

~ *Chris J. Karr*

Nothing beats a holiday treat tasting of Santa Fe wine and tamales, Christmas-style with both the red and green chile sauces. It's a decadent far cry from the skinny deer and stringy coyote my family and I had been subsisting on during our meager holiday celebrations years and decades past.

I waylaid the drunk young man leaving a holiday party after the sun had made an early colorful exit, and it could no longer scald me among the sage bushes, cacti, and yucca plants that dotted the foothills of the Sangre de Cristo mountains in what the day folk called northern New Mexico. As the tipsy youth fumbled with a glowing slab in the fresh darkness, I snuck up behind him and clubbed him unconscious with a decorative rock I found lining a nearby artificial garden.

Until recently, an old Hispanic man tended to this land, but he must have passed on, as this area had been transformed into an uncanny simulation of the surrounding landscape, with new homes sprinkled about that that resembled the adobe abodes that have been popular in this area for centuries, but smelt of new wood imported from faraway lands and strange substances that allowed the day folk to construct this "subdivision" in a fraction of the time that Tewa people built their villages, before the constant brightness and burning of the past few decades.

As my prey sprawled before me, a soft moan escaped his lips. I glanced around me to see if anyone witnessed my stealthy bludgeoning, and I saw that I remained undetected. I dragged him to a dark space between two of the fraudulent mud huts and exposed the artery on the side of his neck. I ran my tongue over the sharp tips of my teeth, opened my mouth, and buried my canines into the pulsating line travelling beneath his ear, and drank greedily. I tasted a delightful tartness from wine he drank to excess, as well as hints of a sharp young spiciness—this must have been the green chile—mixed with a more mature and almost smoky heat—this must be the red. I also caught a hint of fresh honey—my victim had been no stranger to the sopapilla platter.

He was delicious, but I tempered my gluttony and stopped indulging before I drained him completely. The oncoming cold night and his own drunkenness would suggest to those who found him that he passed on after passing out in the cold December elevated desert night. Excited about what I had found, I began the long journey back into the wilderness among the mountains where my family waited for me.

Among the superstitious folk who have lived in this area for hundreds of years, my tribe has been mistaken for the shape-shifting tlahuelpuchi, vampiric witches that hid among the people who migrated to this area millennia ago. When the Spanish arrived with their horses and guns and European beliefs, we were called revenants, vampires, and nosferatu. When the day folk began looking to the skies and stars, and asking who else might be out there, they began calling our handiwork the product of aliens or Little Green Men, despite our clear terrestrial ancestry.

These days, the day folk—those who aren't so preoccupied by fitting us within one mythic tradition or another—call us "chupacabra", which apparently means "goat sucker" in one of their languages, after a careless group of our distant cousins were observed raiding a livestock herd when they should have been a bit more cautious. And to be fair to the day folk mistaking us for visitors beyond the stars, we do have some wily cousins in the north who have leaned into their latest "identity" by creatively mutilating their prey after they finish draining them of their blood.

If you ask seven day folk what we look like, you will receive seven very different answers. We avoid leaving our burrows when the Sun scalds the area with its light, and are generally repulsed by the artificial light that the day folk started drenching their towns and cities in at night, even when the full moon provides more than enough light for even them to see. When we look at ourselves, we see brothers and sisters, mates and offspring with longer faces than the day folk, structurally similar to the coyotes we sometimes consume, but bald without the hair and fur. Unlike the leathery skin of deer or cattle, ours has a more reptilian appearance, covered in scales like the snakes and lizards we occasionally catch and snack on.

Well-travelled witnesses who have caught a glimpse of us have compared us to the ghouls who haunt the old necropoles beneath the ground, forgotten before the day folk crawled out of their ancestral crib and blanketed the world. We have stories of encounters long ago between the ghoul tribes and our own. Where they feast on the rotting corpses of the departed, we sustain ourselves on the blood of the living, and are sickened by the thickening blood of the dead. And while we may both look similar to the day folk and thrive in the night, that's where our similarities end.

Our own legends tell us that we have always lived in these lands, even before the tribes of men crossed over into our world over the Beringia land bridge in the far northwest. We were content to keep to ourselves and give our new neighbors a wide berth, but as the day folk thinned the ranks of our own prey, conflict became inevitable. We began preying upon them in the night, and in return, they retaliated during the day, tearing open our burrows and warrens, and burning us alive with the scalding rays of the sun. The conflict escalated as we wiped out the Olmec tribes in the south, and their remnants and neighbors retaliated in turn. After decades of constant war, we were reduced to a beggar race, pursued into the forests, and subsisted on the wildlife that the day folk had not hunted to extinction or domesticated.

An uneasy truce held as they congregated to their villages and settlements, lighting small bonfires to repel us at night, and we retreated deeper into the forests and wild areas. As new daylight civilizations emerged, my ancestors migrated northward until they discovered a great river and followed it north into the drier mountains and canyons where its tributaries mingled and merged. They encountered a number of day folk on their northern exodus, but they were much smaller and more dispersed than the swelling agricultural nations in the south. Until the arrival of the Spanish, we gave wide berth to the Mogollon and Pueblo villages we encountered and they left us undisturbed in return.

As the sky began turning a purple that preceded the red of dawn, I arrived at a cluster of cactus plants that an older matriarch had transplanted and nurtured to disguise entrance to our family barrow, and to discourage any day folk from investigating too closely. I gingerly pulled a waxy pad toward me, which provided enough of an aperture for me to slip into without impaling myself on any of the spines. Chupacabra have tough hides, but there are still some cacti that are tougher. Slinking into the tunnel quietly, I could smell the results of my family's nocturnal hunt. I caught the scent of rabbit and deer, but no elk. Those were rare. One of the older adolescents smelt of cattle. We would have to have another lesson about the dangers of feeding on livestock and enraging the ranchers who tended them.

But that could wait until tomorrow after the sun set. Weary from my extended excursion, I curled up in my corner, and slept while the hot sun baked the winter ground above us.

A small snout prodding me in the ribs roused me from my dreamless slumber.

"Shakl, Shakl—you smell funny. What did you find?"

One of burrow's younger pups was interrogating me.

"Go gather your litter and sire and bring them here, and I'll tell you," I groggily replied.

He scampered down a tunnel in the warren. Before I knew it, I was surrounded by most of the pups, their sires, and a few grandsires. I recounted my night before.

"Do you remember where the old man outside of Santa Fe used to live and graze his herd of sheep?"

"The drunk one who always smells of tequila and mescal?" a sire asked.

"No, the one that smelt of burnt tobacco and corn."

Those gathered nodded in recognition.

"Well, he's no longer there and his land and sheep are gone. It's been replaced with something called an 'eco-friendly subdivision' and a large village now sits where his herd roamed."

"How can that be? We scouted that location two winters ago—he was still there, even though his herd had shrunk to be less than a handful."

The older pup who had been on scouting duty at the time held up his four-fingered hand. I continued.

"I don't know, but there are now enough dwellings there for a couple hundred day folk. I tried counting them, but their loopy and windy streets and the dwellings' identical appearances made it hard to keep track. They are not yet all occupied, probably more than half are."

An older sire inquired, "How did you get close enough to count? Do they dwell in the darkness?"

"That's *el milagro*," I explained, borrowing the word for *miracle* that I had learned from eavesdropping on Spanish-speaking campers out in the woods. The village is fully illuminated, but the light doesn't burn like the sun or the lamps in Santa Fe, it just tingles. Once I got used to the feeling, I could roam throughout unimpeded."

Murmurs of awe rippled through my audience.

"Why do you smell funny?" I looked down at the young inquisitor who woke me and now demanded an answer.

"I lingered close enough to one of the occupied homes to hear a large crowd gathered within. It sounded like they were celebrating their Christmas holiday early, and the new patriarch of the home invited members of other tribes to celebrate with food, drink, music, and gifts. I lurked in the darkness beneath a window listening, until one of the older male pups decided to leave early and I took him when no one was looking."

One of the den mothers pointed her snout in my direction and took a big sniff. "I can smell wine and honey emanating from you, but what is that spicy smoky flavor? It reminds me of corn and carnitas."

Recalling a conversation that I heard between the day folk patriarch's wife and her friend, I provided an educated guess.

"I believe they call them tamales."

As you listen to my story and begin to suspect that chupacabras are a surprisingly literate and articulate race, you would be partially correct. Before the invasion of the day folk across Beringia, we had our own cities and civilizations. We never adopted writing or scrolls or books, but we had a very rich oral tradition by which we passed on our histories, crafts, and songs. Unfortunately, we were ill-prepared for the arrival of the day folk, and we were driven from our villages and cities when the sun was high and we were defenseless. The tall hominids often built their own cities on the ruins of our own, and some even learned our crafts and sciences from our repositories before torching them. Bereft of our larger communities, our population dwindled and our culture was lost as we had fewer and fewer storytellers to pass our traditions on to the next litters.

Our own burrow is a happy accident of history. Our grand-grand-grand-sires roamed northward of the desert plains into the foothills and mesas and established a warren among the base of a mesa in an isolated area a half-day's journey from the Pojoaque Pueblo situated near the big river to the east. They were far enough away that they didn't encounter members of that village and our grand-grand-grand-sires began building their new warren there.

Shortly after the burrow was established and had produced its first litter of pups, a male member of the white day folk tribe began building a school on the mesa above us, where he would bring in a mixed litter of weak and sickly male day folk pups and the patriarch of the "ranch school" would instruct them in their own outdoor ways. This was always a small group—no more than fifty or sixty around at the time—and our ancestors were able to avoid them easily.

As the founders of our mesa warren began sharing the responsibility of leadership with the new generation of patriarchs and matriarchs, the quiet community above them transformed into a bustling small town of mathematicians and engineers from around the world working on a secret project to end a faraway war. Day folk with guns and metal helmets began patrolling further and further out, intercepting, interrogating, and imprisoning anyone who wandered too close to their village.

Grand-sires who avoided the patrols at night and snuck into the village recall witnessing strange rituals with exotic metals that would produce an unusual warmth and a rare blue flash that would poison and kill day folk the same way the sun killed us. Villagers there were frenetic and energetic, speaking many different languages, as alien to the sleepy Pojoaque village to the east as we were alien to them.

A moderate calm returned after several years, and apparently the white day folk vanquished their faraway enemies. But rather than return to where they came from, many remained and the small village atop the mesa grew significantly in the years to come. As more day folk settled atop and between the mesa and its neighbors, the mesa warren was abandoned as the day folk built roads and buildings uncomfortably close to the burrow. In addition to the buildings and roads slicing through the wilderness, our grand-sires also discovered large metal fences and barriers erected throughout the area. Given that we are natural diggers, these presented no serious obstacle to us and we discovered one large enclosed area with ample wildlife that the day folk shunned.

In my final test to become a scout for the pack—now situated some distance away—over several nights, I journeyed to that ancestral area and discovered a sign with a warning.

NO TRESSPASSING
BY ORDER OF THE UNITED STATES
DEPARTMENT OF ENERGY
RADIATION HAZARD
MATERIAL DISPOSAL AREA C
TECHNICAL AREA 50
LOS ALAMOS NATIONAL LABORATORY

I dug beneath the fence and entered the area and explored the valleys and felt the unnatural warmth emanating from beneath the soil there. I discovered the old burrow there and returned home with a warm rock from that place as proof that I passed my test.

To hear the grand-sires and grand-dams tell the story, the day folk on the mesa would transport clothing, equipment, and soil to the valley where the chupacabras hunted at night and buried what they brought in pits pocked throughout the valley, and leave as quickly as possible, closing the metal fence that surrounded the area. Without humans and other large predators, the local deer and reptiles flourished, serving as our own private hunting preserve.

While they dwelled in warm valley, the sires discovered that their memory and reflexes were improving, and the next litter of pups birthed there—including my own sire—had an unquenchable thirst for learning and knowledge. One pup scavenging through a delivery made the day before discovered a cache of schoolbooks, and used those to learn to interpret and read the signs and symbols that had perplexed us for centuries. I don't know if we are the only literate tribe of chupacabras, but reading is now a basic skill that must be mastered before one can rise to a position of authority in our pack.

"But what about the *luminarias*?" one of the sires inquired.

"That's the best part," I replied. "All of the dwellings *have* luminarias situated along the paths—even the unoccupied ones—but *they don't burn.*"

My assembled audience gasped. I continued.

"I was just as surprised as you. I took one and opened it. Instead of a fire within, each contained a small device that makes light, but the only the tingly kind. Each has a small dial on it that I could rotate to turn the light on or off. I think that they use that to light them up when the sun goes down."

"That sounds like an LED." I looked and spied a youth who had a reputation for spending too much time with day folk books and other printed detritus. He continued. "It's a new kind of light that only emits specific frequencies, unlike the sun or fires or older electric lights, which emit a wider uncontrolled spectrum, including those that burn us."

"Why would they give up their best defense against us?" an older sire asked incredulously.

"They don't believe that we exist anymore. Just as we've lost many of our old stories or replaced them with new ones, they have forgotten—or refuse to remember—that we are still here. When we are careless and they discover those whom we have fed upon, they blame beings beyond the stars or people like them that drink blood and turn into bats."

This last sentence made the younger pups giggle. The youth continued.

"Those that *do* remember us and *do* take us seriously are cast out of their packs or treated like malicious tricksters. They go through the motions of setting up their luminarias, but have forgotten *why* they do so in the first place."

The youth was making a subtle, but very important point. I could imagine him leading this pack someday.

Day folk currently install luminarias as an aesthetic or religious symbol. They find the small brown bags, weigh them with sand, and light a candle within to become an attractive decoration for their holiday season, and even justify the decoration as a luminous invitation into their homes for their seasonal child god.

Their beliefs are entirely nonsense.

Luminarias existed long before their Baby Jesus, and were invented by the old tribes who came into our world with fire. When a fresh new source of prey poured through Beringia into the Americas, chupacabras quickly drained those tribes who lacked a proficiency in harnessing fire to protect themselves at night. Those that did master the bright art learned to set up small bonfires around their encampments in the dark season to keep my ancestors away. We preyed on those who could not defend themselves with flame, such as during the unusually wet period with little dry fuel for fires that enabled my ancestors to wipe out the Olmec warriors before we were driven north into the mountains.

When the Spanish arrived from across the seas in their boats, they also proved to be easy prey until they learned from those that they subjugated to set up bonfires to protect themselves as well. However, the Spanish religion had no room for beings like us in their mythology, so we were cast as demons or largely forgotten, and the priests justified installing their protective wards as an invitation for their holy infant, and not as a barrier to keep us away from their throbbing necks when they slept.

When our numbers swelled, luminarias were deployed throughout the year, but as our tribes dwindled, our encounters with the day folk decreased and they no longer needed luminarias to protect them throughout the rest of the year. However, we still do hold The Longest Night holy, as it marks the point in the year where we are most free to roam in the darkness, and it also marks the time when we should be consuming more for our hibernation through the Season of the Shortest Nights. It is only a coincidence that ours and the day folk's high holidays are only a few nights apart.

The Longest Night began this year on the evening of a day called Saturday, when day folk are a bit more relaxed and willing to stay out later. Our pack crouched in a ditch to shield us from the scalding light emanating from the vehicles entering their new village. We sent a number of scouts into the area as the sun set to do a final count of potential feasts. We had no shortage of volunteers willing to explore a lighted area for the first time without being painfully scalded.

The head scout reported to us.

"We're all back. We counted one hundred and two dwellings and it seemed like sixty-seven of those were occupied. We found eight that were inviting guests in with music and food."

After smelling me after I snacked on the young man, my pack was eager to sip on the blood of those who had been drinking copious amounts of wine and eating tamales and honey-soaked sopapillas.

"And how many are with us?" I inquired.

Word of my discovery spread quickly beyond our pack and neighboring packs spent the past several nights loping across the dry countryside to join us for our own holiday party.

"Our cousins from around Taos showed up first and brought that new pack with them from Española. I've heard that the Las Vegas cousins are around here somewhere, as well as a couple packs from the western reservations. We even had a few straggle in from the northeastern plains. Between them and the Bernalillo packs, we're looking at a little over three hundred of us."

Good. I had worried that we might have too many chupacabras show up or there would be too few humans to feast upon. However, given the number of occupied units, as well as the constant influx of vehicles clogging the streets where the parties were being held, it looked like there would be plenty to go around.

I dismissed the scout with orders to round up any wayward packs and to verify that everyone was in position. Since this was my discovery, my pack moved behind a dark unoccupied dwelling next to the largest and most boisterous holiday party. A few minutes later, I heard a sharp bark, which was the signal from the scout that everyone was in position, and the gates on the roads leading into the new exclusive community had been closed by a gang of adolescent pups to any more incoming traffic.

The music in the dwelling next us went silent. I almost panicked. Had we been discovered? I dreaded that I had led us into an elaborate trap.

Those fears were proven baseless when the music resumed.
Feliz Navidad!
Feliz Navidad!
Feliz Navidad!
Próspero año y felicidad!
That was our signal. I barked twice loudly into the night and heard eager howls around me answer in return. I grabbed a rock from the decorative garden and threw it as hard as I could into the large window displaying a plastic tree tangled in a string of lights and glass baubles. The window collapsed into the house and this was met with shouts and screams. I leaped through window and zeroed in on a portly man holding an empty plate smeared with red and green sauce. He stared at me with wide eyes, his brain clearly unable to process what he saw before him. Before he could recover his mental bearings, I lunged at him and sank my teeth into his throat. Ah, *tamales!* And some wine, but something new with a sour citrus flavor mingled with tequila.

I looked around and saw the rest of my pack enjoying themselves, especially the pups who discovered the children who had been gorging themselves on chocolate, sugar cookies, and candy canes. After I finished my meal, I went back to the shattered window.

I witnessed some distance away a small pack of adolescents who had come in from the western desert playfully pursuing a terrified couple down the main avenue that the dwellings faced. For some reason, members of that tribe liked their meals gamey, tangy with stress hormones. I didn't understand quite why, but made a mental note to remind our pups to not play with their meals, lest they pick up some bad habits. I kept an eye on the small gang until they bored of their pursuit and lunged as one at the couple, finally silencing their screams.

Before I returned to this party to see if I could find a second helping, I listened for a moment. I heard the screams of day folk terror and the triumphant howls of my sated brothers, sisters, sires, and cousins. This was going to be the holiday party that echoed in our stories long after I passed.

After a little over an hour, I heard four sharp barks from one of our rotating sentries signaling that the day folk were close to breaching the closed gates and flooding this hastily erected artificial village. Red and blue lights pulsated and reflected off the artificial huts and a wail of a mechanical siren informed us that we were about to overstay our welcome. I howled loudly into the night, signaling to any chupacabra within earshot that it was time to leave and seek shelter in the forests on the hills overlooking us.

As we loped up the path of a dry arroyo that led back to expanded temporary warren that we had thrown together for our guests, I caught the familiar scent of red chile from the blood-caked snout of a Taos cousin beside me. I looked at her and she smiled. I winked and nodded back knowingly.

"Tamales."

White Elephant

~ *Sydney Sylvester*

'Twas the handwritten letter
That convinced her to come.
So heartfelt and warm,
And so unlike her Mum.

Emma liked having boundaries,
And this one was clear-cut.
For the house she'd called "home"
Had felt anything but.

More than a decade had passed,
Since she'd agreed to appear,
No visits on holidays,
No feigned Christmas cheer.

But the letter that came,
Left Emma intrigued.
Has their misery faded?
Finally left them fatigued?

Please join us this Christmas,
We know we've done wrong.
We just want you to know,
That with us, you belong.

Emma booked the next flight,
Through a budget airline

And found a bar at the airport,
To soothe her nerves with some wine.

And please bring one gift,
It might sound a bit strange,
But we're hoping to do,
A midnight present exchange.

She arrived at their door,
Her mouth dry and throat tight.
"It's just 24 hours,
I can handle one night."

She walked into the house,
Felt a shift in the air.
A welcoming ambiance,
And no sense of despair.

Mum sobbed with delight,
Dad, uncharacteristically beaming.
Her brother claiming he'd missed her?
Emma swore she was dreaming.

The stress she remembered,
Was nowhere in sight.
Each one was dressed up,
Their moods exceptionally bright.

Emma found herself smiling,
Her eyes welling with tears.
She looked at her family,
Their warmth quelling her fears.

Perhaps she was wrong?
She'd judged them too much?
She felt suddenly bad
For never keeping in touch.

Her brother then spoke,
"Sister, please take a seat.
There's somebody here,
That I'd love you to meet."

Then a woman emerged,
Floating in like a gale.
Hair long and eyes dark,
And skin unnaturally pale.

"This is Priscilla,
We're engaged to be wed."
The woman's unblinking smile
Resembled that of the dead.

Emma surveyed her surroundings,
Reconsidering the scene.
The mood now seemed off.
And the house, too pristine.

She looked at her kin closely.
Was it the trick of the light?
Unsettled, she thought that
Their skin didn't fit right.

Smiles strained over skulls,
Beads of sweat starting to sprout,
A deep feeling of dread
Now eclipsed Emma's doubt.

"It's time to exchange,"
Priscilla suddenly said.
And into the dining room,
Emma's family was led.

There were five gifts in total,
One for each guest.
They each picked a number
At Priscilla's request.

And so the order determined,
That Priscilla choose first.
"Hopefully I get to pick,
Whichever one's not the worst!"

Emma suddenly felt
Her limbs stiffen like stone.
Spellbound to her chair,
Her own prison-like throne.

In her peripheral vision,
Using all of her will,
Saw that, like her, the whole family,
Was sitting forcibly still.

"A candle? Thanks Emma!"
Said Priscilla with glee.
"Alright, who goes next?
No one else? Ok, me!"

The next "gift" was a poem,
Handwritten in red.
Priscilla rose to her feet,
Looked at Emma and said:

"Like a log that was felled,
You're run rampant with rot.
Your flagellation, a fungus.
Your self-blame, a blood clot."

The rest of the presents,
Grew ever more strange.
"We did good this year,
There's a hell of a range."

A dead baby bird,
A clown mask, a toe,
A strand of used dental floss
The skin from an elbow.

Emma let out a whimper,
Still stuck in her seat.
She looked up at Priscilla,
Admitting defeat.

Priscilla then hissed,
"Your family's really exquisite.
It's a shame you forsake them,
Never coming to visit."

Using one boney finger
The woman stroked Emma's jaw.
"But now we are family,
Beloved sister-in-law."

Dag It, You Fungi from Yuggoth!

~ Edward St. Boniface

From official intelligence file on Suspect Brown for the Federal Undercover Criminal Knowledge & Espionage Review Service [acronym inadmissible]. Security designation: Strictly Director's Eyes Only.

Following transcript is from a recording gleaned under auspices of the surveillance programme dedicated to tracking and ultimately apprehending the malefactor known as Suspect Brown, a designated subversive, career criminal and urban terrorist. A variety of likely locations across America have been identified as likely haunts of this individual. One of these is the popular Cosmic Necropolis Hotel and Conference Centre and Cryptic Casino situated in Arkham, Massachusetts.

Arkham is well-known for its occultary and Delphic and variously unusual societies and their extensive contacts with other such groups across America. Its academic community works hard to attract audiences for their often obscure causes. Miskatonic University is a major shareholder in the conference centre, and part-sponsors many of the gatherings held there along with a number of associated foundations and charitable organisations.

Suspect Brown's frequent mentioning of and clear familiarity with the Cosmic Necropolis Hotel Arkham and particularly its 'Cryptic Casino' excited suspicion in our surveillance operations as detailed. Eventually the operation was due to be wound up. However, at that moment Suspect Brown himself literally came into the picture, albeit heavily disguised. He was using a previously unknown alias and engaging in activity never profile-anticipated for him.

No less than as a 'warm-up' or preceding act for Sammy Davis Junior himself at a rare Christmas Eve gig, one of the most famous comedians currently working in the United States entertainment and film industry today. Arkham has also become seen as a necessary stop for aspiring and established talent alike on the domestic comedy performance circuit. Artist's niche-space abutting the main stage area was thought to be an excellent venue for overhearing potentially subversive and/or revealing statements.

So it proved.

BEGIN TRANSCRIPT:

COSMIC NECROPOLIS HOTEL AUDITORIUM MASTER OF CEREMONIES (*'Mad Glen Alhazred', audio background)*: "Ladies and Gentlemen and all other nefarious elder cosmic life-forms! Especially our sub-mariner and extradimensional contingent here in fearsome strength tonight! Welcome on this Christmas Eve to a very special show at the world famous Lounge of Death here in The Cosmic Necropolis Hotel, most grotesquely famous hotel in this world and the next! Welcome to and in the name of the Great Old Ones, our owners and patrons whom most of you here tonight know and worship well! I heard our chef has been experimenting with new poisons, especially in the rubber chicken, so some of you may be on your way to that great cosmic chaos already…"

(Enthusiastic laughter and good-natured catcalling and marine bur-bling sounds mixed with electronic static and hissing from assorted presumed nonhuman members of the numerous audience.)

S'B'B *(audio foreground)*: "Thanks for getting me this gig, Mr Davis."

SDjr *(audio foreground)*: "Sammy my dear, Sammy. Normally I would never do this for someone unseasoned in the business. Particularly for a gig on Christmas Eve, a chancy thing in itself. This is a lesser known but important venue to get the word circulating about your act. Which is decidedly untried in my opinion. Especially for this kind of unforgiving fundamentalist cosmic crowd. You did provide me with a considerable and unusual incentive, however."

S'B'B : "Remember what I said, strictly one at a time over six week intervals. That's the only viable regimen for Rangoon Swoon opium or you'll space out forever. Even more than some of that crazy audience out there."

SDjr: "Yes. *Drug Etiquette*, I believe you called it."

S'B'B : "The Chinese have a specific Tau sign describing good manners for getting stoned and whatnot. It looks like a spider that crawled into an opium pipe and saw tarantula heaven."

SDjr: "… Ug? …"

CNHAMoC *(audio background addressing a member of the audience, then whole audience)*: "… Very funny, young man. You do all know that a bad audience goes straight to the divine food cupboard in R'lyeh, don'tcha? I'm your grim reaper host for tonight and boy, do we have a harvest of dead souls doing live acts for you in the lead-up to the midnight hour. One no-hoper deadhead in particular comes to mind. All in the name of He Who Must Not Be Named. Just a little later of course we will have a big name indeed though; that incomparable, internationally and indeed supernaturally funny-guy *Sammy Davis Junior!*"

(Wild applause and pounding of tables from audience and renewed hissing and burbling and electronic noises.)

S'B'B : "Cain't this creepy gaunt guy jest say my name and let me go on?"

SDjr: "Young man, I have to ask you this. Just why are you wearing all those limp rubber tentacles and plastic accessories and a beanie cap with a propeller on top? Even Ed Sullivan wouldn't let that getup pass."

S'B'B *(with dismay)*: "You don't think the outfit's funny?"

SDjr *(sighing)*: "It is, but in the wrong way."

S'B'B : "Half the audience out there are from the Great Beyond or wherever. This should be right up their forbidden zones."

SDjr: "I will not comment on the attendant extradimensional irony."

S'B'B : ". . . Ug? . . ."

CNHAMoC *(audio background addressing member of audience)*: ". . . Young man over there, unchaperoned in the prep school jacket; you have the makings of a comedian yourself. If you survive the night and Santa and Cthulhu's displeasure. Sammy's going to be regaling all of us shortly with some of his recent popular hits too . . ."

SDjr: "Take some advice from an old and ever so slightly bruised hand, my young ambitious sort-of funny friend. Either the audience, whatever their species digs you, or they do not. My term for trying too hard in this respect and irritating said audience is *'Dag'*, as in *'Dagnab-It'*. In short, you want them to Dig you. You do not want them to Dag you; baby."

S'B'B : "So, uh, how do I get them to dig me?"

SDjr: "Good jokes and well-timed delivery and a sympathetically wry personality they emphatically do dig. Weird and freaky outfits are more in '*Dag It, Let's Git The Heck Outta This Unholy Fruit Joint*' territory, believe you me."

S'B'B *(audio foreground, sighing)*: ". . . Bit late now. Gotta go with what I got. By the way, who are all those guys out there who look like stupefied fish? And those oversized zucchinis with the freakout tenebrous wings draped over the tables. That's a kind of Space Beatnik audience I generally haven't seen before outside Greenwich Village."

SDjr: "I believe the aquatic lot are colloquially dubbed the 'Innsmouth Community' hereabouts. The other ones are some gentlemen, or rather things, known as the Fungi from Yuggoth. It's some local extraterrestrial ethnicity. Quite apart from all the other usual aliens. Oddballs certainly even by that standard; but you see stranger specimens at most of the more rural Midwestern gigs. My advice would be to stick to that sheet of *Necronomicon* one-liners I gave you."

CNHAMoC *(audio background, impatiently)*: ". . .You still skulking back there, Mr. Unpronounceable? Get on out here because we haven't got all night . . ."

(Derisive laughter and unflattering comments from a restive audience directed at Suspect Brown as he audibly comes onstage.)

SDjr: "Lord forgive me. The cruelly intentional things I will do for rare and unobtainable transcendental opium derivatives."

(Master of Ceremonies 'Mad Glen Alhazred' joins Sammy Davis Junior in the backstage alcove.)

CNHAMoC: "Mr Davis, I have a very bad feeling about this. Why were you so insistent we put this guy on before you?"

SDjr: "My strange colleague out there suffers from epic delusions of adequacy, my young friend. At least as far as professional comic delivery is concerned."

(Sudden jeering from audience at Suspect Brown.)

CNHAMoC: "Aw geez, he's actually twirling the propeller on his beanie. Where does this idiot think he is, *The Little Rascals*?"

SDjr: "More like *The Three Stooges Meet The Ultimate Gods Of The Cosmic Abyss*, my dear boy. Generally speaking Glen, the worst warm-up act generally favours the next entertainer. If all goes well it leaves the field fertile ground for him. But in this instance I think I may have salted my own earth."

CNHAMoC: ". . . Ug? . . ."

S'B'B : "Gooooood Christmas Eve evening, ladies and germinals! I'm '*Spawn of Yog-Sothoth Throckmorton*', actually. A cosmic gangster come to Earth to fight the mutants and do-gooder religious crazies. Hokay: here goes before I lose my already frazzled nerves. Mary Poppins walks into a bar and says *(Suspect Brown imitating the accent and delivery of actress Julie Andrews)*, 'Good day, my respectable publican. I am chasing some errant and naughty children under my supervision. Have you seen any of my young charges?' and the bartender raps back, 'Baby, as long as you look more or less eighteen, everybody knows the going rates around here . . . .' Yuk, Yuk, Yuk! Geddit? . . ."

(Dead silence from audience.)

YOUNG ADULT MALE HECKLER VOICE: "Hey guy, a lot of us are parents here, you know!"

S'B'B : "Right. Cosmic conservative crowd. All due respect to the wigged-out Yig multitude. Anyway; on with the act. Penguin walks into a bar and says to the bartender, 'Sorry to bother you, but I've lost my brother. Could you tell me if he's been in here?' And the bartender says…"

ADOLESCENT HECKLER VOICE: "…The bartender says, *'Okay, what's he look like?'* Get yourself some new material, old timer. That one's a fossil older than all the weirdo jewellery stuff in the museum at Newburyport!"

(Derisive laughter with pronounced hissing and burbling and electronic noises.)

S'B'B: "Watch it kid, or somebody might melt you down into a pet rock."

AHV: "Sedimentary, metamorphic or igneous?"

S'B'B : "Dagon-ammit; I'll bust your little volcanic ash."

(More derisive laughter.)

AHV: "Mollusk dude, you're a simp. Get back in your shell. My Geography teacher tells better jokes. And 'Flat Earth Fromey' is the most boring teach in my prep school. Azathoth has a better delivery."

S'B'B : "They should never have banned caning and flogging and soul-disintegration trauma punishments at American preparatory collegiates. To resume. Uh, reading from the *Necronomicon* sheet, *ph'nglui mglw'nafh Cthulhu R'lyeh wgah'nagl fhtagn* . . . Boffo cilia fantasies for the big tentacular guy. Now a fun occult story for the more well-read esoteric disciples among you . . ."

AHV: "Disciple? You mean like the Great Enemy Hayzoose and Mother Hydra had back in the day? Betcha our honoured creepy guests tonight the Deep Ones of Y'ha-nthlei know all about them . . ."

(Loud hushing sounds from audience, burblings of some unknown oddly-inflected phrase.)

S'B'B : "Yes, but with the proviso that the general standard of education and intelligence in first century Palestine and post-Deluge old Atlantis was undoubtedly higher. Now this next joke involves a little metaphysical existentialism . . ."

AHV: "You don't mean Jean Paul Sartre, do you? Nihilism and phenomenological nausea ain't 'zackly full of laughs, Droopy."

S'B'B : "Zilch the cod philosophy. Y'know kid, Flat Earth Fromey shoulda jest sent you and your entire class straight down a really deep Plutonian plutonium mine . . ."

AHV: "Mister, your lonely brain cell must be lost in the windowless solids with five dimensions or something."

YAMHV: "We don't understand a word you're saying. This is against the Great Old Ones. And where the heck did you get that freaky hat and jacket? You look like something off a bad episode of *The Ed Sullivan Show*. Those plastic proboscides are an insult to Nyarlathotep, apart from anything else."

(Sudden murmuring low chanting from audience that sounds like a repetition of 'Crawling Chaos' then an abrasive and sudden flare of noise as Suspect Brown violently punches his microphone.)

S'B'B (rapidly, in a fury): "Okay; that did it. Now listen to me, you provincial plebeian worshippers of space slobberers from the Great Beyond Abnormo! All of you square-john spacey satanic scabs sit up and take notice. I am the epitome of Far Out. I am the most crazed of Crazy, Man. You want entertainment? You want diversion? You want laughs? Try my natural protuberant proboscidean gimlet stare and *avoid my fearsome glance if you can!*"

(Suspect Brown yells in rage and whips off his mirrored sunglasses in a frenzy. Gasps and exclamations.)

S'B'B (audibly stamping angrily around the stage): "And no, the thing with the eyes is not a trick. I am BETTER than the spawn of Yog-Sothothery-doobedoo I keep hearing mutant stories about here! With a little bit of muscle twitching I can even force them out further to virtual full hemispheres. Hang onto your collective brain cell, you brainless bupkiss-headed bumpkins! *Boooooooooooinggg!*"

(Spontaneous wild laughter and applause and cheering from audience graduating to full standing ovation for Suspect Brown. Simultaneously a lone man is vocally and physically attempting with great difficulty to cross the graduated table rows towards the stage. On his way the man, accredited agent of [acronym inadmissible] makes his way closer while causing a great deal of nuisance. Numerous expressions of surprise and irritation.)

> **YAMHV**: "Wow. Now that really was funny and scary at the same time. Those were the eyes of *The Blob*."
>
> **YAFHV**: "Or The Fungi from Yuggoth. Like the ones over there trying to act casual, but they can't keep their space-wings to themselves. I've met a few of those creepy veggies at special ceremonies. That creep onstage sounded just like them. Now that I think of it, Senator McCarthy on those old HUAC Hearings Collection records. The freaky nasal hissing is the same too. My dad plays those albums all the time in the basement, when he's not radio-talking to the lethal legumes from Planet X."
>
> **AHV**: "Uncanny. What's that dude up there smoking, old tennis shoes?"

(Sounds of growing audience confusion.)

> **(ACRONYM INADMISSIBLE) AGENT**: "Fugitive known as Suspect Brown! I recognise your voice from briefings on wanted urban and domestic terrorist fugitives. I am a federal agent. You will surrender to my custody immediately!"
>
> **S'B'B**: "...Ug?..."

(Laughter and increased noises confusion from audience, sounds of tables and chairs being shoved aside to outrage and complaints.)

SDjr: "Most certainly this performance is not proceeding quite as I originally envisioned, Glen."

CNHAMoC: "And yet another crazy man's turned up out there. Looks like he's trying to get at your friend. I'd better go and get hotel Security."

SDjr: "Cue the dancers and band on your way. I think it's time I try and save this lamentable evening for us and whatever elder extraterrestrial gods remain with us."

(ACRONYM INADMISSIBLE) AGENT: "Clear the way immediately! I'm a badged representative of [acronym inadmissible] with full powers and I believe that man to be a known and wanted felon. Sir and madam, yes, you, will both of you just please get out of my way . . ."

CNHAMoC (audio background, addressing [acronym inadmissible] agent then audience): "Sir, the Cosmic Necropolis Hotel entertainment staff appreciate enthusiasm from our customers, but not to this extent. Please cease and desist or hotel Security will be forced to respond. And now without further ado audience, the man you've really all been waiting for, Sammy Davis Junior!"

(AI)A: "Anyone within reach detain that man. I'll charge you all as accessories if he escapes! Right, if you won't let me up there I'll climb up. Gangway!"

ENTIRE AUDITORIUM AUDIENCE (collectively, auditory background): ". . . UG? . . ."

(Deafening burst of music from auditorium band. Suspect Brown rushes back to the offstage alcove.)

S'B'B : "Sammy, what's the fastest backstage way out?"

SDjr: "Go through the dressing room main corridor behind us, left at the janitor's closet, right at the public telephone and into the adjacent long passage with the red line straight down the middle. It leads directly to a marked fire door. Go through and you'll be in the back service alley that leads to Derleth Street. Go right and you'll be on Bloch Boulevard. We left your car at the corner with Matheson Avenue. Hang a right from there and Miskatonic Drive will take you over the river and straight out of town. I will make my own way back to my private plane at Dunwich aerodrome where you picked me up. I would not advise you waiting there, since I will undoubtedly be questioned at least perfunctorily."

S'B'B : "Thanks. I'll send you more Rangoon Swoon. I hear the neutronium tarantulas of the Planet Nebae calling me from their diamond webs."

SDjr: "And that sounds like my final surreal cue…"

(Sammy Davis Junior audibly comes onstage to immense and sustained applause launching immediately into his hit 'The Candyman', with distinct clear pronunciation adapting the signature phrase to 'The Cthulhu-Man' with audibly-expressed audience appreciation.)

OFFICIAL POSTSCRIPT:

As indicated in the transcript one of our permanently assigned [acronym inadmissible] agents was actually present during the performance of (date classified), not wanting to miss the chance to see Sammy Davis Junior, and attempted to give chase. Suspect Brown eluded him and clearly had time and opportunity to get clear, probably out of Arkham and Massachusetts entirely.

We might also have a look into some of the more dubious and obscure references being repeatedly made by members of the venue audience and Sammy Davis Junior himself. Apparently the Innsmouth Commission formed in 1928 by a secret Act of Congress for the purpose of similar investigations is still

operational. As is the Wilmarth Enquiry on
the subject of these alleged extradimensional extraterrestrials. Their respective
office contact details in Washington are
appended to this report.

On the Ice

~ *Peter Damien*

Lake Copeland is a little spit of a lake north of town. While everyone mostly does their ice fishing setups on one of the bigger lakes further north or east toward Wisconsin, this lake was where my father and I used to go. It's always been good enough for me.

Tom hung around the edges, looking sullen and unhappy, while I got the trailer aligned on the ice and then slid the ice fishing shack off it and onto the spot I'd chosen on the ice. He helped me haul stuff in there, but only when I asked him or handed him stuff. He wasn't even a teen yet, hell he wasn't even ten yet, and already was acting like he was seventeen and too good for all of this. Hell, he wasn't even supposed to be out here, but my ex called up to let me know she was off on a cruise with her new guy, so Tom was mine for the week, even though she knows this is when I go ice fishing.

He especially got a look when I handed him the big thick sleeping bags I had brought. "We're gonna sleep out here?"

"If we don't, then we got to haul the cabin every night," I said. "It's fine. You'll like it."

He probably wouldn't, but I did.

We got the cooler set up, along with the little space heater, the little cookstove, sleeping bags, and the lanterns.

I had brought out a couple strings of battery powered Christmas lights too, and I spent a bit stringing one of them up outside and one of them up inside. I know it wasn't Christmas yet, but Tom was going to be with his mom for Christmas, and I'm not a total asshole, you know? I don't know if he even noticed them.

I even gave him my favorite thing to do. I handed him the big auger I had and said, "Here, why don't you drill the hole in the ice? Right about here."

He did it without complaining. He was a pretty good kid, on the whole, when he wasn't doing the whole sullen-teenager kind of thing.

By the time I had the lights hung and the little space heater turned up just a little bit, he had made solid progress through the ice. In no time, we had the six inch hole. I got our fishing lines, I showed him out to do the line and the bait—he'd been fishing with me before when he was younger, but I guess he was pretty young back then—and then we settled the lines into the hole.

We caught a couple fish that first day. Nothing big. He caught one, and as his line jigged and pulled, as he grabbed it and worked and hauled the fish out, the kid's face lit up and he grinned in pleasure at it, and yeah that made me pretty happy to see. I used to love doing this with my old man, you know? I remember thinking at the time that maybe if he warmed up to it, maybe this would be something we could wind up doing every year.

We slept in the little shack with the space heater turned low. which led to a bit of an argument in the middle of the night when I caught him trying to crank it up. "Good way to melt the ice we're parked on," I said and yeah I admit I snapped at him about it. But it was a big deal. Anyway he seemed to have forgotten about it by the next day.

I don't remember much of that day. We sat around, we fished, I drank some of the many beers I had brought.

"Can I have one?" Tom asked. I remember that.

"You're eight," I said with a grin, but I handed him a beer anyhow.

"I'm nine," he said, without emotion. "My birthday was last week."

"Sorry I couldn't make it," I said, "I had a business thing come up." And it was true, something had come up at the shop, I couldn't just flake out on my guys, right?

"Yeah," he said.

We sat in silence for a while. I drank a beer or two. He sipped once or twice from the one I handed him, and he winced each time like it was biting him.

I adjusted one of the fishing poles. I don't think he so much as glanced at his that whole day, which, what's even the point of being out here if you aren't going to pay attention to the fishing?

"I heard you got in a fight at school," I said.

He shrugged.

"Heard you hit a kid."

"Yeah."

"You know what your mom would say. You shouldn't be hittin' kids."

"He called me a fag," Tom said, glaring at the beer bottle in his hands. "So I hit him."

I didn't say anything for a bit, then finally, "Look, I get that. But you don't go around hitting other kids okay? I'm serious, don't let me find out you've been doing that again, kid." I said, my voice rising. The way he was just sullenly staring at his beer bottle got right under my skin and scraped on every nerve. I guess I shouldn't have but I couldn't help it.

He just sat there for a bit. I thought about saying sorry, you know, but sometimes you've got to be tough as a parent. My dad wouldn't have said sorry to me after all.

Finally he got up and said, "I'm gonna walk around." He grabbed his coat and headed for the door and he was out before I could say anything else.

I don't know how long it was he wandered around out there on the ice, but he came back eventually and settled into his sleeping bag without a word to me, rolled over, and seemed like he went right to sleep. Well, I kept on sitting there for a while not catching any fish and just staring into space.

No, not into space. I was staring at Tom, at his back as he slept. His sides rose and fell as he breathed evenly in his sleep. Out of nowhere I remembered watching him when he was just a baby, not disturbing him but just making sure that he was still breathing. Everything was so new then, so much simpler. Tom was simpler.

Maybe I wasn't great with babies—I wasn't around much, I had to work, and my ex-wife hadn't yet taken off with the new guy yet—but I did my best. But now? The kid's older, and he's his own person, and I don't know what the hell he's thinking anymore.

Maybe it was the beer loosening up my brain. But what I wanted to do more than anything right then was wake him up. *Talk* to him, really *talk* to him, you know?

But the fact is I don't know what I would have said, or even *how* to say whatever it was to him. Beer can only help so much.

I could've told him I loved him. That was true enough, sure, but you didn't go around saying it. My old man never said it to me, and I turned out okay. And anyway, he was asleep.

And so I said nothing at all to him. I crawled into my own sleeping bag, rolled over, went to sleep. I wasted the bait I had just put on the fishing line before pulling it back out. I wasted the can of beer that I didn't finish. I wasted a lot of things.

The next morning, it was like the sun didn't come up when it should have. It's very dark for a long time, this time of year, but all of a sudden it seemed darker for longer. And a fog had rolled in across the ice.

"You can't even see the shore anymore!" Tom had said, looking out the little window in the door. The weather got him more excited than the fishing had.

"We'll probably wait it out a bit before we pack anything up," I remember saying, not because the fog was all *that* bad but because it was a good excuse to sit and fish a while longer. I was such an idiot.

He stared out the window. I fished. I had a couple more beers. I had a lot of beers that weekend I admit, but not that many all at once, and it wasn't anything that I couldn't handle, it wasn't like I was getting smashed or something. Tom's mom, she suggested without exactly saying it that maybe all the beer was why I saw things. It isn't true. I swear it wasn't that much beer.

After a couple hours, Tom stopped staring out the window and opened the front door. He took a step outside, the door rattling shut behind him. Then he stuck his head back in and said, "You got to see this. The fog's getting thicker!"

I grunted and didn't get up or anything, and so he went back outside to watch it some more.

Something bit the line and tugged on it. I leaned forward in my seat, getting the rod in two hands and began working to reel in whatever was on the end of the line.

Tom came back in. "Dad?"

Whatever was on the end of the line was fighting back. It was a big one, I could just tell. You could feel it through the line. I pulled and then reeled whenever there was a moment of slack, then pulled and angled again.

Tom said, "Hey Dad . . . ?"

"Hang on!" I yelled, because couldn't he see I was in the middle of landing a fish?

I worked at it and I was so close, I swear it was so close that if it weren't for all the ice I would have clearly seen the outline of the fish just under the water. And then out of nowhere there was a mighty yank on the line and it snapped and there it went, the one that got away.

"Dad . . ."

"*What*?" I snapped.

"There's people out there on the ice," Tom said.

"Probably just fuckin' snowmobilers or something!" I snapped again, and I threw the fishing rod down in agitation. His mom used to get mad when I swore around him, said it was *one of the ways I set a bad example.*

But he just stood there quiet and still, and finally my temper calmed down a bit, and so I followed him back outside. This time, he didn't rush out. He let me go first.

I looked around. The fog had come in pretty heavily. You could see the mist of it swirling in the air in front of you like oil on water. You couldn't see any of the shorelines, and we weren't all that far in from the townward shoreline. If you looked straight up, the fog was thin and you could see the dark sky, which still didn't have any morning sun coming into it. I didn't notice that then. I should have.

Then I looked out to the west, further across the lake. Out that way, I realized that the fog was so much more dense. It looked like a summer thunderstorm's storm front, a curled wall of cloud rolling hugely across the summer sky, just before the rain and the hail and the lightning start. It looked like that. And it was moving, I realized as I stared at it, you could see it sweeping across the lake toward us.

And just in the front edge of it, there were people.

There were two people, just shadows against the fog. One was a hunched and rounded shape. One was tall and thin, almost pointed.

I stared at them and felt a chill go through me that had nothing to do with the cold air on the icy lake.

I also realized, after a bit, that they were still too far away for how big they appeared. They weren't at all the size of regular people.

All remaining bits of my temper fled instantly, and I just stood there feeling cold and still. I don't know how long I stood that way. All I know is that when I finally snapped into motion, the fog had rolled much closer and the figures had walked much nearer, and it had all happened much faster than I had expected.

"Get back inside," I said to Tom.

"Who are they?" Tom asked.

"I don't know," I said, "But let's get back inside, and let's go right now. Come on."

I turned and put my hand on Tom and all but bodily pushed him back into the little hut. I shut the door behind us. It had a bolt, to keep the door from pulling open if there was wind, but it had no lock or anything like it.

I watched through the window as the figures drew closer. The smaller, more rounded one, it lumbered as it walked. Alongside it the taller one seemed almost to glide gracefully across the ice. The fog rolled just ahead of them, until soon it was about to engulf our shack.

I can't quite say why I went around right then and turned off the lamp and killed the Christmas lights until we were in as much pitch darkness inside as the world was outside. Only that it felt like the necessary thing to do. In pitch darkness I told Tom, "Sit down and don't move. Don't say anything."

"What is it?"

"I don't know," I said, and I really didn't. But somewhere in the process of turning off the lights, I had realized that I was trembling and that I was actually scared shitless. "But just stay put."

I went back to the little window and peered out from one dark space to another.

The fog bank rolled past us, gentle and constant. Everything was so thick outside that if I had walked a few feet away from our fishing hut, I don't think I would have been able to find my way back again.

The creatures—like hell they were people—kept moving forward at what seemed like a slow pace. I realized that they were going to pass just a few feet away from us . . . but that they were going to pass. The line they were walking in would take them right past us and on across the lake (and toward town, I suppose, but I didn't think about that at the time).

I watched and I had practically stopped breathing. I couldn't stop staring.

As they drew alongside us, I could make out details even through the fog. The hunched and round one was still huge, much taller and broader in every way than a man. It wore a grey cloak that was all in tatters which draped down a long sloping back. The hood was huge, but deep within its shadows I could see two eyes glittering, like they were reflecting light that wasn't actually there. A long white beard came out the bottom of the hood, thin and rough, and it went all the way down to the ice where it trailed away between its feet. And its feet, I realized when I saw them moving forward and thudding against the ice. Its feet looked like hooves. I swear to you, they were hooves. The ice shook with every step it took.

Beside it, the tall and spindly creature. Taller than any man, taller than the creature beside it. It wore a pointed crown upon its head and a red cloak draped about thin shoulders, which hung all the way down to the ice. It had a white fringe along it, and that seemed old and dirty. Its hands came out of the cloak and its arms seemed skeletal. In fact when I saw its face, I thought for a second that maybe it was a skeleton, because it seemed like a skull. So very thin with eyes so sunk into their sockets. Its skin was withered and stretched tight across its bones. It moved steadily without any of the thudding heaviness of the other one.

Both of them, I realized, were carrying large sacks. The tall one had it slung over its shoulder. The hunched one had it dragging from one hand—long, long fingers, jaggedy nails—across the ice. Rough brown bags, each of them large enough to hold several people, and each of them seeming to be full. But the creatures pulled them on without any sign they were heavy.

There was also clanking and I realized that coming out of the back edge of the hunched creature's cloak were long chains, dragging on the ice. Some ended in shackles. Some ended in meat hooks. Some were just broken. They dragged across the ice heavily, leaving long scores across the lake the whole way they had come.

They moved heavily past our shack. They did not stop.

"I want to see," Tom whispered.

And then they *did* stop.

They both turned their heads toward our hut. I saw the sunken eye sockets of the tall one, and I saw the glittering points of light deep in the hood of the hunched one. They stared right at the hut. Maybe they stared right through the window at me. All I know is that it felt like everything inside of me was suddenly a vacuum, and I couldn't get a breathe, not enough to say a word.

And then they began, slowly, heavily, to walk toward our fishing hut.

"No," I whispered.

Panic got me moving again. I stared wildly around the hut for anything I could prop against the door, but we hadn't brought anything really. There was an empty plastic cooler that currently held a bunch of empty beer bottles and weighed nothing. There was a small foldable chair. That was it really.

"Fuck," I said. It was still a whisper. I couldn't get air for more.

I shoved Tom, who was standing close to me still hoping to get a look. He went sprawling across the floor. I realized as he fell that the hole we had cut in the ice was closing itself up, and within a moment it was solid ice again. Frost was creeping up the walls of our shack from the ground up, spider-webbing across everything. Tom lay on the floor across from me, staring at me, but thank god he didn't say anything.

I pressed myself against the door. I didn't know what else to do.

I prayed that nothing would happen, that maybe they would look away, lose interest, and keep going how they had been. I didn't care where. They could go into town and have their way with it for all I cared, just *anywhere* but *here.*

I felt a hand press against the door, and I made a whimpering noise and leaned harder against the door.

It didn't matter. The door swung inward as if I hadn't even been there. I stumbled back and nearly fell but I managed to keep my feet.

They filled the doorway. They were huge, so big in every direction. The tall one had a beard as well I saw, white and bushy and down to the middle of its chest, but it was a beard hanging from a sunk and withered face.

They came inside, and that seemed impossible, but it was as if the walls and the ceiling bowed outward and somehow there was room. They loomed incredibly far above me and around me in every direction. The smell that came pouring off them was of fire, of woodsmoke and ashes, of pinecones and fresh wet earth. It filled the space.

The hunched and gnarled one, it was staring at Tom the entire time. They both were.

Then it was like they shared something with each other. The tall one made a small hand gesture toward Tom, and it turned away and bent to leave the shack. It was like it had lost all interest, that was what it felt like.

The huge and hunched and gnarled one, I could see glimpses of its horrible twisted face deep in that hood, a face that didn't seem to move, like it had frozen into a groaning mask ages before, except for those glittering eyes. It began to open its sack. It was still staring at Tom.

Something in me fired off. Parental instinct or animal instinct, I don't know, but it set fire in me.

I shouted "No!" and then I shouted back to Tom, "Run!"

I lunged toward the hunched being. It was so much bigger. What could I hope to do to it?

It didn't matter. The tall one was still there. When I shouted, it turned back around and peered down at me. And when I lunged forward, it reached out a hand with impossibly long and gnarled fingers. It pressed the tip of one finger against my forehead. The skin was wrinkled and very very soft, like you could push through it if you tried.

And when it touched my forehead, it was like a switch flipped. The world went dark, my limbs gave way, and I collapsed to the ice, and I was unconscious.

I dreamt a little, while I was out. I don't remember a lot of it. But I do remember the important part. God, I remember.

My view was sideways, because even in my dream I was boneless and lying on the floor, rough and cold beneath my cheeks. I could see the hunched creature opening the bag it was carrying. I could see a long chain extending out from it, a hook on the end of it, which curled around Tom—who didn't seem able to move, and didn't struggle—and it pulled him toward the bag, the opening of which was huge and mostly black.

I could see inside of it, from where I lay. I remember that perfectly.

It was full of child-sized wooden dolls. Jointed and boneless and blank.

Tom was just passing the entrance of the bag when darkness took me even in my dream, and then there was nothing else.

I woke because someone was shaking me, and I opened my eyes to find that it was Tom, kneeling over me looking worried and shaking me by the shoulder with both hands. He was saying "Dad?" over and over as he did.

I grunted and groaned. Everything hurt. It felt like I had been hit by a truck. The air still smelled powerfully of woodsmoke and pine and wet earth.

I gradually got to my knees, too unsteady for my feet. But still I managed to focus on Tom, and it took my brain a bit longer to fully grasp that he was here, and that went through me like a shock.

I grabbed him by the shoulders, staring right into his face, and said, "Oh my god. Oh my god. How are you here? I thought they took you. I swore they took you. Oh my god . . ."

He pulled out of my grip, which was too tight.

And he said in a level voice, "Nobody took me." And then he added, "Are you okay, Dad?"

"I don't . . ." I trailed off, just staring at him.

Eventually it was the intense smells that got me, and the sharp cold which brought reality all the way back in. Cold will shock anyone back.

"We have to go," I declared. And I got up, took Tom's hand, and without any other thought, I walked out of the fishing shack and began across the lake, to where I had parked the truck and trailer. We walked in silence. Neither of us knew what to say I guess.

We drove back to town. I didn't take the fishing shack with me or anything that was inside of it.

It probably sunk to the bottom of the lake for all I know. But I don't know really.

I never went back. And as I got ready to drive away, I didn't so much as glance back.

But I kept staring at Tom.

Because I swear to you: something was different now.

It's his eyes that are different. They're the same color and every-thing, but now I feel like there's someone behind them watching me through them, like they're windows now rather than eyes.

Only that isn't quite it. There's maybe something different in his posture, in how he carries himself and how he acts. Like he's older now, or more serious? But is he? Because when I brought this up to Tom's mother, she said that how would I know when I was never around.

In quiet moments when we were alone, I tried to talk to Tom about what had happened out there, what we had seen . . . but he won't talk to me about it. He just shrugs and says he doesn't know what happened. There's no emotion to it. No strong emotion even when *I* get upset about it and, yeah, yell at him about it.

I know this:

I can feel an echo of the fear I had in that shack, when those creatures turned and looked at me. I can feel it when Tom turns toward me.

Sometimes when we're alone in a small room or in my truck, I can still smell those things. The woodsmoke, the pine, the wet earth. Not as strong . . . but it's there. I swear it's there.

No one else can smell it.

Eventually, I was stupid enough to try and explain what happened to Tom's mother. She said I drank too much and that I was making excuses for why I was now avoiding our son even more.

I tried to tell my friends, those I trusted, who I thought would believe me, and it became a running joke. The things I had seen. What else had I seen?

And appealing to Tom didn't help. If I asked him about it in front of anyone else, he just shrugged and said he didn't know really, he couldn't remember anything like that he didn't think. No matter how I pressed. Nothing.

Sometimes whether I'm awake or asleep, I vividly see again that hunched and huge creature pulling Tom in with his meat hook chain. I see the gaping maw of the bag. But more than that, I see those child-sized wooden dolls lying limp and lifeless in the bag, I wonder if one of those wooden dolls came back with me.

❄

ToyＣo's Esoteric Order of the Rescue Pups™

~ *Megan Lee Beals*

David knew the fight was lost when he saw the figure on his kitchen table, next to his daughter's bright blue sippy cup. An innocuous hunk of molded plastic in the shape of a cartoon dog, the eyes blobbed on by an uncaring machine, empty and black and seeping toward the corners in a way that suggested it was bubbling up from within.

"How did that get in here?" he murmured to his wife over his daughter's head as he poured her a second cup of coffee.

"It was in a bag of hand-me-downs from Kayliegh."

David bit his lip before he could disparage Becca's sister or the way she indulged her daughter Kayliegh without a care for how those indulgences might affect the girl's future. They'd argued enough over STEM toys in the past week, and he wasn't ready for another round.

"It's just a toy, honey," said Becca, groggy and grumbling without looking up from her coffee. "She likes it."

David hummed noncommittally into his own coffee. He knew the cartoon dog through cultural osmosis. The Rescue Pups had infiltrated his life like a virus, as unavoidable and unpleasant as a fart on an elevator. Through no effort of his own, he knew the name of the hunk of plastic his daughter Rose was babbling happily to. Rescue Rover hovered dangerously over Rose's oatmeal, and David swooped in to catch her hand before the dog's face took a nose dive for her breakfast.

"He hungry," protested Rose.

The toy was already goopy, and David did a poor job of hiding his disgust. "Oatmeal is people food, not puppy food," said David.

The black pupils of the eyes pulled at his skin as he peeled it out of his hand.

"What is on this?" he asked.

"They're clean," said Becca, but she had to be lying, because the eyes were sticky. He ran the toy under the sink but could not remove the memory of that sensation no matter how he scrubbed.

Rose growled and shouted "Give back!" but he did not obey until Becca spoke his name like it was a warning.

He shut off the sink with too much force, and set Rescue Rover on the table. It stared at him with those pitch black eyes, then was scooped smiling into Rose's juice stained pocket.

"Are you going to sit?" asked Becca.

He sat. He had seven minutes left of the morning before he had to leave for work. His wife set her phone down. He sipped his cup of coffee. They pretended for a moment that it was a good morning, before Rose shouted Rescue Rover's catch phrase and David spilled his coffee on his pants. He leapt up and blotted himself with handfuls of paper towels ripped from the counter, but it was nowhere close to dry by the time he left, and the pants froze stiff in the winter air while he warmed up the car.

"They'll be dry by the time you get to the office. It's really not that noticeable," said Becca. She was trying to be helpful, but it only reminded him of the commute. A full hour there, a full hour back. He couldn't remember the last time he saw his home in the daylight. The winters seemed to darken earlier every year.

"Christmas is in a month," said Becca. She smiled and kissed his cheek. "Then we've got a whole week off together. Have a good day."

He nodded. He'd try.

A week into December, and the entire table was thronged with Rescue Rover's congregation. A multitude of toy dogs in brightly colored hats stood sentry around Rose's plate. "Where are they coming from?" asked David.

Becca shrugged and yawned around her third cup of coffee. "Jen dropped off a bag of them when I told her how Rose was carrying Rover around everywhere."

How had she accumulated so many? Kayleigh was only three years older than Rose, yet the roster of eight Rescue Pups had at least five different editions, and Rover himself was copied over a dozen times, slight variations in the reds, or the design on his fireman's helm. "Did Jen buy all this shit?" David mouthed the last word, sucking the air out of it in apology before he could let the cuss land with any force.

"Rover!" shouted Rose, and she held the initial dog up triumphantly. "Rescue Rover save da day, every day, save da day!"

"She knows the theme song," said David. He knew it was the theme song because it was playing on the gas pump yesterday morning. An insipid jingle that repeated the same words over and over, while an energetic voice spoke on top of it to remind parents that a new line of toys were now available to coincide with the Can't-Miss Movie of Holiday Season! *ToyCo Presents: Rescue Pups Save Christmas!*

"Kayliegh taught it to her," said Becca, and rolled her eyes at him before he could open his mouth to sigh. "Come on, David. She likes it. And Christmas is coming up, and it's the first year she's old enough to anticipate things so I thought . . ."

"I don't want that cartoon in my house."

He hadn't heard Rose sing before. He felt robbed of the lullaby it should have been. Her sweet voice should be warbling over twinkle twinkle, not this tuneless processed corporate slop.

"Our house." Becca's lip twitched. "Or is it just yours now?"

A chasm opened between them, and David felt the floor drop from beneath his feet. Becca paid the mortgage from her accounts before they decided to try for a kid. He knew she hated how they budgeted now. It didn't matter how many times he tried to assure her of her worth, she felt like the money was all his.

"Becca—"

"It's just a cartoon. I thought, if it distracts her, maybe I could have a few minutes of my life back."

David sighed. "It's not good for her."

"Rescue Pups is super heroes!" said Rose.

He looked down at his daughter. Her bright smile with her weird little chicklet toddler teeth. She reached Rescue Rover out to him and pushed the plastic nose into his arm and made a kissy noise and he hated how he flinched away from the strange texture of the plastic. The gummy tack of the nose as Rose pulled it away.

"Rover love you, daddy."

He sighed. "Thanks, Rosie." He kissed his wife. "We'll talk about Christmas, okay?"

"Yeah." She pursed her lips and looked down into her cup. "Yeah, okay." She kissed him back, and sent him out the door.

One week away from Christmas, and the show was always in the background. David put Frank Sinatra's Christmas album on his headphones and tried to feel the spirit, but Rose only wanted to talk about Rescue Pups.

"Are there any games you played with mommy?"

"Rescue pups!"

"Did you get new books at the library?"

"Rescue pups!"

"What are you eating for dinner?"

"Rescue pups n' cheese!"

His wife sighed loudly from the kitchen. "The shaped noodles were on sale, honey. They make her happy."

"I didn't say anything!" He clenched his fist and took a deep breath. When he looked up, Becca had entered the room from where she'd been hiding in the kitchen. She was wearing a pink hoodie with the girl dog on the front, leaping over red block letters that read "Girl Power!"

"Where'd you get the hoodie?" There were eight different rescue pups and only one of them was a girl. Last week Becca was griping about it. He thought she was a feminist. He couldn't be the only feminist in the house. It was too much pressure for a middle-aged white man.

Becca sighed and went back to the kitchen, her voice fading with the retreat. "Jen got me one so I could match with Rosie. It's cute, I don't know."

He bit his lip. He didn't want to fight. He just wanted to see her, even if she was wearing something silly. He wanted to talk to her.

Rose tugged on his sleeve, and he realized that he had not noticed the new pink hoodie she was wearing. "I don't know!" Rose chirped, parroting Becca.

Sinatra crooned about falling snow in his ear, but the soothing properties had worn off hours ago.

"When are we putting up the tree this year?" They had a sad old plastic tree that had survived three apartments with them, but when it was wrapped up in ribbons and tinsel and lights, it felt like Christmas. A private little two-person tradition, now three with their daughter. They set it up last year behind a baby gate, but Rosie managed to fish a light through the bars. David had a picture of her on his desk at work with her mouth around a bright purple bulb, glowing from within, a devious smile in her chubby baby features.

"Rose and I put one up in the kitchen!"

"Roxie Rescues!" shouted Rose, and she jumped up from where they were playing to run into the kitchen.

It was pink. Pink and glittery, decked in primary red ribbon with the rescue pups logo, and David bit his tongue so he would not scream.

Dozens of toys stood rank and file among the pink branches, some pups he didn't recognize from the weeks of infiltration. He reached for the girl dog, Rescue Roxie, on a branch near the top, and it collapsed under the pressure of his fingers and dripped down to resolidify around the branch. He drew his hand away and found it tacky with something that he could not see.

"What's wrong?" Becca asked, but he could not answer her until he scrubbed the feeling from his hands. Her voice increased in volume over the noise of the kitchen sink. "David, you're being ridiculous."

"There's something wrong with these toys." His hands were raw, but the stickiness remained. "What is on them?"

"They're toddler toys, of course they're sticky."

"But they're everywhere! It's inescapable. They were advertising at the gas pump! How many toddlers do you know are filling up at the gas pump?"

Becca shrugged, unconcerned. "It's the movie event of the holiday season, David. Of course they're advertising."

"Movie movie!" shouted Rose.

"I thought we could take her."

"I think this has gone beyond giving you some free time, Becca."

Her mouth clamped shut, and David closed his fists at his side. "I'm sorry."

"Why do you hate it so much?" she asked.

He could still feel the tack of Rescue Roxie melting in his fingers. "You don't see it?" he asked.

"See what?"

She was wearing that stupid hoodie like it meant nothing. He hesitated. "Is it just rescue pups n cheese for dinner?"

Her eyes hardened, but he shook his head. "I'm gonna get us some real food, okay? When's the last time we had tortas from Abuelita's?"

Her face opened to him, in quiet want, in desire, and in that shining moment, he saw his wife as she was before Rescue Pups. "Oh my god I haven't had a good torta in a year."

"Steak and chorizo?"

She practically melted at the words. "With extra salsa."

He kissed her, and he went back into the cold. It was beginning to look a bit like Christmas.

Abuelita's was closed. Not just closed. Shuttered. He could still see the silhouette of their sign, the darker taupe where the sun could not fade against the rest of the building. They left it there like a scab when they plastered the windows in Rescue Pups. A pop-up store for the movie event of the holiday season.

How long . . . ? He tried to recall the last time he went to Abuelita's; it was unfair that in a year the place was stripped of its kitchen, left an open husk for the worm of Rescue Pups to crawl in and pupate. A figure in a full body costume erupted from the plastered doors to greet him with overwhelming foolishness.

"No, I—" He shook the fuzzy paw that Rover offered him and broke away. "Did the torta place move?" The street was empty of possible new locations. There were tax offices and real estate offices, more empty buildings than those combined, and every window was dark.

Snow was just beginning to dust the corners of windows, the frozen sidewalks, and he stuffed his hands in his pockets. The world felt silent. Empty save for the glaring light of ToyCo.

"You feeling hungry, buddy?" From behind Rover, a young man with pointed silicon ears and a Rescue Rover Red elf costume waved to get David's attention. "We've got a Holly Cholly Churros stand inside. The Rescue Red Berry filling is pretty good."

David shook his head. He was looking for steak and peppers. Bread without sugar. "I need something real."

The elf shrugged. "It'll get you by while you look for a place that does tortas."

He hated the logic, but the elf was right. His stomach was growling and if he called Becca now to ask when else she might want, they might fight, and he was more likely to say something stupid on an empty stomach.

"They're free with a purchase of twenty-five dollars or more."

The giant Rescue Rover held both thumbs up next to the rictus smile stitched onto his fabric face, then he and the elf went back inside. David sighed followed them into the vacuous light of the pop up store.

Abuelita's was scrubbed clean, and in its place was a cathedral of hard plastic and florescent lights. Any trace of the restaurant it had been was drowned beneath white paint and suffocated in vinyl decals. It smelled of sugar and burnt cinnamon, and there were play alcoves built for each of the eight pups, where children could kneel at little tables and worship their favorite character.

Rose would love the place.

And she would love the movie.

It wasn't the worst thing, to want happiness for his little girl.

He gathered a few toys into the basket that appeared in his hand. A Roxie Rescue Plush, the new motorcycle that she's sure to ride in the new movie. And when he sat the basket down to sate his hunger on a greasy pack of vibrant red churros, he figured it was not so bad.

She'd grow out of it someday.

"How long have they been making Rescue Pups, anyway?" David asked at the counter. He was running his hands over the stack of red hoodies displayed there. They were so soft, and the little embroidered dog over the heart was subtle. He could probably get away with wearing it to work.

"What's that, sir?" asked the elf.

"Like, when did this start?" He pulled off the tag and handed it to the elf to ring up as he pulled the hoodie over his head. It was cold outside, and the hoodie was soft, and he'd match with his daughter and his wife, and wasn't that enough? Wasn't it good to get along?

"We've always been here," said the mascot over his shoulder. "Welcome."

"What?" David pulled the hood down to hear better, but his head felt lonely without the fabric cradling it, and he quickly pulled it back up.

"I asked if you wanted to buy tickets for the upcoming movie. Presales come with a free popcorn!"

"Uh, yeah. Movie event of the season, right?"

The elf grinned widely. "The reason for the season, am I right?"

He nodded as his phone buzzed. It was Becca.

"Are you getting food?"

Shit. "Abuelitas was closed, but I picked up some things for Rose at the Rescue Pup's pop up store that was in its place."

"Really?"

She sounded happy. He ventured further. "I'm getting us tickets for *Rescue Pups Save Christmas.*"

"Oh that sounds like fun. Listen, you don't need to bring home food, I just ate some of Rose's dinner, and I can make you a grilled cheese or something . . ."

He shook his head. "No, no it's alright, I had some snacks here at the pop up store. I really don't need anything."

"You sure?"

"Yeah." He took his bags from the elf at the counter and gave Rescue Rover a fist bump on his way out the door. "I feel great." He kissed into the phone, "See you soon," and hung up.

Snow was falling heavier now, and it was beginning to look like Christmas, with bags of toys in his hands, a warm sweater around his neck. He put on his headphones, but Sinatra didn't feel right. He flipped through his downloaded music, and there at the top, freshly downloaded, was the Rescue Pups theme.

The phone felt sticky, but that was probably the sugar from the churro. Or the Rescue Red Berry filling that looked so dark it could have been blood. Nothing at all to worry about. He had an event to get ready for. The Movie Event of the Season.

Merry Kissmas, Love Cthulhu

~ *Lauren Taylor Bak*

Madison Duchamp didn't believe in Christmas miracles; she believed in Q4 deliverables.

At twenty-nine, she was already the Junior VP of Branding Optimization at a multi-national corporation. Her calendar required a master's degree in logistics to interpret. She had it all: a corner office, a gluten-free diet, a five-year plan.

What she did not have was patience, a stable relationship with her mother, or a boyfriend.

This last scarcity, according to a bevy of aggressively cheerful girl-friends, made her life a failure. She needed a break, they said. A reminder of what "*really* mattered," as if her promotional timelines meant nothing.

Then, her Uncle Rudy died.

It was a tragic and extremely mysterious accident; the local police assured Madison that no one had been at fault. Anyone could have, and apparently *had*, fallen under their own snow-blower and, to put it delicately, "painted the barn."

The document bequeathing Rudolph Statler's estate to his estranged niece had been notarized. Once she signed the papers, the property was Madison's to dispose of as she wished. She was thinking either *Airbnb* or *controlled burn*, depending on the level of dilapidation.

She thus found herself on an involuntary sabbatical, being jolted through the countryside in a taxi that smelled like pine Car-Freshner.

Sneehaven, population 1,276 and declining—often in the middle of the night, if one believed those silly websites that reported local cryptid sightings—was quaintly nestled between snow-dusted hills and dense forest. Deep in the Poconos, the town was touristy during the holidays and deathly quiet the rest of the year. Madison had visited once as a child, when Rudy and her mother had been on speaking terms.

"Nearly there," the driver said, flicking on the windshield wipers. Snow was falling in fat flakes. He hadn't spoken since the turnoff from the highway.

"Can't wait," Madison muttered, tapping out an email that would be flagged by HR as being "overly aggressive."

She barely looked up as the taxi rumbled past a freshly-painted welcome sign in festive red and white. Tagline: *Where Every Day is Christmas!* It featured a jolly snowman and a cartoon deer that, Madison noted with professional horror, had far too many antlers. Someone needed to update their ad campaign, stat.

Madison turned away from the picturesque views of pine trees and white-capped mountains to scold her assistant over Slack. He had forwarded the Branson account to *Kyle*, who couldn't find the heart of a brand if you FedExed it to him.

"You staying in town long?" the driver asked.

Madison glanced up from her phone. The taxi crept past a cluster of quaint shops strung with twinkle lights.

"Just until I sign the paperwork," she said. "Then back to New York."

"Good," he said rather firmly. "Get out while you can."

Madison was startled. Surely, that was rude? It had been a while since she'd been back to Pennsylvania, but she remembered the townsfolk being hospitable.

"Excuse me?" she snapped belatedly. But he was already pulling up to the curb.

"Here's you."

They had stopped outside a large Edwardian house with a lopsided porch. A wreath hung crookedly on the front door. Madison squinted at the address.

"This is thirty-four Pineview?"

"Yep."

"Charming," she said, dripping with sarcasm.

The cabbie barely waited long enough for her to retrieve her overstuffed suitcase from the trunk before he peeled off, spraying her shins with street-greyed slush. "Asshole!" she yelled after him, raising her fist like a true New Yorker.

The house had a foreboding look to it, but all Madison could see was dollar signs. A few renovations would make the property ripe for a bidding war. "*Cozy, small-town estate, perfect for a growing family or bed-and-breakfast operation.*" The ad wrote itself!

She grabbed her heavy suitcase and turned to walk up the path—and promptly slipped on a patch of ice.

Luckily for Madison, a pair of strong, warm arms caught her, saving her from a tailbone-cracking fall.

"Whoa there!" rumbled a deep voice.

Madison looked up into the kind of face the Hallmark Corporation cast as romantic leads in cheesy movies: heavy brow, stubbled jaw, eyes like freshly brewed coffee. His flannel shirt smelled like cinnamon.

Jack McCallister was a widower, naturally. Born and raised in Sneehaven, he'd left for college and come home to show off his new associate's degree and beautiful fiancée. Eileen had fit right in; the family loved her. They were married the following Christmas.

A few years later Eileen had died in a baking incident, according to the obituary. The townsfolk didn't talk about it and neither did Jack. He took over the family business after the similarly tragic and sudden death of his father, who had fallen head-first into a bear trap while cleaning the gutters.

"Are you okay?" he asked Madison. She bore a resemblance to his dead wife, who had also been a brunette from the city.

"I'm fine," she said awkwardly, trying to shake off both the made-for-TV moment and his encircling arms. "I've just arrived. My uncle died and left me this house."

"Well," he said, not missing a beat, "Merry Christmas?"

Madison blinked stupidly for a second, then laughed. The lumberjack smiled, showing off a set of teeth that would make dentists weep with joy.

"I'm Jack," he said. "Jack McCallister. I run the Christmas tree farm down the road." He stuck out his hand. "You're Dolph's niece?"

"That'd be me."

Madison shook his hand. Firm handshake, calloused fingertips.

"I was very sorry to hear about your uncle," Jack said. "He was one of the good ones."

Madison gave a polite nod that meant *Thank you, but please don't start crying.* "That's what everyone keeps telling me."

Jack reached for her suitcase before she could protest. "Let me get that for you."

"I can—" she started, but he had already leapt to the top step, like it was full of feathers instead of an aggressive amount of business-casual.

"If you need someone to show you around, I'd be happy to," Jack said over one shoulder. "Sneehaven's very walkable. Lovely mom'n'pop businesses everywhere, and the best family bakery you can imagine. We've even got a sock store."

"A what now?"

He opened the front door with the casual confidence of a man who either had a key or had never considered needing one. "A sock store. Specializes in wool, all hand-made. Great for cold winters." He looked back at her, smiling that dazzling smile again. "You'll love it."

Madison stepped inside the house and was hit by a wave of nostalgia. It looked exactly like it had when she was a kid; she'd slid down those banisters into her Uncle Rudy's arms.

"I'll give you a quick tour," Jack offered, already moving toward the kitchen. "Kitchen's here in the back, there's four bedrooms upstairs, plus the master suite, and the attic's sealed off, of course. Local ordinance."

". . . Right," she said, perplexed. She followed him, smiling with bemusement over the cheerful stranger's familiarity with what was now her property.

The kitchen looked like it hadn't been renovated since the eighties. The fridge hummed loudly and a light fixture above the sink flickered. One of the cupboards was padlocked shut.

"I wouldn't open that," Jack said quickly as she reached for it.

"Why?"

He paused, rubbing the back of his neck. "Long story. Something about a raccoon and a priest. Or maybe it was an opossum? I don't remember. Dolph was always stringing yarns. But whatever's in there is bound to smell *awful*."

Madison raised an eyebrow, but he was already moving on.

Jack took her through a sitting room with a huge fireplace hung with stockings, but no television ("I'm not even sure there's a cable hookup . . .") and a dining room set for a party of twelve ("You know our Rudolph, he was always entertaining!"). There were doilies on every surface, presumably the vestigial traces of Madison's late grandmother. Madison poked her nose into the powder room, the linen closet, the pantry. The air had a distinct old-house chill and everything was dated, but she could work with that. There was charm, original features, and hardwood floors.

As they passed through the foyer, something thumped loudly from above. Madison froze.

"I love old houses," Jack said cheerfully, not even glancing up. "They settle when it freezes and make all kinds of noise."

"Right," she said again.

Jack clapped his hands together. "Well, then. You've had a long drive. Want to stretch your legs before the realtor calls? I can show you around town. It's such a lovely day today, not a dark cloud in sight!"

Madison hesitated. She had emails to send, contracts to re-review, a team of brand analysts who were probably assigning fonts without supervision. But . . .

"Sure," she said, adjusting her scarf. "But we can skip the sock store."

Snow drifted lazily over Sneehaven, which looked like it had been focus-grouped by a team of nostalgic grandmothers and one unusually determined greeting card illustrator. The air smelled like pine, burning leaves, and something sickly sweet. Once they turned off Pineview Road, the houses became cookie-cutter bungalows in pastel colors.

The gazebo in the center of town square was wrapped in ribbon, with a banner reading *Sneehaven Snow Festival* hanging between two posts. A child in an elf costume stood inside it, ringing a bell for the Salvation Army. Madison avoided eye-contact, knowing her purse contained only fifties.

On a bulletin board outside the post office, she saw half a dozen posters for missing pets—cats, small dogs, a cockatiel named Mister Wiggles. Madison wondered, vaguely, if the area had a coyote problem, or if one of those nasty HOA disputes had escalated to rat poison. Something to ask about, if she kept the property.

They meandered past a row of shops, each window festooned with cheesy, hand-painted signs, pine-bough garlands, and more twinkle-lights than were probably allowed by zoning laws. But Madison couldn't help but analyze each display's strengths and weaknesses, noting with dismay the aggressive festiveness of permanent fixtures.

"Your town's holiday marketing is . . . robust," she said, eyeing a snowman-shaped bollard with skepticism.

Jack beamed proudly. "Oh yeah! Here in Sneehaven, we go *all in*. Parades, a tree lighting ceremony, bake-offs, hayrides, sacrificial lambs, carolers, hot apple cider—you name it."

"I love hot cider," Madison sighed, feeling suddenly sentimental. When was the last time she'd had cider?

Jack paused outside a bakery.

"This place makes the best Snickerdoodles in three counties," he said. "And I'm not just saying that because the owner's my cousin."

Inside, a woman with flour-dusted hair waved at them from behind the counter. A row of detailed gingerbread houses sat in the window, complete with frosted shingles and gumdrop shrubs. Madison leaned closer as Jack ducked inside to say hello.

There was a gingerbread church with a candy nativity on its sugar-dusted lawn; a gingerbread pub with a BAR sign done up in M&Ms. Outside the library, one of the little gingerbread men had a shocked expression and was half-buried in red sprinkles. A sharpened candy-cane sword jutted from its chest.

Madison straightened as Jack returned, a bell over the door giving a jaunty jingle. "That's . . . creative," she said, pointing.

Jack glanced at the display and chuckled. "That'll be my nephew's doing. He works part-time after school frosting cookies, but every now and then he goes rogue." His voice turned fond, wistful. "I love kids. My nephew, Henry, is at that age when the world is out to get him, but he still finds the time to make us all laugh."

Madison smiled softly. She wasn't a fan of children herself, but it was refreshing to meet a man who was. Jack McCallister was not the sort of man you met on Tinder.

"I got this for you," he said, offering her a steaming paper cup. She accepted it and was hit with the wonderful aroma of hot apple cider.

They walked on, past the pub and the library, which looked like just their cookie miniatures, minus the dead body. Madison sipped her cider with pleasure. A dog barked in the distance, then yelped, abruptly silenced.

Jack began to talk about his volunteer work at the local no-kill animal shelter.

Madison barely heard him. She was trying to recall the sound of a man's deep, jolly laughter. Was that all she could remember about Uncle Rudy? He had bounced her on his lap like Santa. He'd had a scratchy red beard.

She turned back to Jack. "Sorry, you were saying?"

"I was asking what you think of Sneehaven so far."

Madison looked down at her cup, entirely missing a woman being absorbed by a snowbank across the street. Jack stepped into her line of sight as the woman's hand waved like a drowning sailor's before it, too, was sucked down into the cold Beneath.

The warmth of the cider spread through Madison's fingers.

"It's got potential," she said, grinning. "Definitely needs a rebrand. But I've seen worse."

Jack gave a mock gasp. "A rebrand?"

"Oh, absolutely," Madison said with all seriousness. "There's a difference between charming and trying too hard, and you're juuuust toeing that line."

"Duly noted," he said, eyes crinkling with amusement. "I'll tell the town council at the next meeting. Right after we discuss the mysterious disappearance of all those carolers."

Madison gave him a look.

Jack laughed in a way that made her stomach turn over. "Just kidding," he said. "Don't let me scare you."

They walked on, past the church's cheery wooden nativity scene. From the open windows came the strains of the choir practicing. *Si-lent night, ho-ly night . . .*

"Are you going to be staying in town long?" he asked.

"The plan was just to sign some papers and possibly find a realtor who doesn't flinch at the words 'gut job'. But . . ." She looked at the streets lined in twinkle-lights and the way they made the frost on Jack's eyelashes sparkle. "I might stay a few days. Everyone says I could use a holiday."

Jack grinned. "Sneehaven has a way of growing on people. Maybe you'll fall in love and want to stay." He paused, smile faltering. "Fall in love with the town, I mean."

A cold gust blew between the buildings, stirring up eddies of snowflakes. Madison shivered, wrapping her arms around herself. Jack gallantly removed his overcoat and draped it over her slim shoulders. She was dwarfed by its size and felt dizzy as the smell of *man* invaded her senses.

"Thank you," she whispered.

It was the kind of moment that would have faded into a snow globe if the universe had any taste. The church where every McCallister had been married in the last five generations silhouetted against a darkening sky and the snow-tipped peaks of pine trees; the muffled sound of the choir; the snow falling softly over the living and the dead.

Madison Duchamp was utterly charmed.

"I should head in," she said. "The house is just around the corner from here, right?"

"I'll walk you," Jack said. His hand touched her back lightly as they stepped into the crosswalk. "Sneehaven's a bit of a maze after dark."

When they reached the house, Madison was stunned to see it lit up with lights. Uncle Rudy must have had them on a timer. "Oh wow," she breathed. Her uncle had strung up the eaves and the gables with string lights, weaved them through the hedge and spiraled a cord up the massive fir tree out front.

Jack smiled warmly, the twinkling lights catching in his eyes. "Dolph sure loved Christmas," he said.

"I knew that," Madison replied. Hadn't she?

At the top of the steps, she returned Jack's coat. She felt its loss immediately, missing the warmth and smell of him.

"Thank you for showing me around today," she said in the doorway.

"Of course," he said. "I'm contractually obligated to entertain all my friends' relatives who show up unexpectedly." He paused, stuck his hands in his pockets. "Say, how about you come by the tree farm tomorrow? We're kicking off the annual holiday festival—lots of cider, carols, and hayrides, if the weather holds."

Madison adjusted her scarf nervously. "I think I'd like that," she said. "It sounds . . . festive."

"Great," Jack said. "Come by around ten. No pressure."

"Perfect," Madison replied, feeling an unexpected flutter of excitement.

The next morning dawned cold and bright, which was better than cold and judgmental, the latter being a weather pattern unique to Sneehaven on mayoral election days. Madison changed outfits three times, then went back to the first out of spite. She had an appointment to meet with the lawyer in the afternoon, made over Rudy's crackling landline. Her cellphone refused to hold a signal.

Fresh snow crunched beneath her feet as she made her way toward the tree farm. The GPS bounced around as she tried to follow its directions.

By the time she arrived, the McCallister farm was a cheerful chaos. Children ran every which way, screeching. A school choir was singing something technically adjacent to "Deck the Halls."

An inflatable Santa had fallen (or been pushed) face-first into the snow.

Jack was waiting for her, a thermos of steaming cider in hand.

"I'm so glad you came," he said.

"I had time to kill," Madison said, trying her best not to appear too eager. "The dial-up here barely loads email."

She had spent her evening trying to download an Excel attachment onto Rudy's ancient PC. She'd had to admit defeat, and ended her night curled up in front of the fireplace with the tattered copy of *A Christmas Carol* she'd found by her uncle's bedside.

"Ready?" he asked, offering his arm.

Madison smiled and took it. "Lead the way."

The farm was everything she expected—rows of evergreen trees dusted with snow stretching far into the distance, strings of twinkling lights zigzagging overhead outside the barn, the smell of freshly-baked cookies wafting from a stall nearby. They made a slow lap around the field past rows of vendors selling hand-painted wooden ornaments and "artisan" marshmallows.

From the tree-line came a plaintive bleating. Madison glanced over in time to see two men leading a pair of goats through the trees. "Reindeer stand-ins," Jack explained.

The goats didn't look festive. One limped. The other seemed to be trying to walk backward, tossing its head in agitation.

A loudspeaker crackled to life overhead, threatening to announce something but only succeeding in broadcasting a screeching feedback loop that sounded oddly like a woman screaming. A child near the speaker started crying. Madison rubbed her ears.

"We really should replace the old AV system," Jack sighed. "Want to try the hayride before it's overrun with kids?"

Madison hesitated again—not out of reluctance, but because she wasn't used to saying yes to things without a Zoom call.

"Alright," she said. "Why not?"

They climbed into a wagon lined with hay and plaid blankets. It smelled faintly of the goats. Jack threw a blanket across their laps as the tractor rumbled to life and rolled forward at a pace best described as "contemplative."

"So," she said over the roar of the engine, "do you do this every year?"

Jack shrugged. "Pretty much. I used to come with—" He stopped, looking out over the field pensively. "My sister and Henry. Last year was . . . quiet."

Madison didn't press. The moment had weight, but not the kind that demanded unpacking right away. Jack gave her a small smile. "Anyway. This year's better."

She nodded, and they rode in silence for a while, watching as the world passed slowly by— children pelting each other with snowballs with trajectory of military-grade artillery, snow balancing delicately on fir branches, a man in a reindeer onesie losing a very public argument with a funnel cake vendor.

It was, against all odds, sort of perfect.

The tractor, having made its loop, came to a rumbling stop. Madison checked her watch. "Oh!" she said, "I lost track of time. I'm supposed to be meeting with the lawyer any minute!"

"I'll drive you," Jack said, hopping down and offering her his hand. "They can spare me for a little while."

Thanks to a quick ride back to Sneehaven in Jack's truck, Madison was on time for her appointment with the lawyer. He had commandeered a room at the library to meet her.

"I've taken the liberty of photocopying some documents for you," said the lawyer, a round man her father's age who insisted he be called Bert, not Mr. Lehman. "I've got the original floorplan here, the deed of course, some familial records . . ."

Madison was disinterested with the historical documents Mr. Lehmen had procured, but smiled politely. "And what do I need to sign?" she asked after he had shown her a newspaper clipping about Rudolph Statler's award-winning ice sculptures, the heartfelt obituary that had run in the *Sneehaven Gazette*, and a family tree showing she was distantly related not only to Mayor Witmer, but also the Kauffmans, the Fischers, even Lehmen himself.

"Ah, yes, of course, m'dear," said Mr. Lehmen, opening his briefcase. "Transferring the deed is really quite simple . . . so happy to be keeping the property in the family . . ."

The appointment took less than thirty minutes, but Madison was surprised to see Jack waiting for her by the notice board. He was studying a flyer for a missing cat, but brightened when he saw her.

"The party will be winding down soon," he said, "but I hoped I might take you to lunch?"

She tried to remember the last time a man had taken her to lunch, and couldn't. It was all *Netflix and chill* these days.

"You don't have other plans?" she asked. "Family obligations? Wreath emergencies?"

"Only the kind that can wait," he said, offering his arm.

Jack took her to a diner so old it had a mural commemorating the invention of sliced bread. As they ate delightfully greasy grilled cheese sandwiches, Jack entertained her with stories about the town: the time the plow-drivers went on strike, the year her Uncle Rudolph won a blue ribbon for a pumpkin he hadn't planted. Madison laughed genuinely at one story about a runaway goat disrupting the annual wreath-making contest.

Afterward, they walked two blocks community center, which had been converted into a battleground. "Come on," Jack said. "You haven't really been to Sneehaven until you've suffered through the GCD."

Sneehaven's annual "Great Cocoa Debate," Madison quickly learned, was a tradition in which locals blind-tasted dozens of hot chocolate recipes and then accused each other of sabotage.

By the fifth sample, Madison's tongue had gone numb. By the tenth, she could taste colors. Somewhere around cup thirteen, a fight broke out over alleged marshmallow tampering. Eventually, the final votes were tallied; it a tie between Jack's cousin Edith and Tomas, the diner owner.

Madison was called upon to break the tie. As an outsider, her judgment was impartial. Upon choosing the wrong cup, Jack's cousin Edith declared that Madison had "no palate and probably voted for daylight saving time."

"That's basically a war crime here," Jack whispered, his breath hot on her ear. "You'll be lucky to get out alive."

Madison grinned and nudged him with her shoulder.

Edith stormed off, muttering obscenities. Outside the window, Mayor Witmer's prized pet pheasant vanished into a manhole with a faint "honk," unheard amongst the cocoa chaos.

The next few days passed in a flurry of cinematic moments.

On Saturday, they went skating. The pond behind the elementary school was frozen solid—so they thought. Madison fell often, but Jack always helped her up—once accidentally pulling her down with him into a flailing, laughing heap. A dark shadow passed beneath them, circling. In the hubbub, she put her foot through the ice and soaked herself up to the knee. She thought she felt something slimy snake around her ankle before Jack yanked her free, but the shocking cold superseded everything.

A trip to the sock store was in order, naturally. Jack bought her a lovely thick pair in crème and cranberry, his fingers lingering on her ice-cold calf as he slipped the wool over her foot.

He invited her caroling on Sunday.

Jack claimed he didn't sing, then proceeded to harmonize perfectly with a baritone quartet on "O Come All Ye Faithful." Madison, who hadn't sung in public since a traumatic middle school rendition of "Little Drummer Boy," found herself swept up in the music anyway—mostly because Jack was looking at her like she could rewire the stars to spell his name.

On Monday, it snowed sideways. Jack brought her chili and cornbread, and they ate cross-legged on the living room floor in front of a roaring fire. The lights flickered occasionally, revealing an extra shadow on the far wall, but they only had eyes for each other.

They talked until the fireplace went out. Jack brushed a curl from her cheek, but didn't kiss her. She wasn't sure if she was relieved or disappointed. The old house creaked and rattled.

By Thursday, the world had sharpened into something crystalline. Madison knew how Jack took his coffee. She knew about his late wife, Eileen, who had loved to bake, and about his ambitions to franchise the farm one day. She knew he was still fragile, but he had never stopped laughing, despite his grief.

And she knew—without having to say it—that she *liked* him.

Friday morning, Madison tucked a fifty into the donation box on her way through town. As she waited outside the bakery for Jack and Henry, she realized that she couldn't remember the last time she'd refreshed her inbox.

After only a week in Sneehaven, Madison was finding it increasingly unfathomable that she would soon be returning to a life of spreadsheets and pretending to like quinoa.

Fourteen-year-old Henry burst from the shop like a bat out of hell. Jack arrived moments later, two pastries in a paper bag tucked under one arm, steaming cups of cider in his hands. When he passed Madison her drink, their fingers brushed. Henry charged ahead toward the park, scarf trailing like a victory banner. They followed along the snowy path, talking in low voices as they sipped and nibbled their treats. In the distance, a goat bleated a drawn-out, echoing cry.

When they reached the clearing, the bonfire had already been lit, flames dancing high against the early twilight. They stood close, sharing warmth against the biting cold. Festive music from a nearby speaker mingled with the crackling fire.

Jack's eyes found hers, and before either could overthink it, he leaned in. Their lips met softly, the world narrowing to that one perfect moment, a kiss that tasted like cinnamon sugar.

If they'd been looking, they would have seen a ropy tentacle quietly reach up from a sewer grate and wrap around the midsection of Annie Fischer's little Yorkshire Terrier, Mittens. He disappeared with a faint, almost apologetic yelp—like a squeaky toy experiencing existential horror—dragged into the dark Beneath.

But they didn't notice. How could they?

They only had eyes for each other.

"This town," Madison sighed, her breath clouding between them. "It's magical." Snowflakes swirled romantically, as if choreographed. Jack pulled her into a slow dance as children ran loops around the fire. Annie Fischer wandered aimlessly with a trailing leash.

Madison Duchamp had come to Sneehaven to offload a house and maybe a little childhood trauma. But now she found herself wishing this moment could stretch on forever. Or at least through New Year's.

She and Jack made love in front of the fireplace that night, wrapped in wool blankets and the warm, dizzying certainty of new love.

Afterward, Madison lay still, tracing the outline of Jack's ribs in the flickering firelight. Snow tapped lightly against the windows.

"I can't believe I was going to leave," she whispered.

Jack kissed her temple. "You're not, though," he murmured, his voice sleepy. "Right?"

"No," she agreed. "I'm exactly where I'm supposed to be."

There was no warning. No sound. One moment she was there, skin warm, breath steady. The next: gone.

The blanket slumped where her body had been. A curl of steam rose from her mug. A low *skrrrrk* echoed beneath the floorboards followed by a faint, satisfied burp.

Jack sat up. He stared at the space where she had been, blinking once. Twice.

Then he exhaled.

". . . Dammit," he said softly, rubbing his temples. "Not another one."

He stood, stretched, and tossed a new log onto the fire. Padded barefoot into the kitchen, where a padlock lay on the floor. Jack reattached it to the lower cupboard, shaking his head forlornly.

Behind the cupboard door, something shifted wetly, as if resettling. Outside the house, the snow kept falling.

❄

Fire is the Winter's Fruit

~ John Klima

Winter on campus used to be consistent, bitter cold, icy sidewalks that left you sweating and freezing when you got to class ten minutes late, and wind that both took your breath away and made your eyes water. Now, December more often than not meant unseasonably warm temperatures with occasional miserable wind and rain and only rarely hostile cold. You didn't know if you needed shorts or a snowsuit to get through the day.

The worst were days where you needed both.

This particular Saturday started pleasantly. Students walked around campus in shorts and sweatshirts, vestigial memories of summer backyards holding back impending finals and hours of study like so much grill smoke.

The day cooled slowly, like a reverse frog in a pot. By dinner time, students still in shorts were perfectly miserable from the chill in the air. Errant wind gusts dropped the air temp below freezing.

By the time students left their dorms for late-night studying or even-later-night partying, it was full-on winter. The threat of fighting through snow and ice made many students think twice about going out drinking. Still, for most, the imperative to drink was too strong to ignore.

Everything changed for Steve and his roommate Todd when Jack, Steve's best friend from high school, arrived during breakfast. Recently laid off, Jack was tired of his parents badgering him to find a new job. He remembered Steve bragging over Thanksgiving weekend about endless beer and beautiful girls at college parties. Jack decided to see this wonderland for himself.

Sadly, Steve's tales were mostly lies as he felt compelled to look cool to Jack when they ran into each other at the late-night diner frequented by people their age.

Steve and Todd spent the day attempting to entertain Jack. If Jack had also been in college, he might have realized that visiting so close to finals was a bad idea. Jack also never considered calling Steve and instead he just got in his car and started driving.

Steve intended to use the weekend to write a paper that was suffering under his typical procrastination. Todd's weekend project was reviewing old labs to get ready for his chemistry final.

Steve decided there was no way he could work on his paper with Jack in town. Todd thought he could skip out of any responsibility in babysitting Jack, but Steve didn't want to do it alone. Nevertheless, the two made attempts after breakfast to do some schoolwork. Eventually, Jack complained so much about sitting in the room and doing nothing that the pair tossed their scholarly ambitions to the wayside and headed out to see what was going on.

Jack was miserable to be around. Something that Steve didn't remember from high school. Jack didn't like movies or tv, he hated museums and libraries, he didn't even want to go downtown to look at used books or vinyl. Steve couldn't figure out why Jack thought visiting would be fun. Jack didn't want to do any of the things you could do at college during the day. They wandered aimlessly around campus and were a nuisance to themselves and everyone around them.

One thing Jack liked was looking at girls. College girls didn't have time for Jack's boorish behavior. Steve and Todd were horrible wingmen. They were doomed to fail before they even began.

Luckily for the three of them, it was St Nick's weekend and there were parties all over campus. There was an unofficial Solstice celebration—early by a few weeks, but students would be home on winter break when the actual solstice happened—that the fraternities were throwing as a shared party.

The guy across the hall was rushing a fraternity and gave the three of them special bingo cards for the fraternity parties. Each fraternity had a unique stamp. Completing a bingo gave you different prizes ranging from free entry to parties, free shots, free beer, free bottles of booze. Basically, more drinks.

Most of the fraternities and sororities on campus lined a single street. Huddled groups of students scuttled up and down this street, moving from one party to the next despite the cold. The adventurous souls who dressed in costume for the Solstice celebration struggled keeping their outfits in one piece as the winds ripped off the lake.

Experienced partyers went to the east end of fraternity row and worked their way back to campus. That way as they drank their way through a series of parties, they would be closer and closer to home as the night progressed. Inexperienced partyers—the group which Steve, Todd, and Jack belonged to—go to the closest fraternities first and moved further and further away from home as they got drunker and drunker.

The three made up for their inexperience with enthusiasm. The first fraternity was excited to see three young guys with bingo cards. The trio didn't know, but the bingo cards were a recruitment tool. Steve, Jack, and Todd filled out name and phone number on the card before they got their first stamp. The cards were collected at the end of the night and the fraternities discussed the merits of the potential members at a meeting in January after the winter break.

Steve and Todd sat off to one side, sipping watery lite beer. Jack tried to chat up different girls, but they were only interested in guys who were already in fraternities. Jack said something about the girls being stuck-up bitches a little too loudly, and the trio slunk out of the party as best they could and headed up the street to the next soiree.

Things started better at the next party. When the bingo cards were shown, the fraternity members swept the boys into the house, gave them a house tour, did a shot of something gross called Malört, and delivered them to a crowded room, beers in hand. The boys had a bit of a buzz going, so they quickly drank their first beer followed by a second. While waiting in line for a third beer, they noticed the party had no girls at it.

After a brief conversation, they abandoned their places in line and headed for the door. Members of the fraternity stopped them and wanted to talk about the value of joining their house would have on their academic career. They mentioned a network of alumni that could get them into job interviews and favorable recommendations for advanced degrees.

The fraternity's argument captured Todd's attention. If joining a fraternity—and this fraternity specifically—was beneficial to his time at the university, who was he to not at least listen to what they had to say? Before he got led into a back room to sign a bid card, Jack grabbed him by the arm and pulled him outside.

The trio trudged up the street to a third location. Steve and Jack leaned into the wind, but Todd walked backwards looking at the fraternity they had just left. He didn't know at the time if it was a missed opportunity, but as the evening wore on, he knew he should have stayed.

The third location was a catastrophe from the start. The frat bros didn't want to let the boys in as there were already 'too many sausages at the party.' They relented with the appearance of the bingo cards. Then Jack bumped into a sorority girl when he turned around abruptly to get their bingo cards back.

The girl spilled home-made punch all over her light-colored dress. This brought a swarm of over-muscled fraternity guys who pushed the trio around. One of them tore up their bingo cards. The girl was quickly surrounded by sorority sisters who all called Jack an asshole.

As was typical, Jack gave back what he got. Jack got into a shouting match with the muscled frat bros. A lot 'motherfuckers' and 'bitches' were thrown back and forth as well as several homophobic slurs. In a pause between shouts, one of the girl's friends told Jack that he was making an ass of himself and he should just go. Jack flipped her off and took a step towards her.

That was when Steve and Todd physically manhandled Jack out of the party. They were blocks away from the fraternity when they realized Jack's coat was left behind.

To circumvent the approaching tirade, Steve said that all the fraternity parties were lame. He knew of a better party at someone's house. Jack looked from Steve to Todd, and Todd quickly agreed that he also knew about the party.

Jack asked what they were waiting for, shouted that the fraternity was full of cucks, and headed the wrong way up the street. Steve and Todd got Jack turned around and they walked towards their dorm. The lack of a plan could be dangerous; Steve and Todd wondered what might happen when Jack figured out there was no better party.

They walked along the train tracks on the south edge of campus. The tracks were out of the way, but they cut a clearer path back to the dorms. Theoretically this should give them a swifter path home. It also had the benefit of having fewer people than walking on the streets. That meant they didn't have to keep Jack in check. They could just let him rant to the clouds.

They shared their two jackets among the three of them. Mostly Steve and Jack swapped, but Todd helped out occasionally. Mostly Todd wanted to keep his coat on and get home quickly.

There was the problem of Jack continually asking where this better party was and whether it would have hot chicks. Steve and Todd gave vague answers. Jack's continual need to rant about the fraternity parties meant that he didn't really listen to what Steven and Todd said.

Eventually they could see the tops of the dorms over the trees and Jack became suspicious that there wasn't a party.

Steve insisted there was another party. A better party. No frat guys, no stuck-up sorority bitches. But it was on the other side of campus. Jack liked the sound of that. Jack also thought it would be good if he could find a chick to hook up with.

Todd muttered that he hoped that she was willing to bring Jack home with her because Todd wasn't having Jack and some strange girl in his room.

Steve and Todd walked another fifty feet or so before they realized that Jack was no longer with them. They turned around and saw Jack, with no coat, looking at a man sitting in front of a fire about ten yards away from the train tracks. To Steve and Todd's horror, Jack smiled and walked towards the man.

Steve ran back and grabbed Jack's arm and asked what he was doing. Jack said he was going to ask about a drink. Jack claimed, with false authority and more than a little bigotry, that homeless people always had alcohol on them.

Todd said they couldn't be called homeless anymore, they were unhoused. Steve asked how Jack knew this man was homeless. Steve also lied that they had alcohol in their room. There was no need to do something stupid.

Jack shoved Steve and shouted that he was sick of getting jerked around. He was sick of everything going to shit. He was sick of getting lied to. He was going to get something more to drink and he didn't give a fuck if Steve stayed or left.

Steve and Todd shared a look but neither knew what to do. Todd was ready to leave the two to their own devices. He barely knew Steve and he didn't know Jack at all. He hung back while Jack and Steve approached the man sitting in front of the fire. The man fed a birch branch into the fire from an unwieldy pile next to him. There was a mixture of milk crates and broken-looking folding chairs arranged around the fire.

The man looked up and gave the boys a grin that showed a lot of long, crooked, white teeth. He exhorted that they should join him at the fire. He paused and added, all three of them should join him.

Steve and Jack turned and saw that Todd was now the one fifty feet away. Steve mouthed *what the fuck* at Todd who shrugged. The three walked towards the fire.

The man introduced himself as Harrison and urged the boys to find seats. Everyone sat on a different side of the fire from each other. The fire was large and primal. Something that looked like a movie studio's approximation of a caveman's fire.

Harrison added three more pieces of birch to the fire and asked how the evening had treated the boys so far.

All three spoke at once. Jack said the night was shit. Steve and Todd said it was ok. Jack narrowed his eyes at the other two but said nothing more.

Harrison laughed and said that from the way they looked, the night hadn't gone well. Maybe not quite shit, but definitely not ok. He said the boys just needed better company. If you had the right company, then you could just stay in place, share some drinks, and have some laughs. The night took care of itself.

Jack said that Harrison sounded like he knew what he was talking about. Every place they went was filled with assholes and stuck-up bitches. You had to pay for the booze and then some jerkwad doled it out to you to make sure you didn't take too much, too often. Jack didn't need some frat douche telling him how to drink.

Harrison made some sympathetic sounds, reached down beside him, and came up with a bottle instead of a piece of birch. He took a long drink from it and then passed it to his left.

The boys took the bottle in turns and drank the bitter, acrid liquid without pause or complaint.

From hand to hand, the bottle sloshed its circuitous path. Four sets of hands, then five. The small gathering around the fire grew by one.

Harrison fed more birch into the fire, increasing its intensity. Soon the boys were sweating. Jack forgot his lost coat. Steve wished it was colder. Todd didn't think about his warm bed at home.

No one said anything about the person dressed in a puffy winter coat, face hidden in a deep hood, who appeared next to Jack.

The bottle emptied and Harrison produced another and shared it around, passing it to his right.

Five sets of hands.

Then six.

Seven.

More and more and more sets of hands joined the group. It seemed impossible that the space could hold so many people. Some hands were bare. Some wore mittens. More than one wore gloves. Some hands were clean, others filthy.

There was nothing weird about people materializing out of nowhere.

The only odd thing was that whatever was in the bottle never tasted better no matter how drunk they were getting.

Jack wondered if Harrison had a stash of alcohol that he could steal from and then head back to Steve and Todd's dorm room. Except, now there were so many people sitting around the fire, he could barely move without jostling someone.

Nestled deep in Jack's brain a quiet voice wondered where all these people had come from. But there was so much noise around the fire and so much liquor inside his stomach that the quiet voice had no real hope of being heard.

Jack noticed that he and his friends were skipped with the latest pass of booze around the fire. He tried to grab the bottle, but he moved too slowly. The bottle was in front of him and gone before his hand was barely out of his lap.

Despite the bottle moving on, Jack continued to reach for it. He fell off his seat and landed on the ground so close to the fire that its heat hurt his face.

Dark and unsettling laughter filled the air. Not the laughter of friends. Not even the laughter of acquaintances. It was the laughter of something that took pleasure in your misfortune.

Jack tried to protest, but he struggled to form words. He looked around the circle of people, and the only faces he saw were Harrison and his friends. Everyone else had some sort of hood or hat or scarf that covered their face.

Jack eventually got himself to a seated position, but he wasn't sure if he could get back to his seat.

Harrison smiled and asked if Jack had been a good boy this year.

Before he could answer, the people around the fire stood up and threw back their hoods, revealing their faces. Every single one of them had goat horns sprouting from their heads. Jack saw that what he had taken for work boots were in fact hooves. Their mouths were filled with large, sharp teeth. Jack gaped as he watched forked tongues drip out of ugly, red mouths.

Jack scuttled away from these half-demon, half-goat people. He ended up next to Harrison.

Harrison grabbed Jack and hoisted him to his feet. Jack struggled, but Harrison's grip was too strong. Harrison whispered in Jack's ear that he heard that Jack had been a bad boy this year.

There was something different about his voice. Jack twisted in Harrison's grip and saw that the man was a larger version of the demon goat creatures around the fire.

Some of the creatures pulled out chains wrapped around their waists. Others smacked birch branches into their palms. Several of the creatures rolled out three barrels to the edge of the firelight. The boys struggled but were chained easily and laid over the top of the barrels.

Harrison lamented that they didn't have an actual pillory with them anymore, but the barrels worked just as well.

Harrison leaned over the boys and said that if they wanted to scream they could. This would probably be the most painful thing they'd ever feel in their life. He also admonished them to be good from now on. If they weren't, he would be back at Christmas to take them away permanently.

❄

You'll Be Home for Christmas

~ Colleen Anderson

Like an itch he could not scratch, Christmas snuck up on Pete. Throttling it into submission gave him joy of the season. He pulled on the worn suit with fake fur matted like an alley cat's. He rubbed his nose from the musty odor and stuffed a couple of pillowcases and old rags into the cavernous front of the velour coat the color of a murdered seal. Snapping the metallic buttons shut and tightening the licorice-shiny belt, he slid a switchblade into his back pocket. Another nestled into his boot, and one up his sleeve. He'd only managed to keep from being worm food this long by being one step ahead.

Under his breath, he sang, "You better watch out, you better not shout . . ."

He grabbed the rusty metal stand with its slotted plastic ball for money, looking like a stupid alien spaceship. The damn jingly bells protested until he jammed them in a pocket.

His apartment expelled him into a side street. His breath misted against night's obliterating dark. The main drag, and drag it was, swallowed him in five minutes. People in overpriced coats bustled from store to store, to a coffee shop or wine bar. The blinking rainbow chaos of Christmas lights jeered back.

Pete knew it for a sham, a shiny wrapping that hid the scabby underbelly of assholes and pretentious pricks who walked by a wrinkled man with bristly stubble leaning against a brick wall, his hand wavering back and forth with a stained Styrofoam cup. No charity there.

Scratching under the snake's nest of synthetic white beard, Pete put a five in the guy's cup, then set the stand down at the coffee shop's corner. He shook the brass bells. "Ho, ho, ho. Merry Christmas." He smiled at people carrying bags and packs bulging with festive BS. "Ho, ho, ho, give to the needy."

Little grannies and suits with too much money dropped their coins, plinking like cheap change. As if they were actually doing any good. They'd go home, put their feet up on their oh-so-special furniture, sip expensive brandies and feel they had helped some poor slob. They were the worst type of hypocrite.

As a stevedore on the docks Pete made good money, but this Christmas crap soured him. He'd done fine without any goody-two-shoes gifts while surviving the merry-go-round of drugs his parents rode until one died from an OD, the other missing in action. Then the endless foster home charades—he knew the good cheer for a fake. Everyone would return to being shitheads for the rest of the year. Most people did a pretend goodwill to mankind thing, all the while sleeping with their neighbor's wife, cheating their customers, or beating their kids.

He just gave these people what they really deserved. No false cheer here. "Ho ho ho," he called out, and the ball filled with money.

Three times Pete dumped money into one of the pillowcases before he decided his belly had expanded nicely. He folded up the tripod, tossed the rags from the suit, and sauntered away.

He stopped in front of a store window and checked his reflection, his dark brown face disappearing and leaving the crap beard reflection. Maybe he could meet some nice gal in a club later on and have a few beers and a dance or two. That's one thing Pete loved; dancing. You could show your true soul then, let the pretenses down.

Pete walked past trendy stores where the price of a pair of shoes could feed a family of four for a month; purses that, if bigger, could house the same family; useless tech gadgets served the place of medals for those who had never served their country. People swarmed the interiors, careless with their money because they needed it less.

He waited on a little side street, his tripod and ball balanced on his shoulder. A woman came along, wrestling with various bags fluffed with tissue paper. She nearly walked by Pete.

Pete called out as he slid the blade down his wrist and into his hand. "Hey, Ma'am."

She turned, surprise widening her eyes, then she smiled. "Oh, I didn't see you." Her arms suppressed burgeoning packages, but she managed to open her purse and pull out a wallet.

"The whole thing will be fine."

A stillness came over her, just like a rabbit caught in the open. Her head snapped up, sending her short hair bobbing. "What?"

"Time to spread the wealth, some of that old Christmas spirit, if you know what I mean." Pete casually played with the blade.

She opened her mouth and Pete said, "I wouldn't yell or like, call for help, you know. You might get hurt."

The woman blinked her eyes rapidly and looked at her wallet. Her hands shook as she tried to pull her money out.

Pete leaned forward and she jumped. "Here, let me help." He plucked the wallet from her unresisting hands and liberated the bills. She just stared at him when he handed her back the wallet. "You have yourself a merry Christmas." He disappeared before she even had a chance to react. He wouldn't have hurt her anyway. Not his style.

That woman had needed a dose of reality. Maybe he'd give some of the bucks to the SPCA. Now cats and dogs, they had true good-will. They always loved and never hurt you. Which reminded Pete that when he returned home he'd have to take Spike for a walk before slipping into downy dreamland.

Two streets down from yuppie heaven two kids toted enticing bags. Since when did kids have enough that they could squander it on others? He'd never had money for even a single toy car; just twigs, garbage can lids, and whatever discard he had found in the trash.

The gangly girl with short scruffy hair looked about fourteen; the boy, all wide-eyed and full-cheeked innocence must have been ten or so. Pete walked up. "Hey, kids, let me help."

He plucked a bag from the girl's arms and started rummaging through the tissue paper.

"Hey! What do you think you're doing!" The girl tried to grab the bag. Pete turned away. "Give that back!"

He pulled out some socks, and then a fancy bath oil with dead flowers in it. "I'm just doing damage control. Looks like you've more than enough. I'll take this," he stuck the bottle into a pillow-case.

"Hey!" they both yelled.

Pete dropped the bag back in the girl's arms and grabbed one from her brother. He flicked the blade out with his other hand. "Uh, uh, uh, you don't wanna cause trouble with one of Santa's elves. Remember, he's making a list. Naughty naughty."

He rooted through the bag sporting *Toyland* in bright colors. "Oink oink. Look who's got too big an allowance. Oh, co-ol." He pulled out a boxed action figure. "Power Fighter. Does he really fly?" Pete set the bag down, took a quick look around, then ripped the figure out of the box. He posed its arms over its head, ignoring the whimpering brats, and threw it towards a winter-bare tree. The figure bounced among the branches and stuck.

The boy cried, "That was for my little brother. Give it back."

Pete spread his hands. "Don't you kids know that Christmas is about sharing? God bless us every one, and all that."

The boy sniffed, "The real Santa's gonna get you for that, you big bully."

"No, Bobbie, don't—" began the girl.

Someone came out of a house down the street. The kids started yelling.

"Bye, brats." He loped off, zigging through some alleys before removing his beard.

He ran laughing, slapping his leg. When enough distance muted the brats' cries, he stopped to suck in sweet crisp air. Checking over his shoulder for pursuers, he walked on.

"Ooof!" Air whooshed out. A solid wall of human with crinkly silver hair stood in front of him. "Sorry, dude." He began to move around when a big meat claw of a hand clutched his forearm. The steely-eyed guy who looked like an old biker gone to seed glared at him.

That grin felt as if all the ice in the world slithered through Pete's veins. He couldn't even shiver but stared, unease clamping his gut.

He patted the man's broad shoulder, trying to wriggle his arm free. "Hey, man, sorry, didn't see you. Merry Christmas."

A deep rich voice rolled out of the man in the sturdy parka of deep burgundy with something like wolf fur trimming it. "So, you've been playing Santa."

Pete shrugged his shoulders. "Guess you could say that. All for the Christmas spirit, you know."

The guy's eyes gleamed too brightly in the streetlight. "You believe in the Christmas spirit and Santa Claus?"

"Sure," Pete laughed. "It's brought me good luck." He grinned, then scratched at his arm, checking that his blade, sharper than the icy air biting his ears, was ready. "Hey, can you let go?"

"No."

Pete truly looked at him. "Look, I want no trouble. Let's just call it a night."

The stocky man could have blocked a doorway, his mass seeming larger. A sun could not have melted his smile. His teeth gleamed like ice cubes as he said, "It's not over yet. You still have work to do on the old 'Christmas spirit.'" He laughed then, but it wasn't a rich *Ho ho ho*. It came out more of a *huh huh huh*—throaty, belly deep.

He dropped Pete's arm, but Pete couldn't move. Some sort of hypnotism or something. "Hey, man! Let me go. I didn't do nothin."

The silver-haired biker circled him, peering closely into his face. "Do you know me?"

How had he missed the guy's resemblance. "Gee, you must be St. Nick," he replied with enough sarcasm that a brick would have got it.

The guy bared his teeth. "That's right. You can call me old Nick, patron saint of children and thieves. But only the ones I like." He paused and dug in his pocket, pulling out a mint that he unwrapped and stuck in his mouth.

It clacked against his teeth as he muttered, "Used to be called Wotan . . ." Then his bright blue eye speared Pete. "I have a job for you."

Pete's stomach roiled. He still couldn't move his feet. *What the hell?* "I have a job."

Old Nick smiled. "Did I say you had a choice." His fist zoomed at Pete's face.

The throbbing pulled a groan from Pete. He rolled over, his mind slowly pushing through the haze. What had he done last night? Rubbing his jaw, he winced, the sharp stab snapping him awake. The ceiling had things hanging from it—what were they? Dried leaves . . . plants and . . . were those rabbits?

Pete sat up slowly, shivers twitching him, tightening his limbs as he looked around the foreign room. Walls made of logs mortared with something gray, a long table, shelves, a cast-iron stove.

Standing cautiously, he looked at a solid wood door. When he opened it, he saw a long room, simple pine shelves lining it, stacked with neatly packaged items, and many tables in rows. Was he in an Amazon warehouse or Costco? Pete looked back into the rustic cabin and noticed another door that blended into the log walls.

He swallowed, his throat constricting, and stumbled to that door, pushing it open. *Gotta get home!*

Frigid crystals stung his eyes, crisping his nostrils. Wind roared, nearly knocking him over as he looked across a flat white landscape that starkly shone against the night sky. Stars gleamed so brightly that it looked like salt spilling upon the land. "What the fuck?"

Pushing against the gale, Pete walked to both front corners of the cabin, and ran his hand along the rough wood as his eyes teared from the scouring cold. In every direction, nothing but snow and a barren plain greeted him. Shivering with teeth-juddering cold, Pete succumbed to the inner embrace of the foreign cabin.

"Enjoy the view?"

Wiping his eyes, still shuddering, Pete peered at the figure standing at the stove. He already recognized the voice. The frightfully solid figure of Nick poured two mugs of coffee.

"Y-you kidnapped me. Where am I?"

Nick arched his eyebrow as he turned and handed Pete a green ceramic mug filled with steaming coffee. "I think you know. Sugar and cream are on the counter."

Fear burned the winter chill from him. "Listen, you freak, take me back to Vancouver, or I'm calling the cops."

"Cops?" Nick shook his head, chortling as he sipped his drink. "We police ourselves here and I'm the local law enforcement."

"Where the hell have you taken me? Northern Alberta or Arkansas or something?" He'd seen enough creepy movies to know nothing good ever happened in a frozen wasteland.

Old Nick stared, a very hot, blue-white fire in those eyes. "Much farther north. Feel free, call whoever you'd like."

Pete fumbled for his phone, calling 911, then work, his friends. Nothing happened, although the bars showed he had enough juice.

"Welcome to the North Pole."

Numbness stole over him as he finally accepted the bizarre reality. "Look, whoever you are, I'm sorry I robbed those people. I'll give the money back, never bother anyone again if you just take me back."

Nick sat at a round table made from a slice of tree trunk. He put his feet up on a wooden stool and sighed. "Too late for that now. You made my naughty list."

"Oh come on!" Pete nearly splashed himself with the coffee and set it down. "There are people that do way worse. Why didn't you grab them?"

The old biker poked at a tooth with his pinky nail, then sucked his teeth noisily. "There are other forces for them. But you, my friend, have a special quality, and you went after children, who are under my protection."

"Fine. Whatever. I'll make it up to them. Just let me go!"

"You're part of my team now. My Black Pete."

Pete paced in front of old Nick, resisting the urge to crawl on his knees and beg. "But my dog, there's no one to take care of it, and I already have a job."

Nick grinned like a tiger. "You help me out tonight and you'll be free, until the same time next year."

"Tonight." Pete looked toward the curtained window. "You mean now?"

Draining his mug, Nick gave Pete a look as if he were an idiot. "It's the North Pole; it's dark all day. We start in three hours."

"Um, okay. Wait!" he called out as Nick walked toward the warehouse door. "What day is this?"

"Christmas Eve," Nick called back.

Pete drained his coffee and wished he had something stronger.

Bigger than a Cadillac, maybe even a tank. Pete could not believe that they were literally going out with one white horse—a monstrous, nearly elephant-sized, white horse—hitched to the sleekly polished, wooden sleigh. Swaddled in an Inuit style, cinnamon caribou-skin parka, he didn't feel the cold but didn't look forward to flying through a winter sky. "You really deliver toys to every girl and boy?"

Nick, clad in the richest forest-green velvet, with thick grey fur rimming the cuffs and bottom of his ankle-length coat, patted the horse's flank. He hopped up into the other side of the sleigh. "Not everyone. They must believe. Their parents rarely notice the one gift I leave in the pile. Used to be different centuries back, but I have other roles. Climb in."

Pete pulled himself over the high edge. "Shouldn't you have reindeer?"

Nick clicked his tongue and the horse trotted over the crunching snow. "They're for later."

The sudden lurch threw Pete against the seat as the sky leapt toward him. He didn't realize he was screaming until Nick's loud laughter cut through the keening. He kept his eyes squeezed shut until the swirling queasiness settled.

Gripping the front of the sleigh, he peered over the side at the white landscape skimming by below. The northern lights rippled green and red as the sleigh soared higher.

Nick pulled out a laptop from under the bench seat and brought up a list with two columns. He pointed first to the short, left column and then to the right. "Naughty; nice."

The first city looked foreign. Pete had never travelled much. They landed on a wide street between older buildings with arched windows. "Where are we?"

"Starting in Finland." Nick hefted a large black bag as tall as the horse and bulging with items. He pulled two other empty red bags out and handed them to Pete.

"But won't they see us parked right here?"

Those impenetrable eyes glinted. "No."

At the first building Nick touched the door and it clicked open. They entered every apartment and home as if no locks existed. Not once did they encounter anyone awake. Did the whole city sleep on Christmas Eve?

Pete swore that they'd been going through the streets for at least two hours—how were they going to get to all the cities everywhere in one night? His stomach growled and Nick shared the many cookies and treats left out.

They entered a modern, sleek building of glass and polished aluminum. A night attendant sat behind the desk. Paying no heed, Nick walked by, his green coat swirling. The man stared at his screen, never looking up. Pete tiptoed after Nick as they took the elevator. "He didn't see us? What's up? Can't he hear us?"

Nick laughed, making Pete uneasy. "Not unless I want him to."

As he opened the door to an apartment, he nodded toward Pete's empty sack. "You're going to need that here." He moved to the small tree decorated in white lights and red wooden reindeer, placing two gifts wrapped in green paper. Then he walked toward the bedroom. He opened the door to the first one where two boys slept beside each other. Next, he opened the door to a room with a girl, slightly older than the other two, her blonde curls covering her face. Nik nodded Pete forward. "Put her in the sack."

"What!"

Nick left the room. "She's been naughty. Put her in the sack."

"But I can't!" he whispered.

Nick looked back. "You will. I have all night and you cannot break free."

A force compelled Pete forward. He tried to push away, to run, to will himself to stop but he couldn't. He picked up the limp girl, about eight, and dropped the red sack over her, knotting the end and then hefting it over his shoulder. She never woke or cried out. He followed Nick out the door.

As the night progressed, he gathered four more children. Then they returned to the sleigh, the black sack of goodies empty, and sacks of kids stored in the back.

Pete had to first carry the children to one side of the warehouse. Rows upon rows of beds lined a simple room with only a few had children sleeping in them. Too tired to ask, he deposited the kids, then fell into his own bed in the log cabin.

When he awoke, the eternal night had not changed outside. Nick had already dressed and put a plate of bacon and eggs with toast in front of Nick. "Eat up. We have more to do tonight."

Pete plowed into his food, sipping coffee to clear his mouth long enough to ask, "But we only hit one place and Christmas Eve has passed."

"Oh, it hasn't passed. And won't until I will it…once I've finished my route."

Pete choked, spraying coffee and toast down his shirt. "You—you can stop time?"

Nick didn't answer, just buttoned his great green coat.

His appetite gone, Pete put his cup down. "And I have to help you only on Christmas Eve."

Nick's laughter seemed to shiver the cabin walls. "Don't worry," he roared, slapping the table, "you'll be home for Christmas." He left the room, his sinister mirth remaining.

It took a week just to visit the households in Finland. Pete helped feed the horse, cook meals and gather children into sacks. Thankfully, the naughty children, as Santa determined them, were few enough.

They moved on to other countries, slowly working west, following the course of the night. And throughout, night stood still in a perpetual Christmas Eve, every person but Pete and Nick in stasis.

The more sleeping children Pete gathered, the more uncomfortable he became. They remained asleep for the first month—at least he thought it a month—time became elusive when it didn't move. Then one day—one interminable night—he followed Nick into the dorm. The children roused like robots suddenly animated, yawning, rubbing eyes, looking around in fear or wonder. Some started crying, others yelled until Nick waved his hand and leaned on the railing overlooking the room.

"You know who I am, don't you, kids?"

They nodded, wide eyed, a few giggling and looking around.

"You're here because you made the naughty list; not the naughty I-hit-my-brother, or I-didn't-eat-my-turnips. No no no." Nick wagged his finger and every child stood as still as possible. "Oh no, you're at the top of the very naughty, on your way to hell list. Now the only way to get off this list and see your families again is to do as I tell you."

The few children who had been there at the beginning showed every child their chore and how to pack toys in the warehouse. One freckled-nosed boy missing a front tooth yelled back, "You can't make me do anything. My mom's a lawyer and she'll sue your ass."

"Pete," Nick said, while staring at the boy. "Time to do your part. He needs a lesson."

"A . . . a lesson?"

"Like yours. He must follow the rules. Discipline him." Nick handed Pete a black stick of heavy wood.

"No way." Pete shook his head, backing toward the door at this back, fumbling with the cold brass knob. "I'm not beating on some kid."

White eyebrows arched above Nick's cold eyes. "You were happy to steal from them."

Helplessly, Pete flapped his hands. "That was different. I was just evening the status quo, taking from those who had too much, but abusing them is different."

The compulsion took over. Nick pressed the club into his hand and his fingers clamped around the hard-grained wood.

Pete resisted with all he had but the invisible force propelled him toward the stairs. The kid continued to yell and curse. Pete found it wasn't hard to wallop the brat's ass a few times.

Pete soon learned that Christmas Eve is forever. He notched the wooden floorboards beneath his bed, just like one of those silly caveman cartoons, marking off the days. Every time he awoke he helped that evil bastard Santa load the sleigh, feed the horse, discipline the kids—there were no elves—and deliver presents to different cities. When they finally started toward North America, Nick switched into the red coat and pants, trimmed with luxurious silver fox fur. They stabled the horse and hitched up the reindeer—as nasty-tempered buggers as Nick.

Pete had tried running away a few times, but time would not reassert itself without Nick willing it.

Nick had stopped coercing Pete to punish the brats. He endured the routine, though it creeped him, his skin still crawling. The foster homes had been hells he couldn't leave, and this felt too much the same. The hapless kids had little choice. A very few were definitely psychos and he took a certain righteous satisfaction in thumping their asses, saying, "Seriously, I'm doing this for your own good. You don't want to end up where I have."

Every sixth day, Nick allowed everyone to rest, but with an endless wasteland of Arctic temperatures, not even a tree to puncture the sky, and no bars on the cell, or a TV, Pete could only scour pans, fix broken pipes, and clean up. He took to watching the kids work.

After another boring trip dispensing gifts, he talked with the better behaving ones. Imani had kicked a kitten, but only after it scratched her, her mother blamed her for the glass in the driveway that caused a flat tire, and her friend Colette stopped talking to her because Asha had candies. Adam, the freckle-faced brat, had been left alone so often, without any attention, so that he stabbed the butler in the leg with a pencil.

The next time Nick demanded punishment, Pete felt like the monsters in the foster homes who had scrubbed half a bar of soap into his mouth, shoved him into a closest, or alternately, locked him out of the house in the winter until late night. He was turning into his worst nightmare, and ole bloody Santa fucking Claus was just as bad. The kids were only cogs in the toy delivery machine.

Pete pushed his bed aside, pretending to clean, but he counted all the hatch marks. Seventy-two sets of five. They only had South America's west coast left.

Nick came in from outside, the wind howling behind him, a dervish dance of winter and windy fingers pushing into the space. He brushed snow from his shoulders.

Pete passed him a red mug painted with a green Christmas tree. "We're five days from a year, since last Christmas Eve. Surely, I've done enough. Time has to move so that everyone can enjoy their gifts, right?"

Old Nick laughed, the closest ever to a true Santa laugh, but he kept going, tears springing from his eyes. "Heh, oh you'll get most of the year off, to see your family, pat your dog, see friends, but then you're back on the job." He slapped Pete's shoulder. "Your punishment isn't over."

The next city they landed in, while Nick placed gifts under a silver tinsel tree, Pete grabbed a bottle of scotch and vodka. After that, he stayed bombed for a week.

He stumbled down the steps to the warehouse as the kids wrapped gifts, placing them in sacks. Waving the vodka bottle about, Pete yelled, "Hey, kidsch, listen up. Welcome to Santa's hell. You get to go home in just a few dayssh. Yeah, it will be a year of being a schlave but if you smarten up your ashes, you'll never see this white-haired prick again. Don't fuckin' be naughty and you'll never have to suffer this, and you sure as hell don't wanna be here as an adult. It's mush worsh, mush mush worsh."

Pete fell to his knees, crying, the empty bottle clanking on the concrete floor and rolling away from him. He sobbed and sobbed. He just wanted to be with Spike, curled up watching a movie.

Two small hands patted his shoulders. Pete just cried harder.

The little boy with bowed legs from the Philippines had shoved one of the gifts down the toilet the day before Pete's vacation. The slim black club found its way into his calloused hands. He stumped down the stairs toward the shivering child. The boy, maybe seven, stared up at him with brown eyes swimming in unshed tears.

Pete's stomach flipped. He'd become part of Nick's regime, in survival mode but in the meantime selling his soul. He couldn't touch another child. Hot acid surged up his throat and he puked.

Turning to that imperious prick on the landing, he said, "I don't give a shit if I'm here for eternity. I won't willingly strike another child. You can beat me in his place, but I won't do it."

The silver-maned devil stared down at him. Pete would be happy if he never saw another gift again in his life. But he would not become the worst of his childhood, not anymore. Most of these kids would return to their lives, only knowing their time with St. Nick as a horrid nightmare.

For once, Nick didn't chortle or laugh. A thaw seemed to come to his eyes, warming to the blue of a summer's day.

"One act of kindness, genuine kindness, was all it took to change your fate. You're a slow learner, Pete ole boy."

Pete woke up in his bed, Spike licking his face. He rolled over, out of the bed. Then he grabbed Spike's long Spaniel ears and rubbed them against his face.

"You and me, Spike. It's our day."

Christmas came and went very quietly though Pete dreaded that sinister Santa would drag him back.

Pete pulled down the mask protecting his face from the biting cold. The familiar landscape looked as alien as the first time he'd seen it, except a calm blanketed the flat scape of ice and snow. The other five members of the team set up tents as he checked over the ATV and the snowmobiles. The expedition of scientists had come to the Pole to study the climate and Pete had signed up as their Sherpa.

He'd lived one year in one long, horrid night. This was a far cry from liberating people of their Christmas cheer. While the others did their research, he'd search out that factory, sure that having lived under the veil of magic that he could find it again. He checked his own sack of goodies, packed at the bottom of his bag. Hammer, crowbar, saw, a thin black club, duct tape, rope and other items. This time he'd meet Santa on his own terms and bring the kids home.

Snowflake

~ *KB Willson*

Bacon. Sweet, smoky, and succulent. The scent of holiday mornings, when a full English breakfast would set him up for the business of the day. A smell as luxurious as it was inviting, drawing him from sleep, filling his head with images of warmth and comfort. So why did he feel so cold? He tried to stretch, to roll, to pull the duvet back across his shivering body, but his arms and legs were pinned to the ground. Beneath him lay nothing but cold, hard earth, its icy fingers reaching deep into his bones. Shuddering, he opened his eyes onto a clear night sky framed by the tops of tall, black trees; a darkness thick as velvet, pierced by a thousand glimmering stars.

Something blocked his mouth. It tasted of cloth but was hard, like a ball, and pushed his tongue to the back of his throat, making it hard to swallow. A lesser man may have been inclined to panic, but Dave was not that kind of man. Still, the obstruction presented a serious problem, given that the smell of the frying bacon had sent his salivary glands into overdrive. Somehow, he needed to get his bearings, and to work out what the hell was going on.

The wind was getting up, carrying both the aroma of the crisping meat and the warmth of the fireside across his body. Raising his head as far as he could, the flicker of the firelight confirmed what his senses already knew: he was lying, pinned down at his wrists and ankles by heavy iron stakes. And he was naked.

Craning his neck from side to side did little to help, as the fire was somewhere beyond the crown of his head, and there was no way he could catch sight of it from where he lay. Only the heat on the breeze let him know it was there at all. That and the subtle crackling shift of logs as the flames consumed them. Now he was fully awake, his mind flipped into action. Who had brought him here? Who had set the fire? And most importantly, who was cooking bacon? Surely that indicated there was still someone here. He had not been left alone. He tried to call out but, with the gag in place, could scarcely manage a muffled, squeaking rumble at the back of his throat.

Another odour came to him then, on the stiffening wind. Plastic. Burning plastic. Turning the tantalising freshness of the bacon into a thick, sickening, toxic stench that burned like acid in his nostrils. A racking cough seized his chest and, unable to escape through the blocked exit of his mouth, tore through his throat, racing along the only unrestricted airway until it exploded from his nose.

"Ah, you're awake . . ." came a voice from above his head. A female voice. "Supper's almost ready."

More muffled, inaudible squeaking. Pulling against his bonds, he managed to tip his head backward until the top of the figure came into view. Her back was to him as she hunched over what he supposed must be a skillet. The fire beyond cast her into shadow, but by straining hard he could make out a heavy, hooded fur coat which gave the woman the appearance of a crouching bear. For a moment, he entertained the idea that she may indeed be a bear, and that this might be part of some weird hallucination, or a particularly vivid dream; but the pain in his wrists and ankles was all too real and besides, there were no bears in Berkshire.

His head returned to looking straight up, the strain on his neck of attempting to see behind proving too much to sustain. In the patch of sky above him, the stars were disappearing, as heavy clouds moved across the heavens. Despite the residual warmth from the fire, he was chilled to the marrow, and his back and buttocks were numb. How the hell had he got here? He forced himself to think, think back to the events of the previous day. The previous night. He had gone to a bar—not one of his usual haunts, he fancied something different, what with it being almost Christmas—and had downed a couple of pints. The barman seemed pleasant enough and they chatted, bemoaning the state of the country, and generally putting the world to rights. There were hardly any other customers, aside from a man sitting at a corner table and a group of young-sters noisily doing shots at the far end of the bar. And the woman. He remembered her particularly because she looked so unlike the sort of woman who might go to a bar on her own. A country pub, maybe, but not a bar like this, in a run-down area of town.

They had got to talking, and he'd bought her a drink: white wine spritzer, as he recalled. She was so far out of his league that he assumed she was joking when she asked if he wanted to move on, to go somewhere else. She had her car outside—a neat little Ford Fiesta—and once they were in and belted up, she'd produced a hip flask and asked if he fancied a freshener. The smell of her perfume was intoxicating, and her smile cut straight to his soul. Real class, that's what she was. Real class. With a toast to the rest of their eve-ning, he had taken a long, deep swig. After all, it would have been ungentlemanly to refuse.

He couldn't remember anything else.

The flickering light increased about him, and he realised that the bear woman must have moved away from the fire. He could hear her approaching, soft treads on the forest floor. It was her, the woman from the bar. He sighed with relief—at least it was a friendly face.

"Hope I've done it how you like it," she said, looking directly down at him, "I seem to remember you saying you like it crispy." She held a soft roll in her hand, with piled meat protruding from the sides. He watched helplessly as the hot grease dripped from the edges and landed on his naked stomach, the sudden sting making him flinch. Kneeling beside him, she reached across with her free hand and pulled the gag free from his mouth.

"What the hell's going on?" he spat. For the first time he was aware of the taste of blood in his mouth. "If this is your idea of sex games, I've got to tell you you've picked the wrong man. I like my women submissive. Always have. Now get me out of this so I can get some clothes on . . . I'm bloody freezing."

"You need to eat your sandwich first, Dave, after I've sweated over the campfire to make it for you." She put the bread to his lips, and he took a bite despite himself. It tasted incredible. He hadn't realised how hungry he was. When had he last eaten?

"You'll laugh at this," he said, through the bread roll, "but for a moment back there, I thought you were a bear!"

"That's funny, because I was thinking you were just like Goldilocks."

"What d'ya mean? Are you taking the piss?"

"I'll tell you later," she said, staring straight at him.

"What happened after we left the bar?" he asked, holding his anger in check, just beneath the surface. "I can't remember a thing."

"We went back to your place," she said, without expression, "to pick up a couple of things. Then we headed out here."

He swallowed his mouthful. "And where's here?"

"Oh, somewhere in the Scottish Highlands, I think. I just kept driving until I found a place I liked the look of."

Dave spluttered. "What the . . . Scottish fucking Highlands? What the fuck are we doing here?"

"Control yourself, Dave, there's never a need for bad language. Just finish your sandwich and I'll explain." She put the bread roll back to his lips, but more harshly than before, the crisp bacon scraping painfully against his gums. He bit off a chunk, more to relieve his irritation than to appease his hunger.

"Truth is, you're not a very nice man, are you Dave? I've looked at your account: BaitTheBulldog123 . . ."

His throat suddenly dry, he began to croak a rebuttal, but it seemed she couldn't hear him. He needed to clear his mouth of the bacon sandwich which stuck to his teeth and the inside of his cheeks.

"You knew my son," she continued, as he tried to swallow, "or at least, you knew *of* him. He was a fine young man, Dave. If you'd got to know him properly, you would have probably liked him. Everybody did. I'd brought him up right, you see, Dave. To care. To want to do good in the world. To look after the most vulnerable. To fight against injustice. To take a stand."

"In other words, a fucking snowflake . . ."

"Yes, Dave . . . as you so eloquently put it . . . a fucking snowflake. You know, I've never understood why people like you use that word as a pejorative. A snowflake is one of the most wonderful things on God's earth. Each one utterly beautiful, utterly unique. It is a masterpiece of natural design, its complexity and its intricacy breath-taking. So yes, that was my son. A beautiful, complex, marvellous human being. I told him, when he first confided his hurt to me—the way the trolling, the constant cyber bullying, made him feel—I told him how wonderful a snowflake was, how he should own it, be proud of it. But he couldn't. And the threats and insults just got worse. In the end I pleaded with him to come off his phone, to delete his accounts, but his generation wouldn't know what to do without it. It's like a drug. So he continued, and so did the abuse, chipping away at him, driving him downwards, a terrifying spiral towards darkness and despair. Until . . . until . . ."

She broke down now, tears flowing like a river, her breath shaking from her in deep, catching sobs.

Dave gave a dismissive snort. "Liberal horseshit. Sounds like he was a right mummy's boy. Obviously needed to grow a pair . . ."

"Shut up!" she screamed, lashing out at him with the toe of her boot, again and again. "Shut up, shut up, shut up! *I'm* speaking now!"

He recoiled at the pain. No-one treated him like this: no-one. Once he was free, he'd see that she paid for this—big time. "You mad bitch! What d'ya do that for?"

"He's dead, Dave! Don't you get that? He's dead. You killed him!"

"Fuck off… I never touched him. No idea what you're talking about. Give me back my clothes and I'm out of here. I'll make my own way back. I'm not bloody riding with you, and that's a fact. You're fucking mental."

The stars had gone now, replaced by clouds as heavy and as dark as funeral shrouds. The fire sputtered in the wind, which was whipping leaves and small sticks along the ground at a furious pace. Breathing hard, he glared at her from his prone position, spread-eagled on the ground, his eyes full of rage and hate. *Just let me get out of this*, he thought, *and she won't know what's hit her.*

In the face of his anger, he fully expected her to crumble, to give in to his demands, to beg his forgiveness. Certainly, he was in no position to use physical force, but he knew from experience just how intimidating his sheer presence could be. They always gave in, in the end—and he had no reason to believe that this piece of bleeding-heart, liberal pussy would be any different. Yet to his complete surprise, she sank to her knees and leaned across him, her face just inches from his own.

"I'm sorry, Dave," she whispered, her voice like steel, "but your clothes were the first thing on the fire. Along with your phone and your laptop. I had intended to take them to the police—to prove what stuff you were into, all the neo-Nazi filth that you share online, and how your campaign of harassment had led to his death—but then I thought, what could they do, really? I wouldn't get justice for Peter, and you'd more than likely get off scot free. So I hatched another plan."

Her face radiated confidence—confidence and loathing—and for the first time since regaining consciousness, Dave felt his own innate self-assurance seeping away. Desperately changing tack, he tried to reason with her, protesting his innocence and turning the blame onto her and her son, but she pulled the gag back across his mouth and rammed the ball home.

"Oh I fully appreciate your viewpoint . . . it's Peter's fault, not yours. He shouldn't have been so sensitive. It was just banter. You didn't mean anything by it. It's no crime to be proud of your country . . . I've heard it all so many times before, and I'm sick to the eye teeth of it. Peter's only crime was to stand up to you and your cronies, and by God he paid the price for daring to challenge you.

"You asked me why I thought of you as Goldilocks, and then got angry because you thought I was accusing you of being a *girl*. But it's not what gender she is, but what she represents . . . a certain type of behaviour. You behaved *exactly* as she did, except that in the story, nobody dies. Not like in real life. In real life there are consequences, Dave, but you gave no thought to that. You just stormed in, viciously intent on taking down anyone who dared to voice a different view of the world, and in the process, you violated everything that was most precious to me. You entered my home, through the insidious, creeping bile of your social media platform, and laid waste to my life. Goldilocks ate their food, broke the furniture, and then lay happily sleeping it off, oblivious to what she'd done. And that, Dave, just about sums up what you've done to my family. You have destroyed us, and you simply don't care. Well, enjoy your sleep, Mr Bulldog, because it's going to be a long one."

The confusion in his eyes accompanied one last attempt to wrench himself free, but it was a waste of precious energy. Sweat pricked his forehead, only to freeze where it was. The temperature had plummeted in the last few minutes: the fire guttering, almost dead. He watched helplessly as the woman raised herself from his side and picked up the skillet, wrapping the coat tighter around herself to stave off the interminable cold. Dave trembled uncontrollably—with the cold, certainly, but there was genuine fear now too. He saw the skillet and closed his eyes, expecting the coup-de-grâce. It didn't come.

"There's a blizzard coming," she said, looking at the heavy sky. "If you're lucky, hypothermia will get you before you are suffocated, but either way, you won't be found until the spring thaw. Up here, once the snow starts, it's set for the winter. Unless a wild animal senses you, a food source beneath the drifts. Maybe the bears will win out after all . . ."

Dave tried to scream at her as she turned away from him and started into the woods, but the gag made it impossible. He writhed in his bonds, pulling with all his strength against the iron stakes, but it was no good. They were solid. Peering through the gathering gloom he saw her stop and turn back to him. There was no hint of triumph on her face; just the simple satisfaction of a job well done. "I bet you're wondering about the bacon sandwich," she said, her voice raised over the howling wind. "Truth is, every condemned man deserves his final meal, don't you think? After all, we're not savages."

And drawing the hood of her coat tightly around her face, she vanished into the darkness, as the snow began to fall.

❄

What the Heavens Rede

~ *EB Helveg*

Now mark, my brothers, what the heavens rede
Of dangers rimed with blood and blooming pyre,
For ancient dread is borne by ancient seed.

When snowlines into ashmelt blend and bleed
That one becomes the other and expires --
O mark, my brothers, what the heavens rede.

Enthusiastic beasts with fervid need
Our fevered dreams and schemes consign to fire.
An ancient dread is borne by ancient seed.

Crepusculescent shadows hear you plead,
Though every fetid breath with death respires.
O mark, my brothers, what the heavens rede.

Behold our hunted souls that slaughter freed,
A tithe to Hell eternally and prior;
For ancient dread is borne by ancient seed.

That muted peace thereafter one should heed
As warning tenebrific, swift, and dire.
O mark, my brothers, what the heavens rede,
For ancient dread is borne by ancient seed.

❄

Sin-Eater Claws

~ *Tobby Hagler*

I'm eight hundred years old, and I just tripped over a pile of firewood.

My hoof cracks, my sack snaps forward, and the little bastard I'm chasing is now three roofs ahead, laughing.

My knee clicks. That's new.

I hate this part of the job. The running. The chase.

But he stole from an old lady, spat on a beggar, and kicked a blind dog.

So yeah. I'm gonna catch him. And he's going to taste good.

You don't kick a dog.

I'm not climbing anything, I'm too old for that. But I know where he's going. They always go home—home to cry to their mutter, who welcomes them with open arms and warm bread.

Not if I can help it. Naughty kids don't get bread. They get the whip—and I'm making sure this one gets his.

I need a better route. I'm already huffing like a bellows full of gravel, and I was hoping to end the night early to see Gryla.

Shortcut it is.

There's an alley up ahead. I'll just—

Oh. Oh, what is that *magnificent* smell?

It's warm and bitter, with a sharp tang that stings the nostrils like skin left too long in the sun. Sweet, fermented warmth clings to the air like overripe meat on the cusp of turning, the way a wound might smell if it dreamed of honey.

Oh, fangs of Fenrir! That smells delicious.

A boy sits on a barrel outside the hovel he probably calls home. Inside, adults yell about money or debts—whatever. Who cares, when something smells this savory and sweet?

Good. He doesn't see me yet. I sneak along the side of the build-ing until he's within arm's reach.

Suddenly, I'm so very hungry.

What kid? What mutter? I'm going to eat this instead.

I must have it.

"Psst."

The kid looks up, probably admiring my magnificent horns. Then down, at something in his hands. An orb. It's the color of a village lit on fire. Vibrant. Intoxicatingly magical.

He digs his claws into it. Okay, can't really call them claws; he's human after all. But he flays the poor thing like I would do to him, were he on my list.

A fine mist of blood sprays into the air as he peels its skin. Sharp-sweet. Wet pulp. Pressure. It reeks like something squeezed until its bones crack into soup.

He looks up again, tearing the skin and tossing it to the ground without a care in the world.

I like this kid.

So I ask, "May I have a piece?"

He says nothing, just tears a chunk from the corpse and hands it over.

I bring it to my nose and inhale. Sticky and bright, but with an edge—like sap, or sweat, or something between.

I press my teeth into its soft body. It stings—sharp, not the kind that enrages me enough to rip heads from bodies, but the kind that invites more. Acid floods my tongue. I'm enthralled.

My eye slits widen and twinkle before I drag myself back to reality. I lick my claws clean as I finish the rest of this delightful morsel. "It's good," I mutter.

The kid nods, nearly finishing the rest of the strange fruit.

With two segments left, he tears one away and hands it to me, shoving the other into his mouth. "Mm-hmm," he mumbles, pulpy flesh still rending between his teeth.

Yelling from inside breaks his thoughts. He folds his arms and stares at the ground, clearly hoping for more of that sun-warmed, musky creature.

I look down too. I notice three of his toes sticking through his socks, but all I can think about right now is wondering if the orb's rinds are also as tasty as its body was.

Whatever it was, it was good. Almost as good as the marrow of disobedient children or those who shove others when no one's watching.

"Thank… you," I say. I don't know why. It hurts somewhere inside, and I instantly regret it.

Yet, this exchange deserves something in return. He did make an offer, after all.

I produce a small rock from my bag. Its yellowish color isn't far from the juicy meat we just shared, so it seems fitting. These are everywhere back home.

It's smaller than his fist, but his eyes open wider than mine ever do these days.

He gazes at me. Wonder, probably. Or maybe gas? Without a word, he snatches the cool, heavy rock and tucks it inside his vest.

"My name is Ansel."

I extend a hand. "Pleasure to meet you, Ansel."

He reaches to take it, but then grabs the dull edge of one claw and shakes it instead.

Smart kid.

Timidly, he asks, "What's your name?"

My pointed tongue flicks against jagged teeth, searching for words he'll understand.

"I'm Krampus."

"Krumpus?" The boy looks at my hands. "Like, krampen?" He suppresses a giggle, but I notice. I should probably flog him for that, but I don't. The word means "claws" in his language, so I don't mind.

I clack them together and grin. I love these claws. So many punished children bear their mark, a warning to the others to behave.

It is such a fitting name. He's clever, this one. He won't show up on my list anytime soon.

I pat his head, very nearly gently.

"Yes," I hiss. "Like 'claws.' You may call me Claws."

❄

Our den lies in the belly of a long-dead volcano, still smoldering in the right places. The path crunches with ash and bones. Mostly decorative. Some practical. Even demons need a quiet night of leftovers and a good book by the fire.

Inside, it's warm—real warmth, the kind that burrows into your joints. That click in my knee finally lets go.

Pelts stack near the hearth. Blankets, too, woven from things better left unnamed. Books spill off crooked shelves in half a dozen languages. One of them growls as I pass. I scratch its spine and it settles down.

Ah! There she is by the fire—half troll, half giantess, all monstrous beauty. My Gryla. The warts suit her. So does her patchwork hair, and that adorable chin tuft.

She smiles when she sees me with those gleaming brown teeth of hers. The same crooked grin that caught my eye back during the Famine. I'll never forget that night. She'd just ripped a priest in half and offered me a taste. It was love at first bite.

Then she eyes my burlap sack—no squirming. "You're late," she says, returning back to her cauldron.

"I took the long way," I lie.

"You didn't bring anything."

"Didn't feel like it."

"You said you would." She points her wooden spoon at me. "'There's a little bastard kicking dogs and stealing pies off windowsills,' you said."

I turn to stare into the fire. Its embers glowed with the same color as that magical creature a poor boy shared with me mere hours ago. I can still taste the sweet flesh. Still smell the zest.

She's right—I did promise that tasty little morsel for dinner. "There was."

"And?"

I don't meet those beautiful yellow eyes of hers. "He… got away."

She curses, grabs a jug of something suspiciously green, and pours it in. The broth hisses. A wonderful stench fills the air between us.

"I've stretched the last child stew three nights now. Barely any taste of wrongdoing left."

She jabs the spoon in hard. "Might as well boil rocks. At least rocks don't go soft."

I swear she muttered something—*like some demons I know*—but I don't see her lips move.

I grunt and settle onto the stone nearest the fire. Heat seeps into my back. My hooves stop aching—except for the new crack from that damned firewood stack.

"You're slowing down," she says. "You're softening. You're getting . . ."

"Say it, troll."

"Sweet."

I admit: that stings. It prickles like the first rays of dawn. Hot needles raining down from angry gods. Enough to send you screaming into a darkened forest for refuge.

Her voice curdles. "You know, Tatterdemalion would never return empty-handed. Tatterdemalion is young. He's flexible. He says he'll give me a dozen yule lads if I ever come to my senses and marry him."

I snort. "Tatterdemalion eats glue and barks at hedgerows."

"Maybe so. But at least he provides." She slaps her spoon against the pot. A single greasy drop falls back into the stew. "You used to bring me disobedient children. The ones who didn't share their toys. Ill-tempered brats—the ones that exploded with sin-packed flavor. Now I get, what . . . he kicked a dog?"

I rise and turn from the fire, my curved horns casting long shadows across the cave. The flat slits of my eyes glow. I clench my claws and howl.

"You. Do not. Kick. A dog!"

Then she softens like she always does.

"You're right, dear. You don't. And that little bastard would've tasted horribly wonderful for it."

She holds my gaze for a moment longer. "Oh, come here, you half-goat, you," she says, waving me over with one thick hand. "You've had a hard day. Let your Little Gryla hold you for as long as you need."

Towering over me, she yanks a blanket from the pile and throws it like a net. It smells like wet bear and old cinnamon. I melt at the stench of her love.

"Sit," she says, patting the floor. "You can sulk in warmth."

I do. I sit and lean into my Little Gryla and let her hold me. Because I'm oh, so tired.

And her stew, even watered down, still smells better than most things. It doesn't just fill the belly—it fills the soullessness inside.

I love this place of ours.

Cemeteries make excellent hunting grounds.

People are always on edge, expecting something spooky to appear—shadows, ghosts, maybe a moan or two on the wind. So they whistle in the dark, feeling brave for facing their fears.

That's the best part. When people expect monsters, they stop believing anything real will show up. Their fear gives way to tradition, a bedtime story wrapped in wool.

And that's when they let their guard down.

Which is perfect. Because I'm not a shadow or a whisper or a chill down the spine. I'm claws and breath and sack and teeth. And I'm very real. And very hungry.

The little bastard I'm tracking isn't afraid. Good.

He's stolen a candle from someone's grave and is now pissing on the headstone like he owns the place. Not the worst offense I've seen, but disrespect for the dead always sizzles nicely on the tongue.

I'm mid-slink, low, talons barely clicking on the frozen ground—then a scream cuts through the dark.

A real one. Frantic, frightened, small. It's been a while since I heard a proper scream.

Oh.

Then I hear other voices, low and menacing. Threatening.

I veer off without thinking. This promises a tastier morsel from the sound of it. Almost as good as when Gryla puts too much bone in the stew and it crunches just right.

I slink between iron fence posts and spot them—two boys, older than the voice implied, grabbing at a girl kneeling beside a grave.

They've got a bag. She's got a basket, empty now, apples scattered at her feet.

"Give it here," one says. "Ghosts don't eat."

"Leave me alone!" she shouts, fists clenched.

"Two for the price of one," I say, stepping out of the shadow.

They turn, frozen.

I flash my trademark grin. Teeth. Pointy red tongue slithering. Sack wide open.

We're going to eat well tonight, Gryla.

They run like the gates of Hell just opened in front of them. If only they knew.

"Damn," I mutter. I lurch forward out of reflex—but a voice behind me freezes me cold.

"Thank you!"

I turn. Slowly.

Naturally, I'm incensed. "What did you just say to me?"

She brushes off an apple, places it back in her basket, and looks at me like I'm safe.

Me. Safe? I won't stand for this.

She smiles softly. "I said thank you."

My foreclaw presses into my chest. "Thank . . . me?"

She nods. "They were trying to take the apples I brought for Mama."

I stare at her, unblinking.

"She's . . . under there?" I ask, gesturing at the grave. "In the ground?"

"Yes," she whispers.

Gryla's beard. "You brought her fruit?"

"She liked apples."

I blink. My mouth does something strange—it stays shut. Even my sharp tongue holds still.

"Would you like one?" she asks, wiping it with her scarf. Then she steps forward—unafraid—and offers it.

"Maybe," I answer. "I don't know."

She adds, "You can have this one. It's the biggest I've got."

"Hmm. They look sweet," I mumble. "Maybe not."

She smiles. "They are."

"Well, I'm not."

"I know."

This is puzzling. Thank me? With sweet apples?

Then—suddenly—why not? I crouch beside her.

She whispers, "My name is Bahari."

"Claws," I say.

"Claws?" she asks. "What are you, Mister Claws?"

"Well," I say, "I guess you could call me a sin-eater."

"A what?"

I grin. "I devour sin."

"Oh. That sounds kind of nice, actually. The world's full of sin, sometimes. We could probably use more sin-eaters."

I chuckle, thinking of the good old days. "Sin's delicious. Especially when it's naughty children—they're the tastiest."

She laughs and shifts, but not away from me. "Okay. As long as it's just the naughty ones. Like those boys."

Mostly, I think.

She's staring at the apple I forgot I was holding.

I press one half to my snout. Gross. It smells entirely too sweet to be food. How anyone *not poor* eats this, I'll never understand.

Absolutely disgusting.

But she's making an offering. I don't disrespect tradition.

I grunt and reach into my pouch. Pull out a pinch of cinnamon. Something else, too—sharp, brown, maybe clove. I split the apple with one claw and dust both halves with the ruddy powder.

She beams as she bites into the candy-flesh.

I follow.

Crap. It's good.

It fills me with such rage that the next village I visit is in mortal peril. It's that sickeningly sweet. Annoyingly delicious. I hate myself for it.

While *not enjoying the apple at all*, I feel something creeping up my arm.

Spider! Crap, I hate spiders. I try to calm myself long enough to swat it, but I keep missing.

"What are you doing, Sin-eater?" Bahari asks.

"Spider!" I scream at her.

Instead of freaking out—like any sane creature would—she shushes me.

She *shushes* me.

In a whisper, she says, "Come here, buibui. Let's move along, shall we?"

She brushes her tiny hand along my arm, scooping the spider up without it noticing. Then leans forward and sets it on the ground. Blows gently. "Run along now, little spider."

My eyes glow, but not with rage. With something else. If there's a word for "respect" in my native tongue, I might try it. Just to see how it feels.

"Don't be afraid, Sin-eater. Not all things that look scary are monsters."

The bits of apple in my teeth don't taste so bad now. I chew that thought for a while before I say anything.

"Do you . . ." I start, then cough—whatever's in my throat won't budge. "Do you want to tell me about her? Your mama, I mean."

Her face shifts—alive and bright.

"Yeah. Okay," she says.

And she does.

I listen. I don't know why.

Maybe it's the clove. Maybe the cinnamon.

Maybe the apples.

I've read her letter three times. Maybe four. The blood ink has started to smudge for some reason.

She says she's gone to bed hungry one too many nights. Says winter shouldn't taste like water and bark. Says Tatterdemalion sings to her now. That his bag is always full, his hearth warm, and he's promised her a dozen Yule lads to raise and unleash upon the land.

She took the rug—the one with my horn still embedded in it from the winter of the avalanche. Took the good cauldron, too. The one that groans while the meat's still alive.

I don't cry. I don't break. I go hunting. I still know who I am. I punish the bad children—and tonight, I'll punish them so thoroughly they'll sing of me for centuries.

I drop into a village I haven't visited in years. The roofs curve like broken fingernails. Snow piles in the gutters, clean and untouched. Smoke rises from every chimney—a cold reminder that mine, once shared with Gryla, has none.

I check my list.

Blank.

No thieves. No bullies. No liars, biters, or covetous little goblins hoarding toys they don't deserve. Not one tantrum. No defiance. No kicking. No screaming.

"Are there no children in this village?" I bellow into the wind and snow.

No. Just a blank scroll and the sound of carolers in the distance, too far off to burn or flay. This night keeps getting worse.

I mutter, "Come on. Give me one. Just one disobedient bastard. One bully. I don't care—just something naughty!"

A snowflake lands on my snout. I slash at it. It knows what it did wrong. Apparently, the only blood I'll smell tonight is my own.

I kick the brick wall beside the bakery. It doesn't give. Of course it doesn't. My already-cracked hoof throbs.

"FUUU—!"

And that's when I hear it: "Did you say fudge?"

I turn.

A boy stands in the snow outside the bakery, bundled in too many layers. Only his hands are bare. And blue. He's holding a tray of cookies like he's offering tribute to an angry god. He blinks at me, completely unfazed.

I almost don't care that he's not on my list. I need a win.

"I like fudge," he says. "But cookies are better. Especially with milk."

"Milk," I repeat. "From cows?"

He nods.

Then it hits—my stomach tenses. Something rises in my chest, into my throat. I think I'm about to retch all over his cookies.

But then I don't. My stomach ripples. My shoulders bounce—slowly at first, then uncontrollably.

I roar from somewhere deep down inside

But it's not *my* roar. It is, but it isn't. What is happening to me? At first, I think I'm possessed, but then…

Wait.

I've seen children do this before. I'm . . . ?

It takes over. I give in, I don't think I have a choice. My chest begins to seize, but I don't fight it. I allow it to continue. I lift my face to the sky and yell a bellowing laugh. My sides burn with fire that's strangely enjoyable. My eyes burn with salty water, though I have no clue where that's coming from, but it's not so bad once the sting has worn off.

The kid giggles back.

Compose yourself, Claws! I think.

When I finally do, he asks, "What's so funny?"

"You would eat those." I tap a recently sharpened talon on the metal tray with a wonderful, spine-tingling scrape. "With . . ."

"With milk. Would you like some?"

I try not to convulse again. "You drink . . . fluids? From an animal while it's still alive?"

I shiver.

It's so unnatural. Cruel even. I love it.

"Where can I drink this liquid from a living beast?"

"I can bring you a glass from inside," he offers, waving toward the bakery.

My horns won't fit through that door, but the idea of shattering glass as I enter is . . . appealing. "I'm listening."

He holds the tray up and asks, "Hold this, I'll be right back."

Before I think, I take it. He's gone in a flash.

I lift the silver tray of brittle, nauseatingly fragrant discs.

I nearly spew on them for real. But then . . .

Maybe just one?

I gingerly squeeze one between two claws. It crumbles to the ground. It's even more fragile than a bully who cries the first time someone stands up to him—or when I show up to end it for good.

One more try. I slide one into my maw with a single claw.

It's warm and soft. But the edges bite back with a crunchiness like they were forged in a fire. Gross.

The sweetness hits loud and treacly… but then steps aside.

Something darker follows, bitter, but rich.

The chips melt like cooled blood that's somehow still hot; sharp and smooth all at once.

Disgusting.

There's salt, too, but just enough to be confusing. Enough to make the sweetness feel like it belongs there, like it has a place there for now.

I chew slowly, suspicious. It doesn't taste like innocence. But it's balanced. Alchemical, even.

I don't like it.

I take another bite.

Just to confirm my hatred for it.

The bell rings. The baker's son reappears, holding a glass of white fluid.

"Nothing!" I bark, mouth dry from my second cookie.

"Do you like them?" he asks.

"No. They're awful, and you and your father should be ashamed." I take a third to show him my disgust.

"I can leave the whole tray if you want."

I don't answer. He sets it down on the stoop anyway, then stands there watching me like he's expecting something. A riddle. A curse.

I crouch instead, patting my pockets, but they're empty.

"Sorry, child. I have nothing to offer in return." My voice creaks. Imagine—a demon unable to fulfill his contract once an offering's been made.

Gryla was right.

"What would you ask of me?"

"Oh, nothing," he says, beaming.

This kid is mocking me. I'm going to slice his—

That stupid smile. Why is this wretch so innocent?

I stare at the tray. One more wouldn't hurt.

I sit, collapsing against the side of the bakery with a thud hard enough to rattle the shingle bearing the name of the proprietor.

What have I become?

"Are you . . . Okay?" he asks, hesitant.

"Yes," I hiss.

"I'm a really good listener. My dad says so."

I sneer. "I don't want to talk, child."

He lifts the milk. "This might help."

The thought of drinking a creature's fluids—especially while still alive—does cheer me up. I take the glass and pour it down my gullet. As far as a chaser for vile cookies goes, it's refreshing.

I smash the glass on the cobblestone street. "Do you have more of this extraction?"

He flinches. "Um . . . yes. But only if you promise not to break the next glass."

"Oh. Sure. I can . . . spare it."

Moments later, after I've stolen another terrible cookie, he brings a second glass of cow's sap and sits beside me in silence.

After a while, I mutter, "I'm not here to talk." I pause, ashamed. "I have nothing of value to offer you."

"That's okay," he replies. "I didn't want anything. You just looked like you needed a cookie."

"What?" That's not how transactions work, especially between his kind and mine.

"I like giving people cookies when they need one."

"That's . . ." I have no words. If he doesn't want something from me, what *is* his angle?

"Is this a trap?"

He turns to me and says, "No, silly. Sometimes it's just nice to give something to someone. Especially someone like you."

This is unnatural. I don't like this feeling. I need to stop him.

Before I can, he adds, "it's nice to be able to help some, you know. Or give them something just to let them know they're appreciated."

He's wrong, but I don't argue.

I realize something. He's small for his age. He gives things away—disgusting things, sure—but the kind others might try to take. He's soft, and fleshy, and wouldn't stand a chance in mortal combat. And those unprotected, cold, blue hands . . .

Weak.

That's it! Now I know *exactly* what he needs.

I lean close and whisper, "Child, if anyone ever bullies you—if anyone lays a hand on you—you call my name."

Unsure, he asks, "Your name?"

"It's Claws. I'm a sin-eater. I devour the sins of little children."

He snickers. He points at my claws. "Because of those?"

I click them an inch from his nose, grinning.

He beams. "It's a pleasure to make your acquaintance, Sin-eater Claws".

"Nice to make yours—?"

"I'm Caleb."

"Caleb, if anyone bullies you—call my name. Understand? I'll come and eat them in front of their families."

He tilts his head. "That's… really mean."

I blink. "So, eat them in private, then?"

He laughs. A real one. Joyful. Warm. It startles me more than any scream ever could.

He slugs my shoulder—I guess it's a slug, I didn't really feel it—and says, "Oh, you."

We don't talk after that. I don't tell him about Gryla. Somehow, I think he knows. Children are strange like that.

A voice from inside calls. "Sorry, I've got to go. Abba needs me." He scampers off.

I don't say anything. But I pick up one more cookie for the long, quiet journey home.

Hmm. Strange.

Giving gifts for the sake of giving can be . . . nice.

If you tell Gryla I said that, I'll devour you whole.

❄

I'm not doing this to spite Gryla. She's Tatterdemalion's problem now.

I'm not doing it for the children either, if I'm honest. They're soft and confusing. The kind ones? Barely edible. But something about how they give—with no contract, no leverage, no gain—is lodged in my ribs like a shard of frozen bone I can't reach.

To pull this off, I'll need a disguise. I can't afford to ruin eight hundred years of reputation on a whim.

I return to the cave. It was ours once. Just mine now. But I can still smell her kinderstew.

It's as empty as I remember, but I know where to look. Behind a pile of unread books, I find one of her old cloaks—the red one. The color of blood is my favorite. She always looked so good covered in blood.

Focus, Krampus. Focus.

I try it on.

It hangs off me. I'm no half-giant. I stuff the sleeves with damp rags and bits of straw. Then I drag my sack across the floor and begin to fill it—not with children, for once, but with things they might need. A few tokens. A few surprises. Some carvings. Some fruit. A doll made from fine bones woven together.

Last comes the hat. That stupid, glorious, pointed red thing I won off a necromancer in a game of chance that may or may not have ended in flame. I shove it on, covering the horns well enough. I look ridiculous. But they won't know it's me, and that's the point.

Good.

I'm all set.

First, I sneak into Ansel's house. His socks are drying on a rack near the fireplace—threadbare and ragged. I mend them with demon-hair thread, careful not to unravel the spellwork that keeps them warm. I laugh when I see the gold rock hidden under his bed—yes, I'm still a monster, and we always crawl under children's beds no matter what. Mind your business.

One more gift seems right—something with weight. I scrawl a rune on the floorboard beside the rock to grant him fortune. Then I stuff three oranges into the socks and hang them back with care.

I take one last look at this hovel. I hope he strikes it rich one day. Somehow.

At Bahari's windowsill, I leave a spider charm carved from ash root and wrapped in fine silver thread. It's so ugly. She'll love it. Beside it, three apples glisten in the moonlight like hearts no one dares to steal.

Beneath the charm, I tuck a scrap of dark leather etched with a single rune—not flashy, and not meant to dazzle. Just old magic she won't understand until she's older. It doesn't promise protection or power. It simply means: *heard*. Not everything needs fixing. Sometimes, it helps to know someone's listening.

And at Caleb's doorstep, I find a tray already waiting.

Cookies and milk. No note.

I struggle to find something worth giving him. For whatever reason, I leave a rolled-up pair of mittens. It's not much, but his kindness deserves to be returned.

It's tough to find a gift for the kid who has everything—kindness and generosity.

After all, kindness is the only thing that keeps you off my list. And once your name appears?

Prepare to be stew.

Perched on a rooftop, I watch smoke rise from every home as the eastern horizon warms to a glow. My sack is empty, but my coat is warm.

Below, through a cracked window, I hear voices.

"Where'd you get those mittens?"

"Sin-eater Claws left them."

"Sinterklaas?"

"Maybe that was it. But look! They fit perfectly, they're exactly what I needed. I love them."

I grin, horn to horn.

"Sinterklaas . . ." Close enough, I guess.

I pull the red cloak tight as the sun's angry rays shred the last comfort of darkness. They stab into my skin like a thousand burning needles.

I bolt for the nearest forest, head low, hooves cracking frost beneath me. And just before I vanish into the trees, I throw my voice across the rooftops, howling loud enough to curdle butter and wake babies:

"Ha ha ha! Enjoy my gifts to all, which is to live another night!"

As Red as Any Blood

~ *Jack Stein*

They're driving along for a good sixty minutes before either of breaks the silence. "Shut up so I can hear the goddamned GPS," he'd snapped, so she had.

She'd kept her mouth shut when the cool robotic voice repeatedly chanted "Please proceed to the highlighted route" every 300 feet down the gravel road from her grandma's house till it finally met a road that existed on the map.

She'd kept her mouth shut when the simulacrum instructed him to "turn slightly left to stay on Bogg's Hollow Road" at a five-way intersection. She'd stayed silent even as he misinterpreted the instruction and bore left onto Cold Creek Lane instead, like everyone always does the first time.

And she'd kept her mouth shut when a gentle chime announced that the GPS had updated their route to take a thirty minute detour down what it called State Route 834 but she and everyone else around knew as Byron Carver Parkway. He could have just cut through Mr Carver (Jr)'s access road to get back on track. But then he shouted "Shut up, bitch!" at the implacable female voice of the GPS exhorting him repeatedly to "Make a u-turn," and she thought better of breaking her silence.

So now she simply stares out the window as he drives in circles. Eventually he finds his way to something resembling a highway and the GPS falls into obedient silence too.

He's older than her. Next to him she almost looks like a child. "Your parents are gonna think I'm a cradle robber," he'd teased when she'd asked him home for New Year's. She'd giggled and tugged playfully at his salt-and-pepper goatee before wrapping her arms around his neck and reassuring him in soothing tones that her family would love him.

He's the one who finally breaks the silence to curse at the fuel gauge. "Find me the nearest gas station." It's not a request. It's barely even addressed to her, just a command spoken aloud with the expectation that whatever hears it will respond. But she jumps at the chance to please him with a quick answer delivered with artificial cheer.

"If you take a left at the end of the lane, there's a Beeline about ten minutes down the way." Eager to anticipate his next request, she reaches for his phone to give new instructions to the GPS.

"You don't even have normal gas stations out here?" His tone is curt. He's still not looking at her. Still, it's something. She clings to the hope that maybe he's unthawing a little. Maybe he'll keep talking to her. Maybe this time he'll listen. So she babbles on the neutral topic she's been presented.

"Well, technically it turned into a Valero about five years ago, but the guy who ran it never finished taking down the old signs and everyone around here just keeps remembering it as the Beeline."

He grunts. "That's stupid. Just because you ignore it doesn't change the fact it's a Valero now. What do they print on their receipts?"

Her only option is to be agreeable. "I guess I've never noticed."

"Figures." Palpable contempt paints his tone in odious yellows. She's saved from having to defend herself further by the neutral voice of the GPS informing them that they have arrived at the not-a-Beeline.

It's bitterly cold when he opens the door. She hefts herself out of the car and tries to pull her coat close, but the buttons won't quite reach. "I'm going to go pee."

"You don't need my permission."

It's only four in the afternoon, but here in the shadows of the mountains the light is already dimming. In just the short time it takes her to hurry in and out of the icy bathroom, the air has begun to bite at her fingers and burn in her joints.

He's waiting for her inside the car, fingers tapping impatiently on the steering wheel. She knows she ought to hurry, she knows he hates to wait, but as she crosses the parking lot the last light of the day catches the Beeline sign just so and she sees an elder bush growing in the ditch at its base. Broad, green, and thriving, one huge spray of white flowers blooms under the ray of sun in defiance of the midwinter cold. A flight of fancy takes her and she trots over to the ditch, even though the cold seeps through her half-open coat as she does.

Tiny star-shaped flowers cluster like lace, like snowfall. Defying the midwinter chill, they twinkle in the ditch. The memory of a story tugs at her, some Old Christmas tale her great-grandmother once told, and she feels a sudden urge to hold the flowers in her hand.

The car growls as he pulls up beside her and brakes with unnecessary force. "The hell are you looking at?"

She points at the delicate, impossible flowers, deep in the ditch, calling to her like they've bloomed just for her, and she knows what he'll say, but she asks anyway. "Will you pick them for me?"

"Get your own flowers." His brusque voice shatters the moment, and she feels silly for asking. It's just an unseasonal weed growing in a dirty ditch. "Get in the car."

"Okay," she mumbles, trotting quickly around to the passenger door. They drive away without another word, leaving behind the little miracle to fade into the lengthening shadows.

He shoves the receipt towards her. "What does that say?"

It takes her a minute in the dimming light to make out the text. She doesn't have to ask to know what he's driving at. "It says 'Valero.'"

"What did I tell you?" His tone is triumphant, as if this is irrefutable proof that he has won something that wasn't really even an argument to begin with. "Calling it a Beeline is just ignoring reality. That's your problem."

A hill rolls by. The car dips around a curve, delving into mountains each steeper and darker than the next, already fading to black at the edges in the meager light of the setting sun. Around another curve and the median is gone. Around the next and the shoulder is, too.

"Carl, I swear I didn't cheat on you."

"So you're telling me it's mine?"

The road dips into a trough and another hill looms high, a road cut flying by. The hill eclipses what remains of the sun, dragging a shadowy veil over the road. Another curve and the hill is past, but the darkness remains. She doesn't have an answer for him that he'd understand.

"I wouldn't lie to you."

It's not highway road cuts now that swallow them up but rolling, wooded slopes opposite overgrown ravines. With each hairpin turn, the field of vision contracts. Weak grey light delineates only the closest tree trunks abutting the road, but beyond a rapidly-shrinking diameter, darkness has taken whatever lies beyond.

"Carl, I love you."

Darkness swallows the road. Now even the edge of the road is invisible. No moonlight breaches the enveloping mountains. Beyond the impotent beam of the headlights, there's nothing but a black so deep that you can't be sure the world doesn't stop existing at the edge of that little speeding pool of light.

". . . You can see better if you put your high beams on."

"Don't tell me how to drive."

He's driving well below the speed limit now. Even after he finally switches on his high beams, he still can't see round the hairpin turns. When the ravine's on his right he grips the steering wheel tighter. There could well be a gentle slope or a clean grass shoulder, but in the pitch black it may as well be a sheer drop off a cliff. The unknown begins to gnaw at the edges of his nerves, stirring a primal fear of heights that sends him clinging to the center lane divider.

Blinding light floods his vision in a sudden burst and he jerks the wheel reflexively, nearly running his wheels off into the void. By the time the other driver has the time to lower their high beams, they've already passed, leaving his nails cutting into the steering wheel and his heart beating faster than he wants to admit. In the still darkness, a soothing voice announces like a clock chiming the hour: "GPS signal lost."

She waits for hours, waits until she can't wait any longer. But her throat is so dry and her thirst is so strong that now it's all she can think about. She can't see his face anymore in the dark and she knows he's surely still angry, but she can't fight the need growing in her body any longer.

"I'm thirsty. Could we stop soon?"

"I'm not buying you a soda just so you can stop to pee every thirty minutes." He's not driving more than twenty-five miles an hour now as he creeps through the hills and flinches from the ravine at every turn.

"Please, could we just—"

"Where the hell do you think I'm gonna stop? There's nothing HERE." He might be right and he might not; by now it's been two hours since the GPS stopped working, and longer still since they've passed any kind of artificial light. They could pass two yards by anything in the pitch black night and not see it.

The longer that thirst nags at her throat the more she starts to seethe, pricked and prodded by the ash on her tongue. This isn't right, this isn't fair, this isn't what she was taught. Her child's father ought to care for her, shouldn't he? Hot tears start to well and she turns her cheek to the ice cold window to smother them. She won't cry in front of him again. But she's thirsty, oh so thirsty, and she would take anything to slake her thirst. A drop of rain, a scoop of snow, a mouthful of bone-chill cold water dipped from a creek with her own numb hands—

A jolt and a cry and a slam of the brakes cut off her tears. Her hands fly to her belly. His clench at the wheel. The shock dries her eyes an instant as they skid to a stop, just feet from a branch strewn across the road.

He curses, pounds his hands on the wheel, throws the car into park. His hands might be shaking so he pounds his fists into the wheel again; his heart might be racing so he bellows out a wordless scream at the tree.

But all she can see is the silver gleam. The slithering strands, alight in the headlights. Undulating in the tiny pool of light, pulsing out of the black night to shine slick and wet for just a moment before rippling back into the void again. Water, or something like it, flowing sweet and clean and cold under the bridge they've nearly just collided with.

Now she's standing, useless, in front of the car, as he curses and heaves and struggles to drag the fallen branch out of the road. And she wants so, so much to scramble down the ravine and dip her hands into the stream. But she can't, not in these shoes, not in her condition.

He finally heaves the branch away. Not quite enough to clear both lanes. Just enough to pass through. "Thanks for the help." Angry breath puffs white in the cold.

She doesn't take the bait. Only stares, and one more time she asks: "Carl, get me some water please."

He takes one look down the ravine at the black, chattering stream, at the steep slope, at the impenetrable black night hiding who-knows-what outside the weak glow of the headlights. At the roiling liquid that stains the rocks black where it splashes across them, and surely it's only water because what else could it be but for a moment he can't be sure, when a hot waft of something like rot suddenly sweeps his face in a feverish exhale—

Then the bitter bite of the not-quite-midnight air returns to chill him to the bone. He feels the ache in his knuckles and the burn at his cheeks, and his skin might be crawling so he snaps at her fiercely. "Get back in the car."

She complies without a word, and they leave behind the stream to vanish fully in the inky darkness.

They ought to be half way to Roanoke by now, ought to have at least hit Highway 81. But the clock creeps closer to midnight and they haven't seen the light of human civilization in hours, haven't even seen a road sign since before they passed the creek. He keeps on driving—what else can he do?

Slumped against the window, she stares out the glass, unsleeping. She buries her hands in her coat; the cold winter air has grown so bitter that the car's heater can't quite keep up. So she huddles and shivers and thinks of the warmth of her family, dreams of the cheery home and the loving friends that he dragged her away from in his jealous fit. They would be circled at the fireplace now, the young adults still awake to toast the arrival of Old Christmas. They would be sharing wine and bourbon and the last crumbs of leftover pie and the warm glow of each other's company. And here she was. Cold. Parched. Dragged out like a misbehaving child. Scolded in front of her whole family for something she hadn't even done, called a liar and then shoved into the car.

And now hunger starts to gnaw as well. The car keeps on weaving down the winding road, and all she can think of is the meal he tore her away from. Her mouth begins to water for the moist, tender meat rent straight off the bone. The rich, fatty marrow and the rough scrape on her tongue as she licks the bone clean. White rolls, pillowy under her fingers, sopping up every last drop of thick, salty gravy. She thinks of bacon-crisp crunch of cornbread fresh out of the skillet, cracking and grinding between her teeth and oozing with sticky-sweet honey butter that soaks through the bread to drip down her fingers. Her tongue aches recalling the tart bite of cranberries and the way they pop and burst to spill their bitter, bloody juices in her mouth. And she agonizes over the cookies, the cake, the quivering pudding, and most of all the sweet, steaming glory of the cherry pie.

As the car rolls on in the cold, empty dark, it's all she can think of now. The hot waft of air as the pie comes out of the oven. The sticky red syrup oozing from the cross slashed through the crust. That divine crunch when she first slips a knife into its skin, resistant at first but then quickly falling open under the blade. Each precise thrust of the knife spills out a little gush of crimson until the pie gapes open, steam pouring from the gash, and when she slips the pastry knife between the crust to scoop out the first slice and it can no longer hold itself in one piece, the ruby innards spill across the dish. And she can't resist reaching in to pluck one steaming ruby straight into her mouth, hot and sweet and bursting as she bites down on a single perfect cherry.

Now the car pulls round a bend and for the first time all night, the clouds part and the moon shines through. Its light edges the contours of an open field, nestled between the rolling folds of wooded hills. The silver gleam traces a wooden fence, a broken gate, a run-down barn; it graces the backs of a dozen cows and what might be a horse. And at the heart of the field, massive, lush, limbs sagging under the weight of the fruit that hangs from every branch in glossy clusters, stands a single mighty fruit tree.

The clock ticks over, five minutes to midnight—then goes black. In that moment the engine suddenly stops. He pounds on the dash and pumps the pedals but the engine is dead, and he barely grapples the wheel in time to keep them rolling into the ditch as the power steering seizes before he remembers the brakes.

He throws the car into park and pounds his fists into the wheel with a screamed "God damn it!" He flies out of the car in a rage, closing the door behind him with a violent slam. When he gets to the hood and realizes he's forgotten to release it, he drives his fists again into the car. "Pop the hood!" he demands.

Automatically, she moves to obey him. But she can't reach across for the lever with her belly in the way. So now she has to get out of the car too, lumber around the vehicle, kneel down on the frozen ground to find the latch under the driver's side seat.

He's digging around in the car's insides, steam rolling off the dead engine. He hasn't stopped to look around. But she has eyes only for the tree. Something in its languid grace tugs at her. Calls to her. Stokes the hunger that's been growing in her stomach, teases at her parched lips. In the light of the moon, though all else is shades of grey, the clusters of cherries dripping from the boughs shine a deep, decadent crimson.

He's bent over the engine, intent on repairs.

"Carl. Bring me some cherries."

It's such an unexpected request that he finally looks up. "What?"

"That tree. Bring me some."

He follows her pointing finger, at last looking out across the field. At the cows. At the tree. And he's cold, and he's lost, and he doesn't know a damn thing about cars, and he hasn't exactly been holding it in so far but now everything erupts in a spitting explosion of fury and frustration and impotence. He slams his hand into the car and screams right into her face: "If you want some fucking cherries, your god damned baby-daddy can get them for you, you fucking slut!"

The silence that answers is deafening. Before, she'd have cowered, but now something steels her. Something small and hard deep in her core whispers: her child's father will provide. He'll do his duty. He'll slake her thirst and sate her hunger. So she stands her ground. She meets his gaze.

"Okay."

"Okay? You drag me out to bum-fuck nowhere. You make me burn five days of PTO because your hick family thinks Christmas is in January. You show up with your fat fucking belly hanging out and make me look like a fucking cuck in front of all of them. And now I'm stuck here in the middle of nowhere with a broke-down car and a cheating whore and all you have to say is 'okay'?"

She doesn't speak. She doesn't move. She doesn't even blink an eye in the face of his tirade. This is so far from what he expects, so far from how the young, pliable girl he thought he knew has ever responded before. She should be cowering, pleading, begging to placate him. But now she's not doing any of these things: just staring at him coldly.

He doesn't recognize the girl standing in front of him.

And now as the clouds drift back across the moon to extinguish its glow, he's plunged into a darkness deeper than he's ever known. No street lamps. No headlights. Not even the glow of a cell phone. Only dead, crushing black and the primal fear it stirs in his gut.

Out of the darkness, he hears the voice of the girl he'd thought he knew, and somehow he can tell she's not speaking to him anymore:

"Bring me some cherries."

Something massive shuffles behind him with a rush of hot, humid breath in his ear. Instinct takes over and he jerks away in a blind stagger. He can't see a thing, only hears the lumbering rustle. He stumbles away but the sound only grows nearer, heavy thuds punctuating wet slaps and the scrape of flesh on flesh.

It's all around him now. In a panic, he tries to dash for the car, only to realize he has no idea which direction he's facing. Something jostles him, the massive force behind an unyielding wall of flesh nearly taking him off his feet. When he flings his hand out to catch himself, his palm collides with something soft and wet, his fingers plunging blindly into slimy crevices that twitch and flex in response. He jerks his hands away with a cry of revulsion.

Now fear truly takes hold and he staggers ahead. The unseen creatures buffet him back and forth, closing in closer and closer with each step, bruising and grinding and threatening to drag him into the ground. In a panic-fueled dash, he rushes forward with all his strength. Pain reverberates through his leg as something hard slams into his calf but he keeps scrambling forward in a desperate rush. He breaks free from the crush, but the shuffling, snuffling mass keeps lumbering forward. Driving him. Herding him.

But now he's got his feet under him, and his calf is on fire but he can push through, he can trot, he can run. He breaks into a dash. Pain jolts through his leg with every step as he careens ahead, but he's getting away, he's putting some distance between them, and if he can just get a little further maybe he can arc around and get out of the path of the grunting, churning, sulfur-reeking beast--

He hits the ground with a slam that knocks the wind out of him. For a moment he can't feel anything. Then sensation rushes back in a flood of panic, setting his lacerated hands on fire and piercing his ankle with white-hot agony. He scrambles and clutches at the frozen ground, dragging himself forward inch by inch as the sound of the invisible creature shuffles inexorably forward.

He doesn't manage to crawl very far. The tree is right there, waiting for him to grope blindly into its ancient trunk. Waiting for him to cower into the crevices of its massive girth. Waiting to bow down and entwine him in its laden boughs as it obeys the command of the mother of its master's child.

The moon breaks free of the clouds once more. In its silver light, he sees a herd of cows, frozen in place, all facing the East and kneeling in supplication. And at their head, her. And she too falls to her knees, straddling his legs among the curtain of branches that snake round his trembling limbs and pin him in place. One last time, she speaks.

"Bring me some cherries."

The father of her child provides. The tree cracks open his ribs and his insides slither through his useless fingers in quivering ruby-streaked spills as the god of Old Christmas offers up a feast to slake her thirst and sate her hunger. And the last sight he sees is the look of divine ecstasy on her face when she reaches in and plucks one steaming ruby organ straight into her mouth, hot and sweet and bursting as she bites down on a single perfect cherry.

Take Her

~ Bethany Browning

Whether it was kindness or shame, I'd never know. Mother kept reflective surfaces from me for as long as I had been aware of myself. I was forced to search dark waters, dirty windows, polished trays, silver knives for a glimpse of the face that troubled my family. My utensils were ivory. My doorknob, wood.

She'd been thorough.

Why wouldn't Mother meet anyone's eyes when we were in town together? Why did Papa breeze by me as if I was invisible, leaving me with nothing but the scent of his pipe tobacco, a whiff of newsprint, and the fusty aroma of his woolen suits?

When Mother dragged me through the streets, her hand clamped around my wrist like a jailer's cuff, urging me to *hurryhurryhurry,* I'd catch flashes of my face in mud-clouded puddles between cobblestones and the oil-black sides of the Landau before I clambered, knees over elbows, into the carriage. Mother's relieved sigh when we were safely tucked into the cab was an invisibility spell cast over me. She'd tell me to sit low and out of sight, remind me never to speak my last name to anyone.

My sister Johanna once told me, her pearl teeth flashing in the firelight, that my left eye was the size and color of a one-pfennig coin. My right eye reminded her of her own pinky nail, delicate and rosy with a crescent of white across the top. She explained how Mother was repulsed by the patch of wildfire-colored hair atop my head, the way it stiffly reached skyward, a wiry crown. When Johanna was done explaining my ugliness to me, her tongue darted to the corners of her mouth, as if she reveled in tasting the drops of my pain.

I remembered how she sputtered forth into the world; her alarming screeches ricocheted off the walls. Lost in the hustle and bustle of the staff as they conveyed bundles of bloodied sheets down the stairs and glided in and out of the kitchen wielding pails of sloshing hot water, I awaited the verdict. And it was thus:

Johanna, the rose-lipped beauty.

Johanna, the graceful maiden.

Johanna, the radiant flame around which we all fluttered, dusty and dull, like moths who'd lost their way.

As she grew, my sister's voice filled our ears day and night. A tinkle of bells when she was coddled, a skull-stabbing wail when she didn't get her way. Johanna was a hammer-forged axe, sharpened with entitlement and swaddled in plush fur and luxurious velvet.

I eventually stopped speaking. I no longer needed to.

I once overheard Papa telling Mother through lips drawn tight how my 'silent skulking about' gave him an unsettled feeling, as if the walls themselves were listening, plotting, imagining his demise.

"She's naught more than a ghost," he said. "A tiptoeing memory with a heartbeat."

Mother reassured Papa his unease was temporary. Our final Christmas together was nigh, and he should do his best to tolerate my troubling presence in the spirit of the season. She spoke of my future at Dalldorf, as if there was nothing else to be done.

Johanna was destined to make a beneficial match. Mother was as likely to let my existence ruin Johanna's chances as she was to smile kindly in my direction.

What would my life be like, had they survived? My recollection of their faces slips through my hands like Johanna's rainbow of silk ribbons. When the horrors appear before me in the hulking grey hours of winter, I pull my bedfellows close, feel their fuggy breaths on my neck, twist their hair between my tiny fingers, and remind myself I only did what I had to do, what anyone would do if they were offered the same options.

If I'd used my voice earlier that day, to question Mother, Papa, and Johanna about the brewing snowstorm, my world would consist of hard walls, cold rooms, sharp implements, terrible rules, abandonment. I'd heard other children singing about Dalldorf, a common nursery rhyme used as a chant during a game of chase. The song was meant to menace little ones like me, and I wasn't immune to its threats.

> *Climb the walls, now, there you go.*
> *You're strapped in tight you can't say no.*
> *Feel the thoughts leave through your head,*
> *And leave behind a puddle of dread.*
> *The pink flowers bloom when the sticks are picked,*
> *Your mutter loves you, but your mind is sick.*
> *Your dada forgets you quick as he can,*
> *The lunatic child isn't part of his plan.*

What if I *had* said something? Or written a warning on a piece of paper? Would I have proven my worth, changed their minds, convinced them to keep me close to home and hearth? Shown them I wasn't made for the asylum?

Impossible to know.

Our yearly carriage ride through town, past the cemetery, up and over the hills, and deep into the forest to select our tree was the glimmering pinnacle of my year. The smells of baked spices, dancing lights, merry music, and spectacular sights of Christmas promised enough enchantment to carry me through the suffering of the joyless months before and after.

I put fears of the weather out of my mind, and my family disembarked to the Christmas tree farm on the mountain. As the Landau jostled through the snow-covered roads, I was greeted by trees dressed for season, their boughs bent under the weight of fresh snowfall. Icicles adorned fence rails like jewels. Smoke rose in gentle puffs from gingerbread houses.

Johanna's non-stop nattering about the merriment that awaited her during the Christmas season made it impossible for me to fully immerse myself in the soporific swaying of the cab, the pastoral scenes unwinding outside the window, and the soft sound of Papa's snores.

I couldn't wait to free myself from the carriage and breathe in the sharp winter air. Johanna continued her merciless chatter as she darted off to locate a tree that met her stringent standards.

At first, fat, soft flakes of snow flurried around us. My parents meandered through the orderly rows of spruce, fir, and pine, listening to Johanna pronounce whether one tree or the other was 'too pointy,' 'too tatty,' or 'too shaped like Frau Birne.' I fell back. The sight of the fresh trees lined up like soldiers saluting my sister dredged up my envy and stirred my irritation. The persistent *whackwhackwhack* of the axe sent a quiver through my bones.

The wild, tangled forest, just outside of the bounds of the farm beckoned to me instead. I left my family behind and ascended the hill into the surrounding woods.

Could I ever escape to a place of pure silence, out of the filthy city where Papa was important, Mother was sad, Johanna was demanding? Was I truly doomed to the asylum or could I find a way to escape?

Then, a rustling.

I thought my worn shoes were squeaking. The soles had grown thin, and the leather was peeling. I wiggled my feet and heard nothing more than the muffled crunch of snow underfoot.

I leaned an ear closer to where I thought the sound was coming from. I heard a tiny 'tweep,' a release of breath, and a vocalization that seemed, for lack of a better description, vexed.

I stepped toward the sounds. The expressions changed and shifted from twitters and clicks to whispered bleats and tiny snorts.

A chill slithered up the back of my neck. My heartbeat pulsed in my ears.

The wind was more insistent with every passing moment. The sky was low and of a grey so dark it looked nearly green. The chill snapped at my ears, my nose, like swatting branches. I heard the faintest outline of my name. Mother's sullen voice—were it a musical note it would have fallen flat—calling me, the sound carried on the wintry drafts, up, up over my head into the mountain range beyond me.

The snow was no longer falling, it was whipping around me, a vortex of icy pricks on my cheeks and eyelids. My vision, already compromised, was blurred. I could barely make out the crudely woven basket tucked under the whipping boughs of a small fir.

This basket wasn't my business. This mountain wasn't my home. The conditions were treacherous, so I made the better choice and turned back to follow what remained of my tiny footprints back toward the farm and the warm carriage where my family waited.

A sorrowful keening knifed through the chaos. Something awoke inside me.

The decision was out of my hands. With the wind at my back proving useful to help convey my small body up the incline, I pressed through the snow toward whatever fate awaited me in the basket under the tree.

I could no longer feel my fingers as I tugged the basket out from its hiding place. I looked inside and discovered two eyes, perfect shiny moons, peering back at me. Its face was long and covered with coarse hair. Two tiny horns had begun to poke through on the top of its head. It flicked a ruby-red tongue at me.

It reached out with its front two legs. For the first time in my life, a creature wanted to come closer. To me.

Naturally, I picked it up. What was this small goat doing out here in a snowstorm?

"Blahhh," it said, in a convincingly goat-like manner.

Some faceless coward had left this misshapen creature here in the snow to die.

I tucked it, squirming, into my coat and trudged clumsily against the bluster and toward the farm as the white out whipped itself into a frenzy. The warmth of the creature's body calmed me enough to continue my journey.

Mother was scuttling Papa and Johanna into the carriage, which had the tree secured to a sled at the back, its branches flailing in the storm. She pulled a blanket out and wrapped me in it before I climbed into the cab.

A small kindness, perfectly timed.

The carriage ride home was exactly as I expected. My sister wouldn't stop talking about that evening's Strietzelmarkt, the dress she planned to wear, and the array of bobs and baubles she hoped to receive from St. Nicholas. Papa thumbed through his newspaper. Mother stared out of the carriage window, looking at everything and nothing at all.

The goat squirmed inside my jacket. I noticed a woodsy odor rising from it, so I closed my bundle tighter. I stared out of the window, arranging my face into its blankest expression so they would forget about me. The storm calmed as we descended toward town, and I was able to see the faintest shadow of what could only be a wild deer. I let myself imagine it was one of St. Nicholas's reindeer. Oh, what fun, I thought, nearly cracking a smile and then thinking better of it.

I did notice something odd. The deer's shadow didn't prance away at the juddering sounds of our carriage. It seemed to grow larger, closer. Was it following us?

My cargo shifted and Papa noticed I was wiggling more than usual. "You're not still cold, are you?" His tone let me know not to respond. "You have the only blanket in the carriage. We're off the mountain."

"I'm cold, too," Johanna said, with a pronounced pout. "Why does she get everything while I freeze? She can't tell the difference."

"Hush now, Johanna," Mother hissed. "You won't have to worry about her much longer." She said this last part without moving her mouth.

"Speak up, Mother. It's not like she understands you," Johanna muttered, looking at her hands.

Papa shot her a look. Johanna sighed and stomped the floorboard.

I stared ahead.

The goat coughed.

I coughed.

The goat continued to cough, and every time it coughed, my cough had to be louder, more intense. Wetter.

"She's not sick, is she?" Johanna's horrified tone would have you think she'd discovered me standing over a dead body with a bloody cleaver in my hand. "I can't get sick. Not before the market."

My mother's icy fingers stretched across my forehead.

"Warm," Mother concluded. "Straight to your bedroom when we get home." I smelled the sour residue of the apple cider she must have had at the tree farm. "You understand? Bedroom? No market for you tonight."

Johanna stuck her tongue out at me.

I beamed. What a fortuitous turn of events.

"Straight to your bedroom," Johanna said the moment we arrived at home.

When had I ever refused to comply?

I ferried my new friend through the foyer, up the staircase, across the landing and into my room. I no longer cared about the tree, nor the market, or the merry sounds of off-key carols, kerfuffles over which bow my sister should wear in her hair, or the exasperated tone Papa affected when they were running late.

No one said goodbye.

The lock clicked on the front door, and I heard Cook and Maid grumble amongst themselves for a few moments before the sound of their voices disappeared.

Nothing stirred.

I gazed at my new friend's misshapen face. She gazed back at me, blinking.

I decided to call her Wundershön.

Wundershön sniffed the air. Her ears moved back and forth, grasping for sounds. Like me, she observed her surroundings with all her senses.

She wriggled free from my embrace and scampered away. I watched as she snuffled around the room in a state of frenetic energy. I could discern that she was anxious, but she was also fearless, her movements swift and confident as she considered the velvet drapes and assessed whether she was tall enough to jump onto the bed (she wasn't). She had an unusual way of picking items up and bringing them to her nose rather than rooting around on the floor like a pig or a dog. She seemed to want to walk on two legs, yet she fell onto four legs every time she tried, a sorry state that I attributed to her deformities.

I understood her.

As each moment passed, I fell more deeply in love. She scrambled around under the bed for a while, emerging covered in dust and a few hair ribbons that had been lost ages ago.

She sat down in front of me and growled.

I tilted my head to show that I wasn't aggressive and that I didn't know what she needed. She growled again and lightly butted my hand with her forehead.

I reached out to pet her under her fuzzy mandible. I should have been afraid of a bite or a snap, but I was more fearful of rejection. She leaned her head forward and rested her head in my hand.

She growled again, less intensely, like a purr. She sighed. She hiccupped.

She must be hungry.

I needed a plan for keeping her hidden. Judging from the size of her back hooves compared to her body, it was clear that she was going to eventually be very large. My chest hurt as I realized the inevitability of having to give her up. Papa and Mother would never allow me a pet. Nor would Dalldorf, it goes without saying.

Feed first. Then hatch a plan for us to stay together.

I motioned for Wundershön to stay put. I put my finger to my lips before I opened the door.

She bolted past me with speed I did not expect considering her handicaps. She tumbled down the stairs, tiny horns over hooves the size of a klootscheiten ball. I sucked in my breath and ran toward her on my lightest feet, hoping the ruckus didn't arouse the help.

The spicy aroma of tobacco and schnapps greeted me when I finally made it to Wundershön's side. This indicated that Cook and Maid had decamped to the back garden to indulge themselves before my family returned from the Christmas events.

Wundershön looked at me and shook her head. I reached my hand toward her, and she scrambled away toward the kitchen on all fours.

Was she giggling?

I found her in the kitchen, half-buried in a tall basket of Cook's onions, her back legs kicking, her skinny tail swishing back and forth in the air like she was swatting flies.

Allowing her to devour all of Cook's onions was unthinkable. I made swift moves to remove her, only to find that she wasn't eating them at all. She tossed each onion out onto the floor, where they bounced like miniature human heads. She peered over the edge of the now-empty onion basked. I must have been starving as well, because it sounded like she said the word, 'Mama.'

It occurred to me how strange it was that Wundershön only had two hooves and small mink-like *paws*. It became imperative that I steal into Papa's library before he returned. Perhaps she wasn't a goat at all, rather some forest creature about which I had not yet read? A type of badger? A malformed bear? An over-large weasel?

She seemed content enough sitting in the basket, so I looked around the kitchen to see if there was anything she might like to eat. I discovered a plate of lebkuchen, and I stood on my tiptoes to slide the plate off the counter.

I sat next to Wundershön. I broke off a bite of biscuit and held it out to her. She pulled my hands toward her searching nose, sniffed vigorously, and nibbled. We sat together quietly, sharing Christmas treats and watching the snow swirl in infinite patterns outside the kitchen window.

It was as if the star on the Christmas tree had been placed in my heart, a warm glow filling me from toes to fingertips. Is this what others meant by the Christmas spirit? Was I experiencing joy?

I looked at her unusual furry face, now speckled with cookie crumbs, and had another feeling that could only be described as bittersweet. Was happiness caused by its fleeting nature? I pondered the way opposite emotions needed each other to be true. To be happy one must know what sad is. To know calm one must know tension.

I stroked her head as she lifted her snout and drew a deep breath. Her carmine tongue shot out into the air, fast and confident, and I saw that the end was deeply forked, like a snake's.

"Mama," she said meeting my gaze, her eyes clear and pure as the sound of the screams that came from outside. She pointed toward the back garden.

What a clatter! The shrieks were loud and persistent with a tone akin to winter branches scraping a window. The hair on my arms stood up.

Then, quiet.

Wundershön fixed her eager eyes on the garden door. She bounced on her hooves.

Despite my desire to run and hide, I motioned for her to stay where she was. I stepped through the mudroom and carefully cracked open the door to the garden.

I saw what looked like two piles of laundry on the ground next to the water pump.

A rivulet of red ran trickled toward my shoe. Cook. Maid. I dared not look at them, but I knew. Their deaths made them appear vulnerable. I was seeing something forbidden. I dared not step closer.

I froze, but only long enough to catch a glimpse of the malevolence that had let loose this display of violence.

The tip of the beast's head was as high as the sill of a second-story window, and its entire being was covered in hair thick as cut piano wires. Two immense, twisted horns framed its sour face, with thorny teeth that jutted out of swollen, dripping gums. A dense aroma, highlighted by the acrid scent of fermenting pine sap, met my nostrils and my stomach lurched. Its tongue, red as a kidney and fast as a flag whipping in the wind, flicked toward me. It cocked its head and leaned toward the crown of my head. It sniffed.

Mama?

I slammed the door shut as quickly as I could and dropped the lock.

Wundershön sat placidly in the onion basket as I struggled to hoist her up the stairs. I heard the wood of garden door ache, groan, and then splinter open and the pounding clobber of monstrous hooves on the stone floor. Unimaginable sounds came from downstairs as I lugged Wundershön across the landing to our hiding place in a closet at the end of the hall.

Glass breaking. Furniture splitting. Unearthly roars, so deep they boomed inside my ribcage. The sound of pages tearing.

The beast was in Papa's library.

As I shivered in terror, sweat dripping down the back of my dress, Wundershön freed herself from the basket and clawed at the closet door.

I did my best to subdue her, but she was determined get out. To save her, I had to do the unthinkable.

I picked her up and stuffed her back into the basket. I slipped out of the closet before she collected herself. She wasn't tall enough to reach the doorknob. Not that she knew how to use it.

Did she?

My disadvantage was clear. I was no match for the creature's size, and it didn't seem repelled by my appearance. I had to be smarter. And braver.

I ran through the scenarios in my mind. I could wound her in some way, perhaps a knife to the knee. That might be enough to stop forward progress until I found a more permanent solution. Poison? That would require ingestion and just how much rat poison does it take to incapacitate… one of those?

I had no plan, but I was compelled forward by what could only be love for Wundershön. I had received a friend for Christmas, and she was my most treasured thing. I couldn't fathom letting her be snatched away by an unhinged demon and what? Eaten?

Numb from my forehead to my heels, I nudged the door to the library. The height of the creature was accentuated by the flickering flames from the hearth. She glowered at me, a devil in her element. I stood my ground for no other reason than I was frozen to the spot.

"It's not fair." Johanna's strident tone snapped me out of my stupor. "You said I could have one and it is Christmas and I've been very good this year."

I turned to face my family. Papa was tut-tutting at Johanna; Mother drew the back of her hand across her forehead as if she'd recently been relieved of an emotionally daunting task. The cold air whisked in, and I shuddered against it. My mouth wouldn't open. I couldn't unhinge my jaw.

The smack was furious and decisive. The fiend had knocked me out of the way, and I crashed into Mother's grandfather clock, setting off a grotesque alarum of bells and shattered glass. Dazed, I lay in a crumpled heap with blood drawing a crimson line down my cheek.

My pampered family was no match for the surprise fury unleashed against them. Mother fainted straightaway, and the monster dispatched with her by tossing her out the front door. I heard the sickening crack of her skull on the brick walk.

Papa's mouth dropped in horror, but no sound came out. Even if he had been able to scream, the sound would have been drowned out by a roar straight out of the hell's deepest trenches. The beast swiped at Papa; its thorny claws strafed his face and ripped his nose apart.

He collapsed, still alive, while Johanna shrieked like a teakettle boiling over.

The blood pumped from Papa's open wounds as his whole body seized and contorted. Johanna, in a moment of sheer courage I shall never forget, kicked the monster in its ankle. The beast delivered a crushing blow to Papa's skull, which popped open, revealing bits of the delicate, sickly-colored matter inside.

Then, it turned toward my sister.

Johanna backed away, tears pooling in her eyes. The animal lifted her by her gold ringlets and pulled her close to consider her valentine face, her flushed cheeks.

"Take her," Johanna said breathlessly as she dangled above the floor. Despite the agony she must have been in, she roused herself enough to point in my direction. "No one wants her. She's deaf and dumb. Destined for the asylum at Dalldorf. Take her. And you, of all creatures, know how good I've been this year. You've made a mistake."

How could I have not realized? Another haunting rhyme filled unfurled in my mind.

> *Take heed, be aware, behave, don't you dare . . .*
> *The demon Krampus has chains to spare*
> *For naughty babes who refuse to behave.*
> *He'll gladly snatch you, make you a slave . . .*

A fairy story, told to children to force them into meek compliance. I'd never thought it was true, but here she was.

I searched the room for an escape, only for my face appeared to me in a shard of broken glass. Deformed features. Impossible hair.

I had options. None of them good.

I managed to hoist myself to standing. I took a step toward them, toward imminent death.

"She's right," I said. The sound of my voice caused an upwelling of feeling in my chest, a mixture of hurt and hope that I imagined was a lot like nostalgia. My inner monologue sounds nothing like the meekness of my physical voice, which had atrophied from years of disuse. The tone was eerily child-like and high-pitched, the texture nearly a whisper. "I have no future. Take me instead."

I could no longer discern if my sister's horror was due to her current predicament or her shock at my ability to speak.

The creature narrowed her eyes and glanced back and forth between us.

"See?" Johanna spoke with resolve, despite the fact that she was noticeably shaking, her feet kicking in spasmodic bursts. "Take her."

In one unforgiving movement, the creature Wundershön called Mama shook Johanna with such force that her scalp separated from her skull. Her body hit the wall with a dull thud, and she slid down it. The beast untangled its claws from her ringlets, and they fluttered to the floor, a grisly wig.

The beast and I stood next to each other, watching her struggle, witnessing her life force flow from her body. The terror in her eyes transformed into acceptance, then dimmed completely, leaving behind two dull, motionless orbs.

There was nothing in the world left to frighten me. I'd seen all I needed to see of this life, including my sister's frontal bone, pink and frothy from the matter that the inside of her skin had left behind.

The demon left me standing there alone, numbly trying to understand my new fate. I retched onto the carpet.

Still queasy, I turned away from the bodies and closed my eyes, with no thoughts of prayers. My mind was an empty jar.

I heard clawing at the closet door upstairs, the sturdy footfalls of a creature who probably had to hunch to make its journey across the landing. The closet door creaked open and then what can only be described as a happy reunion.

I took a deep breath and awaited the beast's revenge. Whatever happened next, I wanted it to be swift.

Mama was behind me. She huffed; the humid expiration dampened the crown of my head. Her immense presence loomed over me like a curse.

I turned to face her, determined to take my punishment with courage.

Mama kneeled. I was eye-to-eye with Wundershön, who was strapped to her mama in a basket, peering over a coarse-haired, rope-muscled shoulder.

"Mama," Wundershön said, her tone decisive.

Mama gave the basket a little wiggle, and I knew I had to do the one thing children feared every Christmas for centuries: I climbed in.

Was it possible we had the story wrong? A monster. A basket. Misbehaving children scooped up by a fiend and spirited off to an unknown but surely terrible fate.

What if the beast wasn't punishing impish children after all? What if the monster took your children because you didn't deserve them?

Krampus stealing evil babes was the cover story. The terrible warnings, the vicious tales of chains and baskets and flaming hot ovens were nothing more than devious machinations designed to blame children for their parents' failures.

Yes, Krampus could take you. The tales is true. But worry not, tiny babe. She'll take you from *them*.

Not to be enslaved.

To be saved.

I crouched next to Wundershön, held her close to me, while Mama spirited us through town, past the cemetery, up and over the hills, and deep into the forest.

No noise but the sounds of the branches bristling in the wind. No smells but the cleanest air purified through primal, fragrant trees.

We arrived in a place where my damaged heart could find peace in solitude, in silence, in merry companionship with others who had borne the same pain I once suffered.

Finally, I was able to see myself as I truly was. My face appeared before me every time I gazed into Mama's face, her wet eyes the size of a blacksmith's fists, shining dark as the coal in the furnace that kept the horrors of winter at bay.

The Cheshire's Killer Cousin

~ *J. Rohr*

At the Buckshot Bed and Breakfast customers are greeted by a charming woman. Sweet and soft as a cinnamon roll, she checks them in then gives a guided tour. Animal heads line every hallway. Each one either her husband or a customer killed, and expert taxidermy kept them all, some might say, unsettlingly lifelike. Perhaps that's why, despite her pride, she draws attention to the furniture. Most of it looks like wood naturally grown into tables and chairs. Then there are the paintings, all originals depicting the prairies, badlands, or nearby Killdeer mountains. None are by terribly famous painters, but she proudly insists native North Dakotans made them.

She always saves the lounge for last. A cozy, wood paneled space with several leather chairs. Retro vintage LED bulbs cast a dim light around the room.

"Dark but intimate," she remarks. "And if you're lucky, our resident storyteller might be by later."

She's referring to Al Williams, who occasionally stops by for a brandy. His visits having become more and more frequent since her husband passed. Al occupies the lounge happily sharing whatever tales customers care to hear. His tongue spins yarns about everything from romance to true crime.

"What kinda true crime?" a young couple inquires.

"The unsolved kind," the old woman winks. "That's what everyone is listening to on their phones, isn't it?"

"It is very popular."

"Well, after you're settled, if and when Al arrives, be sure to ask him about the circus folks back in 1934."

❄

Despite careful handling, use eroded the road map into tatters. The skinflint owner of the circus cut costs wherever possible. So, for almost twenty years ringmaster Isaac Dupree navigated the 20,016-mile route with the same folded paper. The circus's only guide to 216 shows over 8 months. Creases evolved into holes over time. The rattle of the truck always threatened to shake the sheet into bits.

Granted, Isaac knew most of the route by heart, especially short cuts like this particular dirt stretch. Though that didn't change the desire for a new chart. Pennies pinched in one way justified too many in others. The once grand circus was decaying before his very eyes. He sometimes doubted it inspired anyone to run away from home like he once did.

A deep pothole caused the truck to shudder. The violent turbulence bouncing him, slamming his head into the top of the cab. The map in his mitts ripped. The ache in his noggin bothered Isaac less than the fresh hole in the map.

'Dammit, Murray,' Isaac said. 'Watch the road.'

'Sorry,' the driver said. 'I didn't see. It's gettin' dark.'

'I hear ya,' Isaac said. 'But you know our tires can't take a beating. They ought've been replaced by . . .'

Kerrang boom blam! Cut off by a cacophony of thunderous sounds, Murray and Isaac looked back in the sideview mirrors. Isaac felt his heart stop. He saw the truck behind them tumbling along the road. Other vehicles in the circus caravan swerved to avoid the mess. Some screeched to a halt, but many collided with the cars in front of them or began spilling off the road.

No need to be told, Murray slammed on the brakes. The truck barely came to a halt before Isaac jumped out the passenger side. He ran towards the wreckage.

Getting nearer, Isaac saw at least one tire blown to shreds. He figured the pothole popped it on impact. Meanwhile, Danny the Dog boy climbed out of the overturned truck. Blood dripping down his furry face.

'I'm okay,' Danny said.

Noting that, Isaac ran towards the other vehicles. Clouds of dust kicked up off the dirt road made the air hazy. Still, most of the damage seemed trivial. Many of the passengers shook up but okay. However, towards the rear, Isaac saw a potential catastrophe.

He guessed the truck swerved to avoid everyone stopping short. However, the trailer behind it snapped free. That went careening off the road into a ditch. It clearly hit the ground hard. Isaac already noticed several unsettlingly thick cracks in the sides. Then the trailer shuddered.

A roar from within caused him to skid to a halt. Isaac held his breath. The container shook again, and the splits widened.

The image of the creature inside, painted on the trailer, barely hinted at the beast within. A ferocious portrait yet disarmingly cartoonish, Isaac wished the image matched reality. It made customers feel a daring desire to see the creature, but the painted ad barely hinted at the haunting terror induced after witnessing the monstrosity.

Isaac always considered the beast a mixed blessing. It raked in cash, no doubt. Perhaps it even helped them survive the blasted Depression. However, something in the creature's eyes made Isaac worry what'd happen if it ever got loose. And as another shudder cracked the trailer more, this one accompanied by the sound of squealing metal bending, Isaac turned to run.

A terrible snapping of wood sounded. He felt a spray of splinters shower him. However, he didn't look back. He ran faster. His only thought aimed at getting one of the circus's armaments. A pistol or shotgun, any of the myriad weapons for dealing with rough townies. Something to send the sideshow devil back to hell.

Isaac never made it. The carnival creature grabbed him from behind. In the blink of an eye, it tore him to pieces. Then the beast went after the rest of the circus caravan."

The old cinnamon girl closed the lounge door.

"They're all nestled in bed," she said.

Dropping into a chair she closed her eyes. No need to be asked, Al fetched her a Bärenjäger from the drink cart. He poured her honey liqueur before refreshing his brandy.

Accepting the drink he brought, she smiled. Sitting in a chair beside her he held up his glass.

"To you Adele," he said. "Queen of the B & B."

"Cheers."

Some rhythmic creaking started sounding from upstairs. Adele grinned. She figured the fresh-faced couple in room three must be enjoying one another. They seemed the honeymoon sort. Nothing sour in their mix yet. That got Adele thinking.

"Christmas is right around the corner," she said. "I'm wondering if you'd do me a favor."

"Anything," Al smiled.

The crags in his face exaggerated the expression.

"Don't tell that circus story," Adele said, adding as soon as she saw his face fall. "Just for the holiday season."

Swirling his drink, Al nodded.

"If it's what you want," he said.

Adele reached over to pat his arm. She knew he liked the tale. She even encouraged the spine chiller occasionally. However, it sometimes stirred a grimmer atmosphere than guests care for.

"That sour couple in room five was asking about it," she said.

"Skeptical ones I'm sure," Al said. "Didn't seem to buy my *Zip to Zap* story either."

"Can't say I blame them," Adele said. "I sometimes doubt it myself."

Although Al's tongue painted a vivid portrait, fifty circus folk killed by one wild animal, Adele suspected embellishments rather than facts. Wet red all along the dusty ground. The handful of survivors nothing more than tatters, shredded bodies and minds. Granted, she didn't doubt the dead. Al once found old police photos on a weird website. However, she guessed the story owed more to the killer creature never being found than anything else. As such, the incident seeded notions of some savage monster roaming North Dakota.

"What's to doubt?" Al said. "I was there in '69. Helluva riot. Only time the National Guard got called out in the flickertail state."

"And the town of Zap is forever proud of that," Adele said, leading the conversation down another track.

"You betcha," Al smirked.

He started reminiscing about his other college misadventures. She let him ramble rather than dwell on urban legends about a giant cat creeping along shelter belts. Adele sipped her liqueur. Like her seasonal guests, she looked forward to a quiet Christmas.

Climbing out of the ride share, Marvin took a deep breath. The fresh air felt like a divine gift after the prolonged ride with the driver puffing on a blue cheese flavored vape pen. The moment Marvin stepped out, however, the car started pulling away. He ran after it waving his arms.

The car stopped short. The driver rolled down his window.

"Sup?" he said.

"My bags?" Marvin said. Considering the driver's blank expression, he added, "They're still in the trunk."

"Oh yeah," the driver nodded. Marvin heard a pop, and the trunk lazily drifted up. Going around back he collected his luggage. As soon as the trunk closed the driver sped off.

Already starting to shiver, Marvin hurried towards the B&B's entrance. Passing under a portico covered in holly garlands, he awkwardly opened the front door. A tinkling bell announced his arrival.

Stepping inside felt like being wrapped in a warm blanket. Christmas potpourri scented the air. Seasonal aromas of orange, cranberry, nutmeg, cinnamon, and clove. Marvin suspected a homemade concoction brewed on a kitchen stove, not some cold corporate bundle produced in a factory and robotically shipped from a warehouse.

A woman just cresting the middle age hill appeared behind a desk in the front room. Dressed in corduroy pants and unironically wearing a jolly Christmas sweater, she waved as Marvin entered.

"Welcome to the Buckshot B&B," she said. "I'm owner and proprietor, Adele Losendahl."

Making his way over, Marvin introduced himself.

"Oh, you're the winner then," Adele said beaming. "Congratulations."

"Just lucky I guess," Marvin said. "I was at a teacher's conference, there was a contest, and now I'm here."

"Well, we're happy to have you," Adele said.

The clop-clop of heels sounded in the room. Marvin glanced over to see a woman fast approaching. She looked ready for battle in some corporate Thunderdome. She held a smartphone, a finger on her free hand constantly jabbing at the screen.

Brushing by Marvin she went straight to the front desk.

"The internet is down," she said to Adele.

The older woman nodded, "I know."

"Is someone going to fix it?" the young lady asked. "Soon."

"No, it's after six," Adele said turning her attention to Marvin. "After six we turn off the internet doohickey to encourage our guests to disconnect; interact with people."

She pointed at a wooden sign. Rustic letters burned into it spelled out several rules for the B&B. Marvin smirked when he saw #7: *Be polite or be put out.*

"Unless there's anything else, Ms. Franklin," Adele said. "Internet services resume at 7 A.M."

Groaning, Ms. Franklin started to leave. She bumped into Marvin on her way. Swearing under her breath but definitely not apologizing, she soon vanished around a corner.

After depositing his bags in room three, Marvin followed Adele on a tour of the Buckshot. He tried not to look up at the looming antlers and glaring glass eyes. Along the way they encountered a sugary couple in the reading room.

"We're the McCoys," a beaming young woman said.

"We're reading what birds we might see," said her bespectacled husband.

"We're going hiking tomorrow."

"Best anniversary ever," they said as one.

On to the next stop in the tour, Marvin remarked on a Gary Miller painting they passed. Snow amassed by a northwester against an octagonal silo. One could feel the chilly breeze whipping a tattered rope around as well as helping birds soar.

Surprised he recognized the artist, Adele asked what painters he preferred. He mentioned Norman Blaine Saunders and Susan Krieg.

"I'm not familiar," Adele said. "But that's what I like about this job. The conversations expand my world."

As usual, the tour ended in the lounge. In there, they found Ms. Franklin seated beside the fireplace. Three fingers of vodka in hand, she gazed into the flames as if she might stare them down. Marvin certainly believed she could.

"Well," Adele said. "I have to see about supper. Feel free to have a drink before dinner, mingle, and congratulations on your win."

She slipped out of sight. Spotting a drink cart covered in bottles and crystal ware, Marvin went over to pour a little wine. Howling wind called his attention to a frost-dotted window. The snow-covered world outside looked picturesque, though Marvin guessed he only felt that way seeing it through glass.

Then something caught his eye. Snow drifts, thrown up by the wind, seemed to hit something in the shadows. A shape in the darkness outlined by a faint dusting of powdery white. Hints of a massive feline face called a more sinister Cheshire Cat to mind. Marvin stepped towards the window for a better look.

"What did you win?" Ms. Franklin asked.

Her voice caused Marvin to look away from the window. When he turned back, he no longer saw the wispy outline in the dark.

"Do you know *The Wilderness Station*?" Marvin asked.

"No."

Taking a seat nearby, Marvin shared the whole story. While attending a teachers' seminar some of his colleagues, without him around, thought it'd be funny to submit his name to a TV contest. Part of him felt glad since, if any other channel at the motel worked, he might've ended up getting a crate of erotic baking tins.

"I've seen that infomercial," Ms. Franklin said. "They'd do better with a different cast. I don't want to buy a penis cake mold from a grandma."

"Yet it sounds like you want to buy that mold," Marvin said.

She smirked. He felt safe asking what brought her to the bed and breakfast. She hesitated then shared her own story. After ten years bareknuckle busting her way through glass ceilings, she climbed to the heights of the Chicago stock exchange. A recent bout of migraines resulted in the unfortunate discovery she did not have a brain tumor. That could've been cut out. Instead, she required a more ethereal, psychological remedy.

"Long story short," she said. "I need to relax. Work life balance and all that bullshit."

She drained most of her vodka in one gulp. Marvin sipped his wine. Shaking her head, she went to get a refill.

"So," she asked. "What kind of teacher are you?"

"Art."

"Does that mean you've got weed?" Ms. Franklin said, raising an eyebrow.

Minutes later, up in Marvin's room, they set about surreptitiously smoking his stash of Banana Kush. Blowing smoke out the open window, for a moment, Marvin thought he heard an unearthly growl. The sound drifted across the night air chilling him more than the winter wind.

Blaming it on the weed, he stepped away from the window.

"Ms. Franklin," he said. "Would you care for some more?"

"I'm good," she said. "And call me Keisha."

"Pleasure to meet you," he said, snuffing the remains of the joint.

"Sorry about early," Keisha said. "Bumping into you. My mind was elsewhere."

"Water under the bridge."

"Do you know the origin of that phrase?" she asked. When Marvin shook his head she added, "It's related to the idea you can't ever step in the same river twice."

"Kind of like first impressions," Marvin said.

Keisha narrowed her eyes. A dawning realization of his unintentional implication caused Marvin's peepers to widen.

"I'm so sorry," he stammered. "I didn't mean you from earlier I meant—wow, I forgot how good my weed is."

Keisha started to snicker then burst out laughing. Marvin joined her. All seemed right with the world.

Delightful chimes sounded throughout the Buckshot, a melodious assortment announcing supper for anyone inclined. Still a bit bubbly, Keisha came down the steps giggling. Marvin bobbed along behind her. When Keisha froze at the bottom of the stairs Marvin almost walked into her.

"That's him officer," Adele said.

Marvin glanced over to see Adele behind the front desk pointing at him. Beside the desk stood a uniformed sheriff's deputy. The deputy stepped towards the two.

Marvin stiffened. He saw his career as an educator about to end. The cop as executioner coming to kill an art teacher cliché.

"Excuse me, sir," the officer said. "Can I ask you a few questions?"

"Yes?" Marvin said, suspecting his eyes looked as red as the mistletoe berries above the dining room door.

"Did you take a ride share here this evening?"

"Yes?"

"Do you recall anything about the drive?"

"No?" Marvin looked at Keisha.

"What's this about?" she asked.

The police officer proceeded to inform them. Earlier this evening a Mr. Al Williams, on his way to the Buckshot, passed a wreck along the roadside. He stopped to help but found nothing except a mangled vehicle.

"He had a buncha light up ride share nonsense on his dashboard," the deputy said. "So, sheriff figured someone here might've seen him last."

"I guess that was me then," Marvin said. "Although, I can't think of anything that might help. He didn't seem drunk or whatever."

"That is what I wanted to ask," the deputy said. "If you think of anything, anything at all."

He passed along his card. Marvin took it. Tipping his hat at them then Adele, the deputy departed.

Feeling suddenly very sober, Marvin shuffled towards the dining room. Keisha followed him. They took a seat away from the cloying couple feeding each other crème brûlée.

On the table a small stack of vellum menu cards listed the dinner options. Marvin scanned the items without much interest. Comfort foods like fleischkuekle, and cheese buttons sounded good, however, his thoughts orbited everything except food.

"Are you alright?" Keisha asked.

"Yeah, I guess," Marvin said tossing the menu aside. "It just makes you think. If that driver is dead, I mean, how close was I to dying?"

"How close are any of us?" a voice came over Marvin's shoulder.

Turning, he saw a skinny fellow with a bowling ball paunch standing behind him. The man wore a green and red checkered waistcoat. Sucking brandy from a half full snifter, he approached the table as if invited. Pulling a chair over he introduced himself as Allsherjangodinn Williams.

"But you may call me Al," he said sitting down.

"You're the one who found the wreck," Keisha said.

"Unfortunately, I am," he nodded. "And such a sight I have never seen. You're the young fellow who was in the vehicle earlier?"

Before Marvin acknowledged anything, Al went into a description of the scene. The mangled car looked like something slammed into it, shouldering the vehicle off the road. He saw blood all over the driver's side as well as crimson stained snow.

"Not enough for a trail," Al said. "Though if I had to guess, I'd say it was headed towards this place."

The next day Marvin spent most of the morning in bed. So far, he still didn't know what to make of this trip. It started as a prank from coworkers who, despite his best efforts, Marvin found himself increasingly disliking. Although he tried to treat their jabs as good natured, he occasionally wished one of the more bullied goth kids would snap and shoot them during a rampage. Still, this place appeared charming and meeting Keisha slowly made it seem like the joke would be on them—he was having a good time. That is, until he heard about the accident.

Al's vivid description spun images of a blood-drenched pile of twisted metal. For some reason that inspired him to remark about circus folks. Before he got deep into what sounded like an urban legend, Adele arrived to shoo him away. The tale still poisoned Marvin's dreams. Nightmares stirred him like a spoon, agitating him to no end. Even in this picturesque place, ugly aspects of the world remained inescapable.

Around noon a firm knock summoned him out of bed. Opening the door revealed Keisha dressed for the outdoors.

"I'm going for a walk," she said. "Would you care to join me?"

Despite not being very outdoorsy, Marvin agreed. Minutes later, on their way out, Adele called after the two. She asked them to keep an eye out for the McCoys.

"They went out this morning and haven't been back for hours. Tell them I've got piping hot soup waiting to warm them!"

Out the door, the view seemed perfect for a postcard. Noticing footprints in the fresh snow, Keisha suggested they follow the McCoy's trail. Marvin agreed and they headed off.

Crunching through the snow, they chitchatted aimlessly. Mostly they shared snippets of their lives. Each painted self-portraits of people working very hard to ignore their own unhappiness.

They followed the McCoys' winding trail into the Killdeer Mountains. At one point, the couple appeared to go after a set of heart shaped deer tracks. Pursuing their course, Keisha noticed other prints soon followed the McCoys.

"They look like cat tracks," she said.

"Can't be," Marvin said.

"I had a cat as a kid," Keisha said. "She left the same prints in our backyard."

"Okay, but there's no cat in the world this big, right?"

The prints looked larger than an elephant's. Recalling the sinister Cheshire from last night, Marvin hesitated to go on. However, Keisha pressed forward, and he followed. Not long after, they found signs of the McCoys.

A thermos dropped on the ground. Crimson Rorschach splashes all around. A woman's hand stuck out of snow too shallow to hide any body beneath. Broken glasses in a puddle of blood. Red pawprints of a massive cat disappeared into the hills.

❄

The sheriff arrived after sunset. Winter killed the light quick. Night reigned by the time he took statements from Keisha and Marvin. Though he remained skeptical about the cat prints' size, he believed their story. It wouldn't be the first time a wandering mountain lion went after some hapless hikers.

"It wasn't a mountain lion," Marvin insisted.

"I've got deputies taking a look," the sheriff said. "When they get back, we'll know for sure what you think you saw."

As if to emphasize that point, he grabbed the handset off his shoulder. He tried to contact the deputies but only got static.

"Must be interference," he said. "That can happen in the mountains."

Marvin cast a sidewise glance at Keisha. Her grim expression seemed to share his own suspicions. The sheriff stepped away to try the radio some more.

"I'm starting to understand why you got so maudlin last night," Keisha murmured.

"It's my default setting," Marvin said. "Not a popular trait."

"But it makes sense," she said. "Whatever happened, those people are just gone now."

She shivered. Marvin put an arm around her. She pressed against him.

Adele came in carrying steaming hot cocoa on a tray. Chock-full of a special ingredient, she insisted they all drink. Keisha took a mug, sipped it, and raised an eyebrow.

"Homemade peppermint schnapps," Adele winked. "I figured we could all use some."

Still unable to raise anyone, the sheriff tried his phone. Keisha found herself recalling how many rifles hung on the walls in various rooms. She asked Adele if they worked. Adele assured her they did. Each belonged to her late husband, and she kept them as mementos as well as décor.

"I have to see about something," the sheriff said, sauntering towards the door. "Meanwhile, I don't want anyone going outside unless absolutely necessary. It might not be safe."

He stepped out. Keisha pulled away to drift in morbid thoughts.

Marvin stepped to a front window. Watching the sheriff depart, he saw the gumballs on the cop's car silently spinning red and blue. However, between flashes he spotted something in the deep shadows. Red then cobalt, looming at the edge of the light, it reminded him of a Norwegian forest cat. One with a visage that froze his blood.

Shouting, Marvin pounded on the glass.

"What's wrong?" Keisha asked.

As the sheriff turned towards the sound, the enormous cat pounced. It sailed noiselessly through the air, over the sheriff's car, and landed on the officer, crushing him into the ground. Before the cop could react, long claws raked him open. In a blink, the cat shredded him out of existence. Then the creature looked up. Eyes fixed on Marvin, it charged.

Marvin jumped away from the window. The whole house shuddered. A glaring yellow eye filled the pane, staring through the glass.

Adele dropped her mug. A guttural growl covered the sound of its shatter. Soon a slow, terrible scratching sounded. Long nails popped through the wood as the creature clawed at the wall.

Throwing her mug aside, Keisha grabbed Adele. She asked about ammo. Transfixed in horror, the old woman didn't respond until Keisha shook her to attention. Adele directed her to shells behind the front desk. While Keisha went to collect them, she ordered Marvin to find a shotgun. He quickly returned from the dining room with a long rifle. Adele sent him to the reading room, and he promptly ran back with the proper weapon.

Fumbling shells, he dropped more than he loaded. When the monstrous cat shook the house again, Marvin yelped and fired into the ceiling. Sighing, Keisha held out her hands. He gave her the shotgun and held the box of shells for her.

Keisha thumbed in ammo then snapped the double barrel hand cannon shut. Hurrying to the window, she took aim. The cat hissed. Keisha fired. The blast blew out the window, but the cat had already bounded away.

Silence for a moment then clawing again. This time from the dining room. Keisha snatched a handful of shells from Marvin as she ran by. She reloaded on the go before blasting the cat away from another window. This time they heard a bowel loosening bellow as the animal ran off in rage. Blood around the window said it caught a bit of buckshot this time.

This went on for an intolerable time. The cat creeping around the building, occasionally tearing into the walls. Keisha and Marvin scrambling to shoot-shoo it away. Each chance it got the cat tore deeper, often returning to previous spots, widening a possible entrance.

Although Keisha hit the beast a few times, the buckshot seemed to make the monster more determined. They soon ran low on ammo. Adele confessed there wasn't anymore, evaporating the weapon's comfort.

At least sixteen feet high, maybe nineteen feet long, the creature couldn't get inside yet. However, none of them doubted its ability to tear the house apart. Either it eventually ripped its way in or pulled the house down around them. Neither option preferable, the simple fact of the matter stood they couldn't wait this out.

"Adele?!" a voice hollered out front.

"Al!" Adele said.

She raced to the front. Throwing open the door she shouted for him to hurry inside.

"What's going on?" he asked.

The colossal cat came sprinting around a corner. Adele screamed. Al looked over in time to see it coming.

"*Jólakötturinn,*" he whispered in awe.

Then the beast swiped him. The blow slapped him across the lawn onto the front steps. Adele dove onto the bloody mound of meat ribbons that used to be Al.

"I," he gasped. "Always loved . . ."

Tears in her eyes, Adele ripped the shotgun from Keisha's hands. Storming onto the lawn, she saw no sign of the feline.

"Where are you?" Adele shouted.

An unearthly *ekekek* called her eyes to the roof. The great beast stood atop the Buckshot B&B. Crying, Adele fired both barrels, but the cat already sailed through the air, crushing her when it landed.

Meanwhile, Marvin pulled Keisha back inside. He slammed the door.

"What now?" he asked.

They considered calling for help. However, even if someone believed them, that still meant waiting. Already they could hear the cat clawing again. Looking out the front window, Keisha pointed at Al's car. Exhaust spewed out the tailpipe.

"He left the engine running," Marvin said.

"That means we just have to get to his car and take off."

"I'm not much of a runner," Marvin chuckled. "Or a risk taker for that matter."

"And I came here to relax," Keisha grinned. "We can do this."

Nodding, Marvin grabbed the knob. Keisha counted down from three. He threw open the door. They bolted out and Marvin immediately slipped on a patch of ice. He went face first into the ground. Keisha hurriedly helped him up. Continuing to the car, she outpaced him.

Reaching it first, she jumped in the driver's seat. Running around to the passenger side, Marvin looked over in time to see the beast bounding towards him. He pulled on the door — locked.

Panicking, he rapidly rapped the window. He heard the pop of the lock; saw the creature raise a claw. No time to jump inside, he rolled onto the hood. The beast's nails ripped along the vehicle's side, goring wide furrows in the body.

"Hang on," Keisha shouted and stomped the pedal down.

Not sure what to do, Marvin grabbed hold of a windshield wiper. Pressed flat against the hood, he couldn't say how long they drove. Through the car, out the rear window, he saw the beast chasing them, but eventually, they got far enough away it disappeared in the darkness.

"Keisha," he said knocking on the windshield. "I think you can stop."

She hit the brakes. The car skidded to a stop. The quick deceleration threw Marvin off the icy hood. He tumbled along the road a bit.

Getting to his feet, he tossed aside the wiper still in his hand. Shuffling painfully but quickly, he returned to the car.

"Sorry about that," Keisha said as he climbed into the passenger side.

"No worries," he shook his head. "Water under the bridge."

In the distance they heard a menacing caterwaul shivering the air. Without hesitation, Keisha sped away. Slowly, Marvin began to chuckle.

"What is it?" she asked.

"I'm just thinking," Marvin said. "I have to properly thank my colleagues for this lovely vacation."

"Yeah," Keisha laughed. "Tell them you had such a good time they should come up here themselves."

"Sounds like a plan," Marvin grinned.

Deep and Dark

~ *Elad Haber*

In the deepest, darkest stretch of night, we emerge.

From the sewers and broken basements. From the cracks in the foundations of the tenements. From the filthy underskin of the city.

We are thousands of tiny insectoid bodies. Ant arms protrude out of our spider heads and furry flesh hangs off dilapidated wings. We scurry and scamper and scratch over each other, leaving bloody tracks in our wake.

We are a madman's vision of beautiful. A Frankenstein-insect, no two exactly alike. A psychopathic Santa Claus created manifestation.

And we are hungry.

The alarm squawks daybreak. I'm already up.

December 25th. This used to be a day for celebration and cheer.

I remove the chains and spin the lock to the bomb shelter where I sleep in a sub-basement beneath my building.

In the dimlit halls of the basement and the dirty daylight of the lobby, the bodies of the insects and the remnants of their prey litter the floor like confetti after a particularly gleeful concert. Bodies of rodents and stray animals are mounds of flesh and blood, whatever is left after the feeding is done.

In the streets, humans pick up the pieces of the nightly carnage and try, at least for a little bit, to live a normal life. Find food, water, companionship. Their expressions are hollow, their skin ashy and their bodies malnourished. There is one guy with a grungy looking Santa hat.

This is unsustainable. Someone must act. And that someone is me, apparently.

I climb up the stairs to my apartment and enter into what was once was my living space, now transformed into a lab. There are tables set up in the kitchen, in the living room by the windows, in the hallway before the bedroom. I turn on all the lights in the apartments, including the dozens of extra lamps and hastily erected spotlights.

No tree, no presents. No milk and cookies. Sorry, big guy.

In my lab are illuminated the carapaces and disembodied appendages of the bugs. Some of them are splayed on the wall, hung by tacks, like preserved butterflies. Others are half-dissected on a folding table. One table has wires and flammable materials, strewn with warnings.

There are notes written on a whiteboard stolen from a looted office supply store: *Photophobia? Collective thought? Hivemind?*

We know that the bugs were born in the weeks following the nuclear fallout. When the world was night for a week. This was about a year ago, during the saddest Christmas I've ever had. It took a few days, but it seems like the radioactive sewage from the bombed out cities leaked underground and infected the spiders, the ants, the beetles, the cockroaches, and anything else with legs.

When the poison skies finally let up and the sunlight returned (albeit muted and dull), the bugs receded to the underground only to emerge in the deepest darkness. Therefore, light, sunshine, and ultraviolet must be their nemesis. My tests on this have been successful. I can see in the shriveled brown of the carapaces where the light has affected it. But it has to be a lot. Not just a flashlight in the dark, but an underground sun to flood the tunnels.

How do I do *that?*

We feel the night like an itch.

It's an itch that cannot be scratched. It can be probed and searched for and dug with a nail, but it is elusive, pulling away when we push at it, retracting when we finally find it.

There is an interruption in our slumber. The night is not here yet, or if it is, it is not quite the darkness we desire. We would feel it. We would know.

And yet.

Something is coming. Something wet and powerful. We feel the explosions far away, some kind of pent up release followed by a deluge.

There is no solidarity amongst us. No heroes. When the floods fill the tunnels, we wrestle and murder each other to find safety in the cracks between the walls, in the rafters above the churning water, now bloodied with our dead.

Desperate, thousands of us claw our way to the surface.

Once upon a time, scholars wrote of the shifting sands of power. How to grab it, how to hold onto it. Now, in this epoch of after: after-life, after-civilization, after-society, there is only one power I need. Tactile power. Electricity.

We've seen them during the brownouts and rolling blackouts. Lit windows in apartments. That train-engine sound of generators on rooftops.

We're going to need it all.

We set our trap. One shot at this. Improvised bombs in the dams to flood the sewers and every light in the city connected to every generator we could locate. Snaking cables from apartment lobbies to flood lights hastily erected on upright poles. Thousands of Christmas lights in X and Y patterns between buildings.

I feel like a conductor about to start a symphony, except we've not practiced and I'm fairly certain this will end in disaster.

Wait for my signal.

The beginnings of night. A kind of calmness on the streets bathed in eerie purple and orange light. And then a series of rumbles. Children shriek.

Hold.

Rushing rivers below our feet. The sound of a million clawed footfalls. Some high-pitched screaming from the sewers.

Hold!

The sound of the footsteps is a wet crunching that comes from everywhere. A screech, a scratch; everything getting louder. I start to see them, those who survived the flood, clawing ontop of each other to the surface.

NOW.

Flip the switches. Kick off the generators. I swoop my arms up and down. Lights blare to life in the empty streets of our city and from low-floor windows in apartment buildings. Electric fireworks.

It's so bright, I shield my eyes.

The screams of the dying bugs are like music. Like a scratched up holiday song, wailing in a department store. I keep conducting, eyes closed, waving my arms back and forth, a symphony of destruction.

They continue to burst forth from cracks and hiding places. Many of the bugs die instantly from the harsh light but some push forward and attack anybody nearby. Children with LED flashlights emerge and blast them like some high-stakes game of laser tag.

Soon enough, the world quiets. The generators die out and circuits overheat and the lights blink off, one at a time. Christmas is over.

Was it enough? I dare ask myself.

The night gets darker, as it always does.

"The Night I Defeated the Demon of Winter"

from chapter XLVIII of
the autobiography of Sir Gottfried von Berlichingen

~ Chris Baker

I used to tell anyone who could be made to listen that my son Hans was a demon, and I would happily expound at great length upon all the reasons I believed this to be true. The only time I ever regretted saying so was when the actual Demon of Winter, Kramppes, tossed the little brat into a sack and tried to carry him off to hell.

That occurred just before midnight on the fifth day of December 1544, at the commencement of the Feast of Saint Nikolaus. I have no patience for most religious rituals and only observe them to the extent that a man of my station is required to. But I have made an exception for this particular saint's holiday ever since my hand was torn off by a cannon shot during the Siege of Landshut. *(This was recounted in Chapter XII.)*

On that awful occasion, I had gazed with uncomprehending horror at my bloody stump and cried out to Nikolaus. In the instant before unimaginable agony made it impossible to speak or even think, I had begged the saint to spare my life and my livelihood. Not only did Saint Nikolaus vouchsafe my survival, but he also guided me to a skilled armorer who fashioned a metal prosthetic for me. This articulated mechanical hand was nimble enough to grip a quill pen, or a handful of playing cards—or a sword.

That was when the fearsome knight Götz von Berlichingen was reborn as the even more fearsome knight Götz of the Iron Hand!

That was also when I swore by all of Christ's nails and hooks that I would always celebrate the feast day of the patron saint of miracles.

Nikolaus is also the patron saint of the innocent, and I have also had cause to pray for his intercession on the many occasions that I have been unjustly imprisoned. *(These periods were covered in Chapters XXIX-XXXII and XLVIII-LII)*

My enemies are legion, and they have conspired to convince the world that I am a liar, a turncoat, a vulgarian, a rabble rouser, a mercenary, and a greedy plundering highwayman. All scurrilous lies! Except for the last two or three, perhaps.

I paid every fine and bribe imaginable to regain my freedom—a veritable mountain of florins, tall as the Swabian Alps! Though it was my coin that liberated me, I also credit saintly intervention with my good fortune. At the age of 64, I was still hale and healthy, none the worse for wear after hundreds of battles and years of confinement. (Other than that metal forelimb that I just mentioned.)

I retired to live out my days in a castle above the Neckar River and turned my attention from warfare to the making and selling of schnapps. And the drinking of it.

My wife Dorothea enjoyed the Feast of Saint Nikolaus as much as I did and always helped to make the holiday cheery and festive. This is my second wife Dorothea that I speak of, not my first wife Dorothea, whose tragic illness and death I recounted in Chapter XXXV. My new wife had the same name as my previous wife. That was not why I married her—I married her because she is exceedingly pretty, and as clever and resilient as I myself am. But having two wives named Dorothea did spare me the trouble of updating certain legal documents and ledgers.

I told each of my five sons and three daughters that if they were good, Saint Nikolaus would visit us at midnight on his feast day and stuff their shoes full of coins and candy and toys. And my children were well-behaved, for the most part. Except for that insufferable turd Hans.

Hans terrorized all his siblings and bedeviled all of the servants. He stole coins from my purse. He put frogs in his mother's bathwater. He snuck into the cellar and added emetic herbs to the ale.

When I hired a castle priest to instruct my children, Hans repaid me by loudly reciting every piece of Latin profanity he had learned. He did this in the middle of service at Würzburg Cathedral while the prince-bishop himself was presiding. The vividness and specificity of the boy's oaths would have made a Roman centurion blanch.

Hans set fire to the priceless Flemish tapestries in my Great Hall. When caught, he blamed this act of arson on a piglet that he had smuggled up from the pens. (I suspect that this poor creature, who Hans dubbed Herr Oinkhart von Schweinsberg, was also unjustly blamed for a pile of excrement found in the corner of the room.)

All this the boy did in the week leading up to the feast day of Saint Nikolaus in 1544.

I have made myself furious recounting these offenses. My heart is pounding, I am grinding my teeth, and the nib on my quill split twice as I wrote this. I will move on with my story, but I must stress that the instances here cited represent a mere thimbleful scooped out of the vast ocean of the boy's misdeeds.

Every year, I relished explaining to Hans why he had once again been passed over by Nikolaus when the jolly saint crisscrossed the world bestowing gifts on all the worthy children. This was the only form of recompense I ever received for all the trouble the boy caused me. Oh! How it gladdened my heart to hear this little monstrosity screech as he watched his siblings enjoy their candy and toys! Oh! How I struggled against the urge to pound him to paste with my metal fist as he insolently glared at me through his tears!

With all the patience I could muster, I explained to Hans that having your gifts withheld was not the worst thing that could happen to an unruly child on this feast day: Saint Nikolaus has several assistants who are charged with dispensing punishments rather than rewards. I advised the boy that instead of whining about presents, he should instead be grateful that he somehow dodged the harsh disciplinary action doled out by the likes of Knecht Ruprecht the Farmhand, or Kramppes the Demon of Winter.

My son scoffed and jeered. He said that I was spouting nonsense. He insisted that there was no Saint Nikolaus, no Ruprecht, and no Kramppes.

Hans told me—me, his father, to whom he owes everything—that the only person who gives out presents in this castle is a bearded old imbecile with one hand, half a brain, and no testicles. I seized hold of the boy and reached for my chastising cane, which I always kept close at hand for occasions like this. But the child wriggled out of my grasp and fled.

It's written in Proverbs that *Wer seine Rute schont, der haßt seinen Sohn*: "He who spares the rod hates his son." I have never, ever spared the rod. But I must confess that I often still hated my son.

On the night of the Feast of Saint Nikolaus in 1544, I lay in bed eating hard cheese and sausage and waiting for the children to fall asleep so that I could deliver gifts to all but one of them. I passed the time complaining to my wife about the only human capable of vexing me as much as my son Hans—that insufferable monk Martin Luther. I had only met him once, in passing, at the Diet of Worms. But I bore a very personal grudge against the corpulent prig.

You might assume that my distaste for Luther stems from the fact that I was the renowned leader of the righteous and honorable peasant uprising of 1525 *(as recounted in chapter XXVII)*, while the fat monk was the author of a vicious reactionary pamphlet titled *Against the Murderous, Thieving Hordes of Peasants*. But my real issue with this dogmatic Saxon was that he seemed intent on robbing me of every single source of pleasure in my life.

Luther the Joy-Crusher droned on and on about how Christianity had adopted far too much pageantry and spectacle, which are the only things I ever really liked about it. The dour monk dismissed the veneration of saints as superstitious idolatry, even denouncing celebrations like the Feast Day of Saint Nikolaus. He commanded us to refocus our end-of-year merriment and gift-giving around the day that we celebrate the birth of Christ.

Luther the Sanctimonious Scold purported to deliver us all from superstition. But he would have us convince our children that the newborn messiah, still soaked in his birthing juices, leaps from the manger every Christmas Eve and spends his first night on Earth delivering gifts to every urchin in Christendom. I ask you, how is this preferable to the idea of warm, fatherly Saint Nikolaus bestowing his generosity upon us all?

I was so wrapped up in my denunciation of Luther, Lutheranism, and every variety of Luther-ishness that I had not noticed my second wife Dorothea rising from bed. She was looking out the window into the castle's courtyard. "Your son is at it again," she said.

I had barricaded Hans into his room like I normally did at bedtime, and then he'd found a means of escape like he normally did. On this night, he had decided to plunder my armory. The obnoxious wretch was parading around the moonlit, snowy courtyard in ill-fitting plates and chain mail. "You must put a stop to this," said Dorothea.

I could hear his clanking now, and it sounded like he was scraping the edge off of one of my swords that he couldn't fully lift. "I'll let the rogue tire himself out a bit more, so he'll be easier to subdue," I muttered as I sliced another piece of cheese for myself. "Perhaps our holiday gift will be that he catches his death of the cold."

Hans was shouting and swearing and daring imaginary foes to face him in combat. Suddenly, my wife shrieked. The boy's challenges had apparently been accepted by a large figure that emerged from the shadows.

"Götz, bestir yourself!" she cried. "Some strange giant has appeared in our courtyard, and it is making its way towards your son!"

"Why do you always call him my son?" I asked as I rose to my feet.

"I refuse to argue about this!" Dorothea exclaimed. "Hans is being menaced by some hulking shaggy brute!"

I had reached the window by this point, and I could see the figure for myself. It was ugly, and not the mundane sort of ugliness one normally encounters, like Dorothea's sister Elisabeth, or that triple-chinned monk Luther. This thing was clearly not human. It was almost eight feet tall, and covered head to foot in dark woolly fur. It had cloven hooves where its feet should have been.

"It looks like the descriptions of Kramppes, one of the companions of the saint," I told my wife.

"Hans! The Shadow of Saint Nikolaus stalks you!" screamed Dorothea. The boy's view must have been obstructed by my prized helm, which I later found to be irreparably dented and damaged; he was utterly oblivious to the creature's approach.

"Hans, Hans, beware!" screamed my wife. The boy seemed to finally catch sight of the monster. Hans turned to flee, but he tripped over my armor, which was designed for a strapping full-grown man, not a ten-year-old child. The demon continued to creep towards him.

While I fervently believed that Nikolaus had interceded in my life on several occasions, I had always pictured the saint to be some sort of invisible spirit. I had never imagined that he and his feast day companions might be actual physically embodied creatures. I certainly never imagined that I would see one of them with my own eyes.

What a delightful surprise this was!

"The little shit is finally going to get his comeuppance!" I crowed. I threw on my robe and grabbed my metal prosthetic from the bedside table.

"Kramppes always carries an armload of birch switches, which will be employed to thrash Hans mercilessly for his naughtiness," I explained to Dorothea as I used my good arm and my teeth to strap on my iron hand. "I must go down to the courtyard and watch this spectacle from a better vantage point! Don't worry, my wife, I will make sure that the chastisement doesn't get out of hand!"

"You oaf! You fool! Knecht Ruprecht the Farmhand is the one who beats children with switches!" raged Dorothea. "Kramppes is the one who drags them off to hell! He is the Demon of Winter! Didn't you see the great curling horns atop his head?"

She was right—I had confused the functions of these two helpers of Nikolaus. Hans wailed with fright, and I felt a bit sheepish about my eagerness to see a supernatural creature mete out discipline to the boy.

I realized that I would have to act. "Take comfort, Dorothea," I said as I grabbed the cheese knife and stuck it in the belt of my robe. "I will confront this demon who threatens your son. Our son. My son."

I offered up a prayer to Nikolaus, who is also the patron saint of imperiled children, as I strode across the room to the hearth. Then I thrust my mechanical hand into the burning logs and seized several hot coals in my iron fingers, which I used to light a lantern. I returned to my wife's side in time to see the demon seize Hans in its enormous claws. Then I stepped out of the window and fell forty feet into a snow drift.

I was relieved to see that the lantern had not been extinguished by the fall. I ran across the courtyard, following the sound of my son's cries and cursing myself for not remembering to pull on my boots. The deep snow stung my bare feet.

The lantern and the moonlight allowed my eyes to fix upon Kramppes, who seemed to be having some trouble stuffing Hans into an enormous sack. This was to be expected. I knew all too well how the boy was able to squirm and twist so artfully that it was almost impossible to maintain a good grip on him.

The beast fixed me with a baleful stare and flicked its hideous serpent's tongue as I approached. A ghastly sulfurous odor assailed my nostrils.

"You are too late, Götz of the Iron Hand," said the demon in a booming voice that made my blood freeze and my bones ache. "The child is mine now."

"Are you listening to this, Hans Jakob-Reinhard von Berlichingen?" I shouted at my son. "Do you now understand what your detestable behavior has wrought? Do you grasp what this creature intends to do to you?"

"I will ram a spit through this boy, and then I will turn him slowly over the hottest fire in Hell," the demon helpfully explained.

Apparently, Saint Nikolaus was otherwise occupied and unable to answer my prayers on this night. I briefly wondered if I should offer an entreaty to Satan, and remind the Dark One of all the souls I had dispatched hellwards in battle. Instead, I sent up a prayer to the Christ child: Please save my boy, you newborn whelp, or grant me the strength to save him myself.

The demon finally succeeded in shoving Hans into its sack, which I was now close enough to see held several additional children. I decided to try a bit of diplomacy. "Herr Kramppes, I will afford you all of the respect and obeisances due to one who sits at the right hand of a ruler, even if it is the despised ruler of an infernal realm," I said with the most placating tone I could muster. "But I must insist that you immediately produce my good-for-nothing child from your sack and return him to me."

"Ha! Ha ha ha!" said the Demon of Winter. "Götz of the Iron Hand, your temerity is more amusing than annoying, but now I must ask you to step aside. I have many more miscreants to call upon this night, and I cannot tarry."

Verbal negotiation had never been my strong suit. I took several steps towards the creature as I shouted to my son, "Hans! You must endeavor to climb out of that sack, or you will suffer unspeakably for ten thousand years."

"No, not for ten thousand years, Götz of the Iron Hand, or even ten thousand times ten thousand years," said Kramppes as it hefted the roiling sack full of children over its shoulder. "The human mind cannot comprehend eternity, so let me be clearer. The boy's flesh shall crackle and burn—forever. His fat shall render and boil—forever. He will shriek in unendurable agony—forever."

I was now close enough to feel the humid stinking breath of Kramppes on my face. I cursed my son for putting me in this position. "Hans Jakob-Reinhard von Berlichingen, I swear by all of Christ's nails and hooks that if it were up to me, I would happily see you dragged off to the eternal torment you richly deserve," I told the bawling wriggling lump in the demon's sack. "But your mother would geld me if I allowed that to happen, so now I must tear this stinking devil to pieces. But doing so will bring me none of the pleasure I usually derive from violence."

Thus saying, I reached upwards as high as I could and clapped Kramppes in the chest with my iron hand. I had never unclenched its fingers after thrusting them into the hearth—the metal prosthetic still clutched a fistful of red-hot coals

"Aaaaaaagh," said Kramppes. The shriek almost made me forget the stinging pain of my own bare feet in the snow.

"I tried to be polite and negotiate with you, you filthy furry devil," I said. "But now I invite you to lick me in the ass with your loathsome serpent's tongue." I scraped the coals back and forth and up and down on the creature's chest, as if I were drawing a crucifix with a piece of charcoal. I was forced to concede that the creature's previous scent was not the worst smell imaginable—this smell of scorched demon flesh and fur was far, far worse.

"Aaaaaaagh," repeated Kramppes. "I will have your soul for this, you blackguard."

The demon flicked its evil tongue at me, and I grabbed hold of it with my flesh hand. I wrapped this forked protuberance around my mechanical fist once, twice, three times. The coals had all stuck to the creature's chest, but the empty fingertips of my iron hand were still glowing with their residual heat. Wherever that foul tongue touched the hot metal, it sizzled and stuck fast, like a calf's liver tossed into an ungreased frying pan.

"Kurff you, Görzh," screamed the demon. "A ffousand kurffes on you."

Kramppes dropped its sack, which freed up its enormous arms. The monster reached for me as I dropped the lantern and seized the cheese knife from my belt. I began to saw away at the demon's tongue near where it was stuck to my iron fist. The flesh was incredibly tough and unyielding.

"If the Christ child and Saint Nikolaus will not assist me, I call upon you, Martin Luther!" I cried. "Help me send this monster back to hell, and I will pledge eternal allegiance to you! I will endorse every boring pronouncement you ever made about papal indulgences!"

The creature clutched me in a crushing embrace and raked its talons across my back as I continued to slice and hack at its tongue. Out of the corner of my eye, I saw Hans' head emerge from the sack.

Kramppes too noticed my son's sudden reappearance, and in its distraction, the beast briefly loosened its grip on me. That gave me the freedom I needed to finish slicing through the creature's tongue. I fell backwards, no longer tethered to the demon by its protuberance.

I caught my breath and prepared for a second engagement with the monster, which staggered off towards its stack and hoisted it up onto its shoulder. I don't know if I had well and truly defeated the beast, or if it merely did not wish to waste more time with me. But it trudged off into the darkness.

"Never forget the lesson that you have been taught on this night by Götz of the Iron Hand, you foul hell spawn!" I shouted after it. Truth be told, it was more of a *sotto voce* mutter than a shout, and I cannot be certain that the beast heard it. I put that down to wind-edness rather than any discretion or timidity on my part. But I do believe that the departing demon saw me waving my metal fist at it, which was still wrapped with half of the creature's smoldering tongue.

I suppose I could have given chase and attempted to rescue the other children from Kramppes. But it was very late, and I was cold and weary, and the only other child who had managed to poke his head out of the sack before the demon cinched it shut again appeared to be Friedrich the miller's son. And Friedrich's behavior was almost as abominable as that of Hans.

I allowed the wounded demon to make off with the rest of its quarry while I dragged my own worthless progeny back into the castle and deposited him in the arms of his mother.

❄

Dorothea smothered Hans with kisses and tears as I thrust my toes as close to the fire as I could bear in an attempt to restore feeling to them. I swear that if I had been in that snow for another minute, I would have needed two iron feet.

At this point, the entire household, who had witnessed the events in the courtyard but not dared intervene, rushed into my bedroom. I upbraided my men-at-arms for not coming to my aid. Then I ordered them to fetch some lard and herbal salves for the scratches on my back. Once those had been applied and my feet had warmed sufficiently, I limped across the room and picked up a sack of my own, one that I had earlier filled with candy and nuts and wooden toys.

"Gather round, all of my children, and I'll let you in on a little holiday secret," I said. "Saint Nicholas does not bring you presents—I do. And Saint Nicholas does not defend you whelps from the dark creatures of the night—I do. Götz of the Iron Hand makes his own fortune!"

I distributed the gifts to my offspring and felt very gratified by their obvious delight. I even gave some to Hans. Not as many as to my other children who I loved more dearly, but enough to distract the boy from the overwhelming events of this night.

I was proud to have notched one final victory in combat after officially retiring from the battlefield. But I had to concede that I had prayed directly to Martin Luther for his aid just before my moment of triumph. I resolved to be more measured in my criticisms of the fat monk going forward. I even shifted the focus of my household's midwinter revelries from the Feast of Saint Nicholas to the day of the Christ Child's birth.

Still, it must be said that Kramppes, The Demon of Winter brought about a more miraculous reformation in Hans Jakob-Reinhard von Berlichingen than the Lutheran Reformation ever did. My son was a new person after the events of that terrible night, always obedient, attentive, and helpful. I am ashamed to say that I now found him to be somewhat dull.

This transformed Hans even offered to repay me for my ruined iron hand, which corroded away to nothing wherever the demon's tongue had touched it. And on my 68th birthday, he presented me with a large sum of money, an amount sufficient to once again hire the armorer who forged my metal fist. My son refused to say how he acquired these funds. He may well have had a rascally streak in him still, but like his father, he was clever enough to conceal his illicit activities from the authorities.

My reformed son even came to my aid several Christmases later when I was called upon to defend my good friend and drinking companion, the alchemist Johann Georg Faust, against Satan himself. It was Hans who distracted the towering Dark One and tossed me the dirk that I used to stab Lucifer in his thigh while I employed my new gold-plated bronze fist to pummel the creature's two dangling *juwelen*. But I shall save that story for Chapter LXV.

The Ugly Christmas Sweater from Hell

~ *John Tures*

Christmas sweaters, as a rule, are supposed to be ugly by design. But the demon summoned by this sweater was on a whole different level, or perhaps a plane.

"What the hell was that?" the young nurse with the pink spiky pixie cut exclaimed, flying into the last room on the west wing of the nursing home. "We barely had time to clear the hall before that thing came to our area. I don't wanna think about what happened in the rest of the building!"

The young doctor who staggered in after her pointed at Esther, one of the residents, quietly knitting away at a sweater. "Wha-what have you done?" He snatched away the sweater she had been working on, held it aloft, and gasped as he deciphered the strange messages coded in the symbols and squiggles.

"I don't get it," Nurse Meadow with the pink hair looked at the sweater in awe.

"Ah told you people not to get Esther that Ugly Christmas Sweater kit!" brayed Esther's roommate LaShonda from the other bed across the room, turning off the Krampus movie she was watching on T.V. "That woman's plumb crazy! Never follows directions! Probably copied it out of that book with weird patterns her daughter got from that antique store."

The doctor threw the sweater down in horror. "Oh no!" he cried out in his thick Russian accent. "She knitted ancient runes from hell! She has summoned an evil creature!"

"I-is it that . . . the 'Bubba Yaeger' you were tellin' us about, Yuri?"

The doctor snorted in derision. "No, Meadow. It is not Baba

Yaga, as you Westerners call it. She has summoned . . . Sviter Chort!"

"*Gesundheit!*" proclaimed LaShonda from her bed.

"Wha-what's Sviter Chort?" Meadow mumbled.

Esther slowly tried to reach out for her sweater, but Yuri kicked it away. The elderly knitter shrugged and put her headphones back on, flipped the switch, and continued to smile and bob her head to the music of Metallica.

"It is . . . the sweater demon!" he announced.

LaShonda looked at the two staffers from the nursing home in shock. "You Russians got a demon for everythin', includin' *sweaters*?"

"Have you seen my country?" Yuri shot back. "Why do you think I fled to America?"

Then all grew deathly quiet.

"Ah think he killed everyone on this floor," LaShonda announced, while Yuri and Meadow tried to shush her.

"Demons cannot kill . . . directly," Yuri stroked his black beard. "They possess people to do things."

After another moment of silence, Meadow volunteered to peek outside. She dove back in almost immediately. "He's still out there . . . all black, horns, pointy ears, beard, cloven hooves, tail, and the wickedest smile, glowing eyes . . ."

"Anyone still alive?" LaShonda fiddled with her bed remote, bringing her up to a sitting position.

"Just Klepto Kara, swiping everything like it's on sale, and Spagnola, that lazy janitor, workin' himself to death moppin' the floor. They're demon-possessed for sure." Meadow could barely get the words out, trembles overtaking her. "And we're probably next!"

Then, down the hall, the occupants of Room 145 could hear a man and woman having an animated conversation.

"It's probably Simon Charlton, the Director of Marigold Manor, havin' another surprise inspection." Meadow moaned.

"And he has guest," Yuri nodded ruefully.

"As I was saying, Congresswoman Gray, we run a tight ship here at all of our Marigold Manor facilities, cutting expenses and salaries to the bone," the director proclaimed. "We institute a series of fines for workers and higher rates for residents for the slightest infractions to make up the revenue difference."

"That's good," Congresswoman Chelsea Gray, the chair of the House Budget Committee replied. "We're going to need to slash Medicare and Medicaid to justify tax cuts for people like you, and congressional pay raises for people like me."

"We've got to warn them!" exclaimed Meadow, but Yuri clapped a hand over her mouth.

"They're ones who cut your pay for wearing that hairstyle," he whispered into her ear. "And those boots."

She squeaked in dismay, then reluctantly nodded, leading the doctor to withdraw his hand.

LaShonda grunted her approval. "Let those two meanies figure it out."

"I say, orderly!" the director snapped as he rounded the hall. "Do you think it is still Halloween? It's Christmas, for God's sake. You should be in a Santa suit. I'll see to it that you're docked $1,000 for this serious breach of rules."

The demon muttered something which made Yuri tremble.

Representative Chelsea Gray tutted. "Is that a foreign language? Speak English when you are addressing a member of Congress. Let me see your papers proving you are a citizen of this country!"

In a deep guttural tone, Sviter Chort switched to words everyone could understand. "So, you like to cut things? Why not each other?"

Yuri dared a peek this time, then ducked back. "He has scalpel, and she has letter opener now."

He didn't need to explain what was going on anymore. What followed sounded like a UFC Cage Fight in the hallway between the director and the representative.

"Aw . . . too bad," LaShonda said with faux pity.

Meadow ducked behind Esther's bed and frantically scanned her cell phone. "Underworld A. I. says we can kill it with sunlight or starvation . . . or a Nichirin Blade." She gazed up at the Russian doctor. "Yuri, do you have one of those?"

"No," he said in a mocking tone. "Do you?"

"It's midnight, an' I think that beast is pretty damn full too," LaShonda noted.

Meadow returned to her desperate search, as the demon's claws could be heard scratching the wooden door. "Wait . . . it also says Wisteria can kill a demon too!"

LaShonda gave a triumphant smile. "My sister's grandkids just brought me a lot yesterday." Then, to the creature outside their door, she hollered. "Hey you ol' sweater demon. I got a whole can of demon whup-ass Wisteria in here for ya!"

Doctor and nurse seized as many of the purple flowers as they could carry. They flung open the door and thrust the Wisteria at the demon. The dark creature roared as if in pain when he saw what they were carrying. As if on fire, Sviter Chort contorted his body, then seemed to explode.

"We killed it!" Meadow screamed.

"No!" Yuri cried with dismay. "It's changing form!"

The chunks of what appeared to be flesh fell to the ground, then flew toward the door marked "Janitor." Seconds later, several roaches flew out from underneath the door, past the swabbing Spagnola and the knife fight going on.

"Stop those cockroaches!" Yuri commanded.

Instead, Meadow opened the rear door, so that the insects scurried out the back.

"What have you done, you fool!" the Russian doctor blurted out. "You let the demon get away!"

But Meadow smiled for the first time since the sweater demon appeared. "Did I? I think Stormy and Sunny, the two kittens I feed out there, will have quite a feast."

As if to emphasize her point, one of the roaches vainly attempted to squirm back under the door from outside, but a cat claw pulled it away.

Yuri breathed a sigh of relief. "At least we are safe."

Esther shrugged as Yuri and Meadow returned to the room and held up her sweater. Those two and LaShonda proceeded to undo all of her handiwork, ripping up the yarn. So they didn't like her little Xmas sweater. *They're just jealous*, she mused. No matter. Valentine's Day would be coming soon. She would simply knit her grandniece a new sweater, just like the last one, with the funny symbols from the book. *Might warm up things from the cold*, she thought.

❄

Not Just for Christmas

~ Erik Grove

It begins as a five-foot-tall smudge in the dining hall. You have to look at it from the exact right angle with the right lighting and even then you can't always catch it. But if you do, you see something like a Vaseline thumb print on a pane of glass. I can't photograph or record it. I can't prove to anyone else that it's there.

Every time I've seen it, while standing by the coffee machine or the table where they put out a menorah with birthday candles and yellowed Christmas stockings, I know deep down that it's wrong.

No one listens.

"We've got work to do," they tell me and break time ends.

No one ends up on Akeley Island if they've got other options.

In the center of the island— a barren bump of rock and ice in an undisclosed location north of everything else in the world— the Dyer-Lake Research Station (the Icebox to the locals) is more of an exile than opportunity.

There are eleven of us living full time in the Icebox. Most of the staff are scientists doing science things with the particle collider the company has installed deep underground.

"Like CERN," they told me when I got hired. "But without any regulatory *obstacles* to the *scientific process.*"

In the schematics, the collider looks like a really high level in one of those pipe video games where you're trying to get water to go through all these turns and obstacles. I can feel it vibrating beneath the research station, a thrum that meets every footstep, a buzz under my pillow. Every time I ask what it actually does I either get a long answer with a hundred words I don't understand or one of the scientist shrugs and says, "we shoot really powerful lasers at really small things to see what will happen when they blow up."

I'm not a scientist. I'm the kitchen manager. I cook three hots a day, keep the coffee going, and make sure the cupboards are stocked with pop tarts and peanut butter.

What I didn't know before I got to the Icebox is that scientists eat an unhealthy amount of peanut butter. I have seen learned men sink two knuckles into a jar and scoop without shame. What do they think I should do with peanut butter that's been violated like that? Another thing I didn't know before I got to the Icebox is that men like them, rarely think about the consequences.

The kitchen has a cut out between the cook space and the dining hall like in a short order restaurant. From there, I can keep an eye on the smudge while I rehydrate eggs or bring big plastic bags of soup up to temp.

Is it growing? Is it *thicker*?

I keep trying to get people to take me seriously. I make appointments with the station director.

"Maybe the collider is doing it," I suggest. "Like when you put a magnet near an old computer monitor."

The station director steeples his fingers and nods thoughtfully.

"The isolation up here can be taxing," he says.

He gives me an extra day off a week and makes a junior scientist named Neil cover for me.

"I'm not imagining things," I insist. "It's real. You'll see. It's *real*."

When he works in the kitchen on my day off, Neil moves all of my things and empties coffee grounds in the sink like an asshole.

The station director came into the dining hall the first day of December and put on a Christmas music playlist. He put it on repeat and told me I'm supposed to play it breakfast through dinner.

"It's festive," he says. "We all need a little holly jolly."

If anything is going to drive me crazy, it's the same thirty-two songs playing over and over and over again. I'm hearing Burl Ives in my dreams.

I'm pretty sure the smudge doesn't like the music either. It's cloudier, more tangible. I used to stop the scientists before they walked through it but none of them listened. There's only so many ways I can sound the alarm. Now the clueless middle-aged men with too many PhDs stroll through the smudge, unaware. They never notice the strands clinging to them like spiderwebs.

The station director is draped with it when he tells me about the holiday party.

"The men have been working long hours," he says. "They need a release."

I look past him at the smudge. It has developed a new shape. A cocoon.

The station director snaps his fingers in front of my face. "Are you listening?"

"Jingle bells," I say. "Blinking lights and gingerbread."

He leans closer. "I put in a special request for a case of liquor."

The cocoon pulses in time with the particle collider thrum.

"Maybe whip up some boozy eggnog?" The station director winks.

"Sure," I say.

What could possibly go wrong?

The night before the holiday party (I've been asked to light the too-small red, green, blue, and yellow candles on the menorah so its not "*just for Christmas*"), I dream of the cocoon splitting open. A fissure forms, thin at first, then bleeding. Like stone fruit rotting beneath an oppressive sun. The juice pools on the linoleum, dark and stickier than blood, and a hundred fingers claw at the frayed edges, blunt cracked nails straining and pulling. Deep inside the cocoon, from an impossible void within, a cacophony of shallow breathes and rapid heartbeats scrapes at my ears. I hold an old chef's knife, the tip angled down, down, down.

Am I meant to cleave through these grasping digits or the membrane that holds them back?

I wake with Neil standing over my bunk.

"The sink's backed up," he says.

Of course it is.

It's later than I normally sleep in though the only way I can tell is the digital alarm. The sun stopped brightening the dawn here days ago.

I nod at Neil. "Give me ten minutes."

After he's gone and I've pulled my pants on, I find a kitchen knife tucked under my pillow.

Clearing the pipes of all the things Neil tried to wash away occupies my morning and early afternoon. I fill a bucket with coffee ground stained gobs of fat.

I hold out a yellow gloved handful of the congealed but still gritty clog. When I rub my fingers together there's a texture that even through the plastic makes me gag.

"You've been pouring grease down here?" I ask Neil.

Track seven from the Christmas music playlist is playing again. Something something Santa Claus is coming.

"Sometimes," Neil says.

"The drain isn't a god damn magic portal to nowhere." I tell him this not for the first time but he shrugs with a trained Ivy League helplessness I can't begin to relate to.

On his way out the kitchen he stops, staring at the cocoon, as if he's finally caught sight of it. The cocoon has grown larger than a man now. Gossamer strands criss-cross the dining hall.

Neil blinks and rubs his eyes beneath his glasses. "Huh," he says and walks away, whistling along with the omnipresent soundtrack.

I thought scientists were supposed to be observant.

When I've got the drain clear and everything washed up I go out into the dining room and stand in front of the cocoon.

"What?" I ask it, and the Christmas music playlist gives an answer. Something something a creature was stirring.

❄

The scientists fill the dining hall and in less than an hour they're singing along to the those cursed songs and swaying with their drinks beneath strands of twinkling lights.

Outside, there's another storm. A white out blizzard intent on burying us all.

I stand in the covered and heated motor pool with a cigarette while the party sounds spill out across the forlorn island. A few dozen steps outside the compound, the cold and dark can kill. Succumb to it and they'll find your body after the thaw.

I toss my cigarette at the storm and head back inside before my teeth chatter.

The scientists are quiet in the dining hall. I see a few slumped over the scattered tables. I think they're passed out from drink at first but then I see the rest of them on the floor, the thin strands of spit from their drooling mouths connected to the cocoon's web.

The station director doesn't wake when I shake him.

The overhead lights are off. The dining hall is lit in ghastly, twinkling red and green. A mounted television plays a claymation holiday favorite with the sound muted.

I get a knife from the kitchen and turn off the fucking Christmas music.

A sound comes from the cocoon. A wet squelch. The cocoon's membrane strains with something pressing out from the inside. A five-fingered hand.

The possibility that this could be a gas leak, that what I'm seeing could be the trick of a poisoned mind, is not so unfathomable that I can dismiss it. But the more sinister possibility lingers, impossible for me to ignore.

There is something within and it wants *out*.

That pawing hand on the other side of the cocoon's skin curls its fingers and claws its way down, four barely visible cuts open through which I can see stained fingernails, blunt but not without edge. The hand pulls back, and the cuts shine darkly, solid lines of black in the cocoon's ephemera.

More movement inside.

Schlurp. Schlurp.

And then— is that an eye pressed to one of the cuts, searching with jittery intent?

I move toward it, tightening my grip on the knife.

The eye disappears, replaced by a single gnarled finger. The knuckles are bony. the skin slick with ichor. The finger makes a hook and tugs down. The membrane tears like wet paper.

"What are you?" I ask the cocoon.

A deep groan replies. "Ohhhh. Ohhhhhhhhhhh."

The images on the mounted television stutter and pixelate. The screen flashes to black.

"No signal," the screen reads in white blocky font.

The storm has taken out the satellite receiver. There is no one to call for help.

First, one hand's worth of fingers and then another emerge through the widened slit in the cocoon. The hands are not spectral or a smudge in the corner of my vision but as solid, as visceral, as anything I have ever seen.

Just like my dream.

The hands grip either side of the growing hole and tear. A face emerges from between them. Man-like but not *right*. Long straw-like hair circles the eyes and nose, and another jagged gash opens— a mouth.

"Ohhhhhhhhhh."

All I can see are its nubby teeth. All I can feel are its eyes. Fixed on me, knowing me.

I tell my legs to run or my arms to fight. Neither listen.

The hands follow the face, reaching down until they can press their palms to the dining hall floor. The flesh is naked but matted with clumps of hair, glistening with something red and jelly-like.

It is being born, I understand. It is *emerging*. A man, or something wearing the vestiges a man. Not immature but fully formed of muscle and bloat. A rough, quivering tongue traces a slick path around this man's lips, licks at the wisps of wet beard around its edges. His jaw opens wider and wider and wider like a snake preparing for a meal. Within, there are rows teeth. Hundreds of teeth, studding his thick cheeks and running all the way down his gullet.

"*Ohhhhhhh,*" he moans, louder and lower. The sound catches me in the pit of my stomach. A primal bellow like the howl of a northern wind before oblivion seizes you.

I manage enough coherence to see Neil on the floor and make my way to him. I get a grip under his arms and drag him back, away from the birthing cocoon.

The man is a third of the way birthed now and coming faster. His shoulders are out of the membrane, and he has a grip on the seams between tiles. He drags himself, his torso loose, sliding bit by bit.

Neil is difficult to move. He murmurs and twitches on the floor. I take off his glasses and slap him across the cheek.

"Come on, you useless . . ." I say, trailing off when the man from the cocoon stops moving. He redirects toward me.

The man makes a new sound. Could it be a word? His voice is thick with mucus and spittle.

"*Niiiiiice.*"

I hold out the knife. "Keep away from me," I say.

"*Knottttttt....*"

The membrane is at his hip bones now. Bulges that I think are his knees strain the lowest edges of the cocoon.

"*Heeeee.*"

Tears run down my cheeks now and I jostle Neil with everything I've got.

Should I have done more? I tried to warn them. I thought these men, these scientists that treat me like I'm less than them because I make a living with my hands and not my head, deserved a lesson, a refutation of their hubris. But not like this.

I could run. I could lock myself away in my bunk and let this wretched thing fulfill its dark purpose. I could barricade the door and pray it doesn't come for me before a rescue.

The man's body is fattened, more so in his bulbous belly. The flesh around him quivers like shaken aspic when he fully emerges and lands with his face down on the floor. He slips and slides with his hands, knees, elbows, and feet for purchase in the pool of gooey wet that accompanied him. The cocoon—what is left of it—is as deflated as a popped balloon.

The snot leaking from my nose fills my mouth with salt.

"*Ohhhhhh.*" He stands. "*Ohhhhh.*" The teeth in his massive mouth flex and wiggle, each one motivated by strands of muscle. The ones along his throat clack together making a sound reminiscent of dominoes falling into dominoes.

A weakness takes hold of me and I sink beside Neil.

The man wipes down his arms and chest, sweeping off viscera. He drags his hands through his long beard and hair, flicking more goo aside. He returns his attention to me and to Neil. His lips curve into a mockery of a smile.

"*Nice,*" he says and swivels around back to the cocoon. He reaches inside and pulls out a long robe-like jacket and a stocking hat made from what looks like blood-stained chicken skin. He dons the jacket. The bottom goes nearly to his knees and covers—to my great relief—whatever nasty business is nestled between his legs. He sets the stocking cap atop his gore-greased head, skewed to one side.

"*Ohhhh,*" he moans, and the sound catches something in his throat. He coughs and spits out a gob of effluviant afterbirth, then smiles again. His eyes twinkle from the lights.

"Ho," he says. "Ho. Ho. Ho."

He raises a finger to his lips. "Shhhh."

My mind cannot form around this madness. The man from the cocoon is . . . *Santa Claus*? An impossibility, surely. Santa Claus is a mascot, an image from soda pop cans. Not *this*. The being that emerged from the cocoon is an aberrant terror, something unleashed from a distant and awful place. But it is an uncanny— if grotesquely distorted— mimic.

The station director did this, I suddenly understand, with sixteen hours of repeating jingles. A thousand red nosed reindeer and animated snowmen. He marinated the cocoon and the thing gestating within it with the holiday spirit. He bent it into this nightmare because *everyone needs a little holly jolly.*

The wicked, unrepentant monster.

"What will you do?" I ask.

Santa's blinks wet dark eyes. They are blacker than a shark's, blacker than the endless northern night.

"I will know," he tells me. "If you've been bad . . ."

He returns to the deflated cocoon and fishes out a large pair of black boots and a bulging patchwork sack.

"Or . . ."

He chuckles. He hefts the sack over his shoulder and steps into the boots.

"Have you been *gooooooood*?"

The knife slips from my hand to the floor with a festive clatter. I pull Neil close, my arms wrap around him as if he's a comforting teddy bear or a life preserver and we are close to sinking beneath frigid, constant waves.

Santa leaves sticky boot prints on his way to me. He swings the sack around and reaches within. The contents are a sloppy, pungent stew. He produces a train engine carved from inhuman bits of bone. He sets it into my lap.

"Choo choo," he says. He smells of sour beef scraps left to molder from the butcher's table.

". . . Thank you, Santa," I manage.

He pats me on the head and leaves gifts for all of the slumbering scientists. His sack of gifts is boundless and each item he takes from within it is eldritch and formed from bone, hair, and sometimes leathered flesh.

He leaves a doll on the station director's chest, a small androgynous elf-like thing stitched from blueish gray skin. The doll wiggles against the station director and mewls. It makes a sound like a suckling babe and paws at the station director for a nipple to latch onto.

The train I'm holding is warm in my hands, its parts seemingly cleaved from the living marrow of some tremendous leviathan. I set the train down and it moves, rolling on its bone wheels without any help from me, leaving a faltering trail of blood like twinned macabre lines of Morse code.

Santa fills the old stockings with rich, dripping, organ meat and hoists his sack once more to his shoulder.

"And to all a good night," Santa says to me, winking, before he stomps with vicious, unrelenting purpose toward the motor pool and the expanse of ice and dark beyond.

In his wake, the station's power generator falters. The lights go out like the melted menorah candles and I am left surrounded by sleeping men and the sound of stirring forms in viscous bile through the open wound at the top of our world.

Holiday Offerings

~ Brian U. Garrison

❄

If
Krampus clatters near,
you must prepare a tea of clove and cinnamon
and carve a slice of thimbleberry pie.

No,
Krampus will not eat.
He's got heads on pikes like over-ripened lollipops
and if he snacks on other food he'll lose his evil cred.

He just loves inhaling
the warm free smells of Christmas—
this day—

when everything is perfect—
evaporating on Christmas.
The pie fades.

Don't
let your soul escape
unless you are prepared to blindly navigate
the furry, spiral lungs of godly goats.

Wait.
That sounds kind of nice.
A quiet water slide into eternity.
A foggy, homey hug that never ends.

❄

It Used to Get Cold on Christmas

~ Nat Reiher

Del. Yeah, you. With the mouth. Wanna humor your Mama for a bit and join me up on the roof? I've made some of that skinny keto whatsit hot chocolate ya like, kind that tastes like dirt and anti-joy. Put some salt in it, too, like your dad used to. Come on. It'll be a Christmas pow-wow, just us girls. Let your lil sis have the TV for a while.

Why the roof? Because I met someone real big and mighty up on a roof once—we'll get to that, it's why I'm askin, don't rush me—and also because I'm your mother and I said so. I got the ladder propped up. Come on now. Soft on your feet, kiddo. This double-wide's old as Judas and just as reliable. There's a reason we go to the church gymnasium when the clouds start to swirl all angry-like.

Ah. Ain't that something. Nothing like chilly, corrugated metal on your ass-cheeks to wake ya up in the morning. We'll be sweatin bullets by eleven, so drink up the cocoa and enjoy the cool while ya can.

You remember *The Lion King*? "Everything the light touches is our kingdom." There ain't no castles or knights or dragons, but all this? It's ours. Legally. Your great-grandparents—my Gammy Rae and Daddy Vik—bought all this for nickels and dimes back in the seventies. Used to be fifty raw acres of pine tree before that was carved out to make way for crop fields, which ain't never been planted and now never will. There was a barn out here, too, only that burnt down around the same time as the old house did. All we got left is weedy pastures and kudzu.

Wish ya coulda seen it, back when it was something. Believe it or not, we used to get snow out here. Not just shaved ice slickin up the driveway and making ya late for work. Real snow, the kind that stuck. You could bundle it up and throw it. Mostly it snowed on the front half of the year when the real chill-your-blood cold hit. One time it snowed on Christmas Eve and it stuck around. Really stuck around. Ya believe that? A white Christmas, down here in Mississippi, in the heat and the suck.

And there won't never be another. Not out here. We may get snow now and again—maybe even the good sticky snow—but never again on Christmas. One day, the good sticky snow will stop. The shitty ice-shave snow will stop, too, before long. I can see it, just now, clear as day: warm Christmases stacked on top of each other like melting blocks of ice, wife-beaters and tank tops on New Years, humid Januaries and Februaries swollen with warm rain. Power keeps goin out. Not just here, but everywhere. Watching little Sadie open Christmas presents with the fan twirlin and the window open to tempt in a breeze that ain't there.

What's that?

Nothing. Slip of the tongue. Sadie. Nobody you know. Don't pay that no mind, hun.

Anyway. The white Christmas. I was knocking on the door of ten, just a few years younger than you are right now. Me and your uncle Ronny shot out the front door like a couple of bullets, decked out in our mud boots and parkas. It was a fine coat of powder, kind ya see in movies: spotty in places, sure, but ya could stomp in the stuff and look back and see where you'd been. I must've made a hundred snow angels that day, and your uncle spent hours trying to make a perfect snowman. Kept failing because his version of "perfect" included a white cock and balls, which he couldn't get to stay.

"Snowmen ain't got weiners," I told him, or somethin thereabouts. "Don't put no genitalier on him. He's perfect the way he is."

Ronny flipped me the bird, as was his way. He'd already asked Mama for an extra carrot (he'd used one for the nose) but had been denied when Mama surmised what he intended to do with it. That's what Ronny was like. Took Mama all of five seconds to figure out why he wanted an extra carrot.

So the snowman never got finished, at least by Ronny's standards. He was real salty about it. He says, "Harriet, ya little shit, race me to the creek," or something like that, and off we went. He was dumb as a rock and sometimes he spit in my face for no reason, but he was the only other kid for at least half a mile and hell, he was my big brother. He drew me a picture of a dragon one time. Wish I still had it.

We get to the creek and it's frozen solid—still and silent, a thin coat of ice scattering the dim sunlight. You could see the water rushing underneath, dark and cold and trapped. We played rock-paper-scissors to see who goes on it first and I win, if ya can call it winnin. I took a running start and break just as I hit the ice and hoo boy, am I flying, wings out like one of my snow angels, smile as big as the moon.

Any big smile like that on a face as dumb as mine, well, always bound to get smacked off: I fell and busted it and the ice underneath me followed suit. Felt myself slipping backward into the water and it got up to my waist. Felt like being eaten alive. Then there's your uncle, scrambling onto the ice, grabbing my jacket and dragging me back to the bank. Only he gets too caught up in his Superman shit and falls flat on his face. Wham. On the ice. He didn't get back up. But I'm back on the bank, more or less, so I drag him back out onto the snow and then run screaming back for Mama and Daddy.

Ronny spent that night in the hospital. When he fell, I didn't think too much about it, only that we was in a helluva lot of trouble. But Ronny never woke up—his face was an awful mask of hematomas near black as the night, and they pulled his eyelids back, his blue eyes was filled with blood. I didn't know what was happenin then, but I learnt later that he'd suffered a subarachnoid hemorrhage—that's when the blood pools between your brain and all the protective little webs that wrap around it. I wadn't there when the doc said he might not make it, but I seen my Mama when she come out the room. I ain't never seen my Mama's face like that. She looked like she lost twenty pounds in an afternoon and someone had sapped all the color outta her skin. Gammy Rae came and picked up and brought me home while my parents stayed at the ER. Probably because they wadn't very sure he'd make it to morning.

As soon as Gammy Rae was passed out on the couch, I snuck'd out back and spent the rest of the night slumped up against the chicken coop. My dad had strung up some heat lamps inside the roost, so I figured it was a good place to keep warm and keep watch. Eyes on the roof of the house. I'd already propped up a ladder against the back wall, same as I did today.

Look. I was a little kid and my brother had just cracked his head open like an egg. And we still believed in Santa back then. Didn't have computers in our pockets telling us that Santas ain't real and that look at all these sex positions and that Hitler wadn't that bad or some such bullshit. I was nine. I believed in the goddamn fat man.

I know you're not mocking me, Del. I'm just saying. There's a reason I ain't never told ya this story before. And it ain't just about your Uncle Ronnie, who ya never met and never will. It ain't never stopped hurtin. Never will. But that ain't the reason. Frankly, I hadn't made up my mind until this mornin'. Nothin's changed, I just—

Well. I can't hold onto it no more.

Because, Del, after I done waited long enough and even snoozed off a bit, I heard a soft little bang and looked up. There was a man on the roof.

I couldn't see him real good until I climbed up the ladder, and I made sure to go slow so I didn't spook him. He was climbing out of the chimney when I peaked over the edge of the roof. The shingles were still dusted with snow, dark little patches of asphalt pokin out of the ice. Our roof was slanted, but the guy didn't seem to have no trouble making his way off the rim of the chimney and back over toward the edge. I didn't know what he was about to do—there wadn't no reindeer and sure as shit no sleigh, far as I could see—so I cried out.

He turned to face me, and I'll spend the rest of my natural life wishin he hadn't.

His frame wadn't colossal or jolly or saintly at all. He was a thin, withered-looking guy, cloaked up in ragged, frostbitten furs that hung in pitiful little tatters over his scarecrow body. His skin was pale as snow, veined with blackened frostbite like a dirty old map. He had a beard, which I expected, but it was wild and matted with little sticks and glistening shards of ice poking out of it. The lines on his face might as well've been canyons, and his eyes were glowing blue twins. Not like sapphires, mind ya, more like the last little flickers of stars winking out. When he spoke, his voice sounded the way ice sounds when ya throw it in a warm drink.

He says I shouldn't be up here. Says it's deep in the night and the world is too dark and frightening for someone as small as me to be up and about. He says it more like a threat than a warning, which scared me a lot, but I pressed on, cause I had to. He was scary as shit, no question, but just cause somethin's scary don't mean it's evil. Then again, just cause somethin ain't evil don't mean it can't kill ya. I tell him my brother's hurt real bad and might not make it through the night and that if he wakes up right now, happy and whole, I'll never ask for another present as long as I live.

And he considered me, then, the way a baby considers a cockroach first time he seen one. He tells me he ain't in the business of shuffling and unshuffling mortal coils and such. Says his name ain't Santa Claus, neither, and he seems real hot and bothered that I called him that, says he's a hell of a lot older than Christmas. Says the bag of presents is just a coincidence and I shouldn't be readin too much into it.

He turned to leave and next thing I know, I'm on my knees bawlin and screechin so loud I like to woke up the whole damn county. I tell him, well, if ya can't make him well, can ya at least tell me if he makes it? Just tell me if he's gonna be alright, that's all I want. I ask him if he's got the future in that magic bag of his.

Crazy thing is that the old weirdo just stares at me for a long, long time, so long that I think he's gone and croaked right there on his feet. He looked awful tired, then, all dried up and chapped out. I don't think he was lyin about not being Santa Clause. He was somethin a heck of a lot older than a dead German saint.

He'd already left me a couple presents, ya know. Mama and Daddy weren't there to leave any and at that point Gammy Rae barely knew who the President was, let alone that it was Christmas Eve. And every year on Christmas morning, I've kept an eye out. Sometimes there is and sometimes there ain't, but once every few years there's an extra present on the pile that ain't come from me. It's always some shit I didn't even know ya wanted. I think that's what he does now that the ice has started to melt—he lets the parents do most of the heavy lifting, then sneaks a few in there. He does what he can, I guess. Same as the rest of us.

And just when I think he's done stroked out and done for, the old not-saint reached into that bag of his—I heard a sound like wind howling through an old church—and pulled out some fruit I ain't never heard or seent of. Looked like an apple had a baby with a tangerine. Shit made your mouth water, just lookin at it, and when I bit into it, it was like a big fat grape, practically exploded in my mouth.

Course I ate it, Del. Snatched it plum out of his hand and damn near bit into my tongue. It was like drinkin water for the first time. You couldn't look at that thing and not eat it. He said something else, but I was too busy smacking away. By the time I finished it, core n all, he wadn't there no more. I was standin up on the roof by my lonesome, juice drippin down my chin. I called out for him a few times, went out around the property and looked round till I gave up. Took me hours to fall asleep.

When I woke up the next morning, I was crying because my brother was dead.

Rather, I *known* he was dead. Ronnie lay in his hospital cot with his head crooked to the side and his heart monitor singing that long, whining dirge that meant time's up. I sobbed myself awake because I saw it clear as day. Only Ronny wadn't even dead just yet. He'd languish in his coma for six more weeks until he finally slipped away and ain't never come back. Six weeks of me just sitting there, knowing what was coming—seeing what was coming—and not nothing I could do about it.

That's what the frosty bastard on the roof done to me. Gave me a real Christmas whopper.

You're giving me a look, Del. I can read your face like a stop sign and no, I ain't crazy. And I ain't fuckin with you, either. Oh, come on. You damn well know that word by now, I've heard ya say it when ya thought I wadn't listenin. First off, I'm always listenin. So do me a kindness and listen to me now: because that man—be he dream or nightmare or real as a shit floatin in water—damn well did have the future in that bag of his. And I asked him for it. And he gave it.

I saw Ronny die—over and over and over again—for thirty-eight days before it finally happened. It was a little different every time. Sometimes he was alone and sometimes Mama or Daddy or all of us was with him. When it finally happened, it was just Mama and Daddy, cause I couldn't face it. I wanna say I remember his funeral, watchin his casket go into the earth, but I don't. I just remember standin in that graveyard, feelin all numb, knowin and seein and feelin shit I wadn't s'posed to. Like scrolling through your phone and seein spoilers for a TV show ya ain't watched yet: I saw that little boy done disappeared that errybody forgot bout; I saw that blowhard win a third term, flashin that trillion dollar grin and holding up a Bible like it meant somethin to him; I saw those poor kids gunned down in the streets of D.C. and I saw their blood drownin the asphalt; I saw those ladies jumpin off the roofs in New York and Jackson and Chicago and Atlanta and I saw their bodies go splat when they hit the ground; I saw New Orleans disappear and Florida right behind it; I saw the lights go out for the first time. I watched it all then the same way I would watch it all later: through a phone screen, on my computer, through the boob tube at the salon—the world fallin apart in pixels and ten-second videos. All this shit, I seen, and more, the way the world would curl up and burn like a spider caught fire, all before ya was even born.

And that was back then, Del. The shit I see today would burn through your retinas like battery acid.

For a while, I prayed it would stop. Jesus didn't answer me, so I took it up with the man hisself, or at least I tried to. Next Christmas I set up shop back behind the chicken coop so I could catch the sumbitch and make him take it back. But he never showed.

Yes, Del, I went to a doctor. No, Del, twenty milligrams of Prozac with water in the morning didn't do squat. I saw things. They happened. I ain't sick and I ain't lyin.

Play the lottery? Oh, sweet Christ, Del, why didn't I think of that? Never crossed my mind. Not once. It ain't like that, hun. You can't do nothin to change the tracks cause you're already on em. Only difference between me and everyone else is that I see the tracks from up top—I see where they're goin, but I can't step forward and take em apart. Let's put it this way—I seen myself lose the lottery dozens of times.

Well. Not in a ways that matters, anyway. I learned that one the hard way. Hardest thing I ever learn't, right up there with "Don't dickaround on thin ice." Your daddy taught me that, even though he didn't mean to.

I met your old man up at the community college down down in Raymond, back when there was such a place. He was studyin business a couple years ahead of me. I knew he was on my horizon, your daddy—I'd already seen our first date, lazy nights on the couch with popcorn and sodas, long walks down the Natchez Trace sharin airpods and such.

But first time we met, the way he caught me when I slipped out in the hallway cuz of some damn spilt coffee, hell, I ain't never seen *that*. A flash and a fall and a rush in my gut and then a sudden stop and there he was, starin down at me—his big goofy grin and that messy hair of his, that beautifully broken nose and the clothes that were too small cuz he couldn't afford new ones. He asked me for my number later that day—he bought me a smoothie because he said I might PTDS from nearly dyin—and I gave it to him. Not because of the tracks in front of me, but because I wanted to, and that was a shock. I thought I loved him 'fore I met him, only I didn't know what love was yet. It's a chemical thing in your gut and your head and your heart and it lasts forever, but hoo boy do ya feel it in the moment. Hoo boy, does it hit like a drill when it happens fast.

He was easy to love, Del. Your daddy was so damn easy to love.

Did I try? Of course, I did, hun. Of course, I did.

I'd known it was comin for a while. Maybe even before I met him. I think it started as this vague knowin somewhere in the back of my brain, this sorta dim awareness that I'd meet a man and fall in love and spend the back chunk of my life wishin he was still with me. I sensed that loss in some shapeless way and when I was finally close enough to see the tracks—

Well, I tried, ya know? Made him start takin baby aspirin every night, swapped out his Coke for beet juice, even got him to do some meditation now and again. He wadn't a big guy, but somethin was wrong in him that the doc ain't never catch. Used to, folk could go to the doctor once or even twice a year. Now, they shut down so many out here that we're lucky to get in at all, assumin you can afford it. There's a reason I bake Doc Carter brownies when he comes in to do y'all's physicals. It's like strikin gold, havin him so close.

Ya know they're gonna start sendin your blood to the government in a couple years, right? They're gonna say it's a forensics thing, save ya from identity theft and such, but nah, they're tossin out all the shit with a Y chromosome, they're gonna be trackin pregnancies, see, tryin to make sure they have a steady stream of good little worker ants and—

Sorry. I just—

It's everywhere, now. Sometimes the tracks overlap.

Anyway. The beet juice only went so far, I reckon. It did change, though. A little. Not the what or the how, but the when. For a while, it was workin. He was at his office downtown, filin some piece of paper or another when it—

Yeah. That was it for a while, then the aspirin must've done somethin 'cause it changed—for the first time, somethin changed!—but not for long. After that, it happened when he was out in the yard rakin. Then it was the drive-thru at Taco Bell. Your sister's soccer game. A work party. New Year's Eve, watchin the ball drop in the living room. Mowin the yard. Drivin to the store. In the store. Everything I did—every time I made him take a cold shower or forced water down his throat or snuck lisinopril into his coffee— just mucked with the where-and-when of it. The tracks were movin forward whether I liked it or not. I sensed it the same way you can sense rain. There's a smell in the air and a faint pressure in your head and here it comes barreling toward you.

I spent a lotta nights starin up at the ceilin and prayin, scrapin my brain tryna figure out how to save him. I learned words like 'determinism' and 'fatalism' and, well, some other stuff I ain't mentionin. All the while, I saw him die, and die, and die again, some rough deaths, some quiet deaths, some godawful deaths that I couldn't bear stomach.

So when it landed on somethin good, I stopped. I let it happen. I let him go, Delilah. I tried. I tried so long and so hard, but all I could do was make it easy.

That last night, with the s'mores and the hot cocoa and the tent him and your sis built in the living room. We watched *Elf* and ate popcorn till we all felt sick. He fell asleep so calmly that night, so quickly, even though it usually took him a while. I stayed up, lookin at him, hopin to memorize his snore and the smell of his hair. I never fell asleep. I just sat there and held him, even after he was gone. I didn't expect to feel nothin 'cause I'd already seen it so many times in so many places but when it was there and it was real, well, them tracks finally took me to a place I just couldn't go. In my head, it's a dream, like watchin somethin through a hidden eye that's real and not real at the same time. When it happens, it's always too much. When it's tangible, it stops bein a dream and starts bein somethin that makes me plum sick at my stomach— nauseous, painful knots in my gut, I'm talkin, and it only gets worse with time.

I never told your dad any of this, and I think that was my worst sin, in the end. I told myself that I didn't want to burden him with it, that I was bearin a cross and like hell am I passin that baton. I don't see things that way no more. All I see now is fire and famine and plenty of rain. Coasts wiped clean like they wadn't never there. We end up in Illinois, for what's worth. This tin box of ours gets swallowed whole by a tornado the size of the Chrysler Building and ain't fuck-all insurance will cover us. Wildfires burning along the west choking the air and once the Delta drowns, all bets are off and if you want some protein that didn't start out scuttlin under the couch on six legs, you better be willin to grow it yourself. That's what your sister does, you know—farmin a bit further up north near the border, her and her people.

We go with a caravan, all three of us, 'long with little Sadie when she's still a wee pup. I can see you nursin on the trail, huggin her tight under a smoke-choked sky. One night she falls sick and a fella named Curtis gets himself shot snatchin antibiotics from a gov'ment truck. He dies a few days later of infection. And we settle, and stay, and the days grow hotter and hotter then hotter, still.

We still have Christmas. Every year, we all get together in the house—smaller n this one, but it's ours—and we exchange little gifts wrapped in printer paper. Sadie colors hers with crayon, makes em all bright n pretty. We sing songs and hold hands and I tell insufferable stories bout how much better shit used to be cause that's what everyone wants to hear, right, what wonderful comforts that got left behind cause we was too stupid to hold onto them. I see us all sittin in the living room, sunlight burning through the thin glass, hot wind howlin somethin fierce. I see the long, sweltering nights. I see ribs protruding from hungry bellies and I hear the coughin in the dead of night.

Last of all—on my last and hottest Christmas—I see that feller from the roof, only he's even worse off than ever and he ain't too big on talkin. He still delivers presents now and then, but only shit people need—toilet paper, toothpaste, the like. He's all withered and gray and his crystalline bones is showin through the skin. Those starry eyes of his are black and dead and the space between planets. He's all spent up, and so am I, 'cause I can't see nothin past that. Just one last chat in the heat and the dark with the Saint-that-ain't-Nick. Maybe I spit up that fruit and give it back to him. Maybe there's just nothin after that.

And I think bout the world I'm givin ya and wishin I had so much more, but there ain't. It's all dryin up. And as I get closer to that dark at the end of the tracks and all the black and nothin on the other side, the only thing I got is to say that the world wadn't never mine to give, I guess. All I had to give was you, and your sis, and Sadie. You were my Christmas present to the world.

And you're gonna make it, Del.

God, that's your name, isn't?

Delilah. Del.

Right now you're all squirmin' and pink and wet and you're bundled up in white sheets like Baby Christ and, God, I've never loved anything so much. The world wadn't made for ya—it was made for shitheads and psychopaths who live past their use—but you're gonna make it anyway. Because I'm gonna raise you for it and one day we're gonna have a nice long talk on a short cold trailer about how you're gonna make it. All those where's and when's scattered all over everything and through it all is you. Bit by bit, I was buildin ya into something the world wouldn't break. Least, I thought I was. Lookin back on the tracks windin through the past and the dark, I'm thinkin ya built yourself.

I love you, Del. I love ya so much.

Come to Mama, baby love. I can't stop shakin. It's hot as hell and I just can't stop shakin.

Frau Perchta's Handmade Christmas
A Holiday Guide to the Perfect Home

Foreword by Knecht Ruprecht

translated from the German by Kevin Wetmore

~ Kevin Wetmore

Seid ihr alle verrückt? Ihr veröffentlicht ein Buch von Frau Perchta? Und ihr dachtet, Krampus wäre furchterregend—ich schlage Kinder einfach mit einem Beutel Asche, wenn sie ihre Gebete nicht kennen, und gebe ihnen vielleicht einen Stein oder Stock statt Süßigkeiten, wenn sie unartig waren. Sie zerstückelt Kinder, weil sie eine Serviette falsch aufgelegt oder den falschen Faden für ihre Handarbeiten verwendet haben. Wer macht so etwas?

Eines muss ich Frau Perchta lassen—sie ist die fleißigste Frau im Geschäft. Krampus, Sinterklaus und ich, wir haben einen Tag. Sie macht zwölf ohne Pause. Und ihre Tischdekorationen sind hübsch, wenn auch verstörend. Ich meine, sie sieht aus wie eine alte Vettel mit einer Hakennase aus Eisen und trägt einen Stock (an dem wahrscheinlich das Blut von Tausenden klebt). Ja, sie ist eine Hausgöttin, aber eine, die dich für ein unordentliches Haus bestraft. Du bist gewarnt. Frohe Weihnachten und um Himmels willen, putz dein Haus!

K.R.[1]

---

[1] Are you all mad? You're publishing a book by Frau Perchta? And you thought Krampus was terrifying—I just hit children with a bag of ashes if they don't know their prayers, maybe give them a rock or stick instead of candy if they have been naughty. She dismembers children for placing a napkin wrong or using the incorrect thread in their crafts. Who does that?

Introduction: A Frau Perchta Handmade Holiday

Well, it is that time of year again: snow is falling regularly, only a few hours of light penetrate your alpine village each day, and with the coming of Christmas you must bedeck your domicile to be the perfect home for the holidays. Do you need some fresh ideas for holiday decorating? Are you tired of the same store-bought decorations every year? Have your children been misbehaving and your home an unpleasant untidy mess? Does your house lack order, cleanliness, and discipline? We can take care of all of this with a few simple activities, projects, and violent, painful discipline.

Why have décor purchased from a store, same as your neighbors, when a unique, handmade, disturbing and gruesome display is charming and easy to make? In this volume, put together from my many experiences in preparing, decorating, and destroying the home for the holidays, you will find many ideas for a handmade Christmastime that the whole family can alternately enjoy or by terrified by, especially if they are wayward children.

I have taken as my project this holiday season Gudrun, a stocky, spirited little eleven-year-old Mädchen from Kartoffeldorp in the Alps. She is indeed spirited, but rarely listens to her mother, her father should have been taken by Krampus in his youth for all he's worth, and worst of all the little Untier never picks up after herself. While Weihnachtsmann will no doubt bring her candy, little toys, and fruits, she will leave them all over the house. Thus, she is my project to make a handmade, perfect house.

I must give Frau Perchta one thing – she is the hardest working woman in the business. Krampus, Sinter Klaus and me, we got one day. She goes twelve without a break. And her centerpieces are pretty, if disturbing. I mean, she looks like an old crone with a beak nose made of iron and carries a cane (that probably has the blood of thousands on it). Yes, she is a domestic goddess, but one that punishes you for a messy house. You've been warned. Happy Christmas and for the Heaven's sake, clean your house! K(necht) R(uprecht)

Chapter One: Presentation Matters

When I make my rounds during the twelve days of Christmas, cul-minating in Perchtestag, I am always suitably impressed with the simple yet elegant décor many Alpine peasants manage to achieve for the holidays. One need not be a wealthy Burgomaster or Indus-trieller to have a home full of graceful cheer and festive yet elegant holiday ornamentation. If one cannot afford glass ornaments, the skulls of small animals, if cleaned thoroughly and presented taste-fully, arranged in a circle around candles, dusted with an artificial snow made from salt and dead skin can easily impress more than some store-bought geegaw. Did you know glass ornaments were first made in Germany in 1847, but animal skulls have been in use for tens of thousands of years? Traditions are important at holiday time.

Presentation is important. One does not simply gut open one's victim with a sickle or scythe, letting the blood fly everywhere, caking on the walls and covering the floor and simply leave the entrails half in and half out of the corpse. That is what common barbarians do. One carefully punctures the body and slowly moves the implement in a straight line, down through the bowels *[see fig. 1]*. Then one carefully opens up both the chest and the abdominal cavity, and carefully excises the organs. Set them aside—we will use them for other projects; nothing wasted!

Once the body is completely devoid of organs, we fill the cavity with straw, snow, dirt, unspun flax—you can even use pebbles and leaves. The important thing is to fill it completely. Before we seal the corpse, I also like to add some pleasant-smelling herbs or flowers. Your reward for all your hard work is the pleasing scent of Alpine Rose, Simple Leaved Milfoil, Juniper, or Spruce needles throughout Twelfth Night, making your home and your festivities most pleasant indeed!

Use a needle made of iron to then sew the corpse shut. Some folks will tell you a needle of wood or bone will work just as well, but I prefer iron and insist upon it for all corpses I sew shut after eviscerating and disemboweling them. I value tradition above all, but also the iron needle is just more practical and less likely to break than the others.

The stuffed body can then be set up in a prominent position in the home, a sort of centerpiece of any gathering that doubles as a warning. As you can see, I have placed Ulf, or what was Ulf, next to the sideboard in a subtle pose that hints at his strength in life while also reminding others if you do not leave herring and milk porridge on your Pertchen table, or are just wayward in general I will gut you and turn you into well-presented horrific décor *[see fig 2]*.

I see Gudrun has given little thought to the presentation of her poorly wrapped gifts for her family. She still has not finished spinning the flax her mother gave her, and her room is most untidy. I have distinctly heard her mother caution her twice, as is only appropriate, about my coming wrath. We'll check in with Gundrun from time to time to see if she improves her holiday spirit.

Chapter Two: The Perchtentisch

Your Perchten Table should be specially prepared and placed in a convenient area of the home. Alternately, it is perfectly acceptable to place the specific foodstuffs under a tree outside, in the branches of a particularly old tree, or even on the rooftop, to keep it from animals but allow easy access for goddess witches and their familiars to feed upon.

I prefer a simple tablecloth. One can get a small piece of clean white linen and lay it out on a small table. I find the skulls of teenagers or dogs to be particularly adept for use as serving bowls. There should also be a centerpiece that does not call attention to itself but, when viewed, is seen as elegant and tasteful. The head of a deer, perhaps, festooned with ribbons. As you can see here, I have decorated mine with a wreath made of Ulf's entrails. Simply braid them together and then sprinkle with just a little bit of glitter and salt to simulate new-fallen snow *[see fig. 3]*. The salt will dry out the entrails more quickly, but we only need them to last to the end of Perchtentag.

On the table we place herring, milk porridge, eggs, honey, and some bread soaked in boiled milk. These can be rather bland and plain, so I like to make them more flavorful and festive. Add to your milk porridge a pinch of cinnamon, a few cloves, and a dram of Ulf's blood and it really brings out the essence of Perchtenmilch. Again, recall that presentation is as important as the sustenance itself. It's a good thing.

I really like the disembowelment craft project above when someone has eaten foods forbidden on my holy day. It is a gentle but firm reminder that dietary restrictions exist for a reason and a good member of the household follows them without question. So be careful on January 6th, if you place any old thing in your mouth,

Chapter Three: A Clean Home is a Home Ready for the Holidays

While my Ulf centepiece turned out beautifully, I am deeply disappointed that yet again Gundren has not finished her spinning or the other household chores.

I cannot help but notice that the kitchen and dining area of her home also has a slightly acrid odor to it, which no guest should be asked to tolerate. I'm going to take Ulf's spleen and cover it with the flowers from some Alpine Wild Oregano. Most people associate oregano with the dried herb in Italian cooking, but the fresh flowers are a bright purple, pleasing to the eye and fragrant. The purple color is perfectly acceptable—one can create ornaments and adornments without relying on the red and green theme that has dominated our Christmas aesthetic, and doing so often brightens the room and calls equal attention to the more traditionally colored garlands. Simply take a half dozen or so of the blooms and strategically place them on the spleen and place the bloom-covered spleen in a central but not obvious place *[see fig 4]*. One can also use Ulf's liver as I have here to prepare a similar decoration for the mantel.

A new broom should be used in the days after Christmas to clean the home of both dirt and evil spirits. I like to attach St. Benedict's Thistle to a spruce branch. It cleans the room better and leaves the space with a slightly bitter smell, reminding one of the horrors of existence. It also aids the digestion.

Chapter Four: Fun with Flax!

Not everyone appreciates the variety of crafts, linen, and activities you can do with flax. As with most social occasions, timing is everything. The spinning of flax should be completed by Epiphany eve. Nothing is more disappointing to me than unspun flax on the morning of the Epiphany. Thus, flax spinning should begin early in the holiday season to be completed and ready for crafting and clothing making in the early days of January. When I enter a home on Perchtentag and I find unspun flax still on the distaff, my instinct is to cut it, tangle it, really work it with my twisted claws until it becomes unusable in the household, except for wiping one's excrement. I then wipe it with my excrement and leave it as a distasteful centerpiece, surrounded by pine needles and mouse droppings. This way visitors to the home know that a lazy spinner lives there and the dinner napkins and tableclothes will also most likely be substandard.

I also tend to burn the hands of lazy spinners, who then reach for a cloth to put in cold water to sooth their burns, and I often ensure they grab the excrement covered unspun flax to rub on their hands. This is the most economical approach to punishing poor housework at the holiday season and ensuring that excrement-cover flax is both décor and serves a practical purpose *[see fig. 5]*.

As you can imagine, Gundrun's spindle has a great deal of leftover, unused flaz. But as I have said, there is no such thing as unused flax, only flax I have not yet used to wipe my excrement or with which fill your abdominal cavity.

Chapter Five: Perchtentag: I am coming!

With the arrival of Perchtentag (that's January sixth for the unfortunates who do not observe), my patience is at an end. The house is beyond chaotic and messy, and my project has not worked according to the original plan. But regular followers of "Frau Perchta Living" know that we do not let a project defeat us. We consider, we reflect, and we adjust. The decorated ornament mirror that did not work out can still be made into a lovely serving tray, or a heap of sharp glass with which to inflict encouragement to clean. So with the inability of Gudrun to reform her sloppy ways, I now have a new project: a decorative holiday scarecrow that can also serve as a warning for misbehaving children.

Now follow carefully (and remember, all of these projects are also available as how-to videos on my website, so please come see how this one works and how it turns out). I enter the home after the family has gone to sleep and make my way to Gundrun's bedroom. Ugh. I can hardly stand to look at this sty. But that is not the point now—we have a craft project. Remember—variety is the spice of any home decoration scheme, so we will not be repeating with Gudrun what we did with Ulf.

[Follow figures 6 through 12 to create a remarkable table display as I have done here with Gudrun]. It looks extremely impressive and your guests will be enthralled and terrified. If you have a bit of gold paint you can also give the impression that the remains are gilded, adding a touch of class to what might be a more banal display.

Now, when your guests wake up and see this remarkable craft project there will be some screaming—that is to be expected. Don't forget, if one has an iron beak as I do, you can insert it into the abdominal cavity to cause additional pain and mischief. If one does not have an iron beak, any sharp implement from the kitchen will do—the effect is more important than the tool used to achieve it. And again, presentation is key to a graceful and dynamic handmade holiday display.

Sometimes graceless people critique these efforts. "What Frau Perchta works at is so ephemeral!" someone once complained within my hearing. "Your home is clean, presentable and decorated for the holidays, but then the calendar continues." While correct, this individual missed the point of all of this activity. A clean home with everything in its place and a select few exquisite holiday decorations is a feast for the soul of your family and guests. One would not argue chefs' work is ephemeral and therefore useless; one enjoys the delights of the cuisine. One does not merely "feed" as an animal, one savors as a human being with a soul. I explained this to the one who complained while removing his spine through his mouth and using it to create a decorative spoon holder for Walpurgisnacht. The rest of his entrails were fed to pigs while his skull was excarnated, polished, and now is used to serve after-dinner mints at small gatherings in my alpine cave. It is important to not be wasteful with your crafting materials. He also forgot that, because of my work, next year the children who lived will be better behaved, leave a cleaner house, and obey without question. It's a good thing.

Frohe Weihnachten!

CONTRIBUTORS

Colleen Anderson

Colleen Anderson, a Ladies of Horror Fiction, Canada Council, and BC Arts Council grant recipient, has been published in eight countries. An award-winning author, her works appear in *Amazing, Cemetery Dance, Weird Tales*, and Flame Tree's *Moon Falling* anthology. She is a Rhysling Award winner for "Machine (r)Evolution" and a two-time winner of the SFPA's dwarf poetry contest. She is the author of poetry collections *I Dreamed a World, The Lore of Inscrutable Dreams*, and *Weird Worlds*, and fiction collections *A Body of Work* and *Embers Amongst the Fallen*. Her lated collection, *Vellum Leaves and Lettered Skins* is available from Raw Dog Screaming Press. Colleen freelances as an editor, and edits for *On Spec*. She lives in Vancouver, BC where she searches for mermaids. You may find her on the Internet at www.colleenanderson.wordpress.com.

Lauren Taylor Bak

Lauren Taylor Bak is an emerging author of erotic romance and speculative (sci-fi, fantasy, horror, weird) fiction. In another life, she obtained a PhD in English literature, and is sort of an expert on (a very small corner of) the subject. Her work is snarky, shameless, and frequently bisexual; she has recently had stories appear in *Jungle Scandals* and *Tales of Galactic Pest Control*. You can find out more on her website laurentaylorbak.wordpress.com or follow her on Bluesky @laurentaylorbak.bsky.social.

Chris Baker

Chris Baker is a writer and editor in Oakland, California, USA. His journalism has appeared in *Wired, Rolling Stone, Slate,* and *Giant Robot.* He explores the origin stories of the latest trends in the zeitgeist at his newsletter *Pop Cultural Precursors.*

Devan Barlow

Devan Barlow is the author of the *Curses & Curtains* series of fairy tales-meet-musicals fantasy novels, and the collection *Foolish Hopes* and *Spilled Entrails: Retellings*. Her short fiction and poetry have appeared in various anthologies and magazine, and she is a 2025 Hugo Nominee for Poetry. She reads voraciously, and can often be found hanging out with her dog, drinking tea, and thinking about sea monsters. She may be found on the Internet at devanbarlow.com, and on Bluesky @devanbarlow.bsky.social.

Megan Lee Beals

Megan Lee Beals writes cozy and fanciful horrors from her home in the perpetually soggy Pacific Northwest. She lives with her husband, her twin son and daughter, and the family's formally feral cat. When she isn't writing or chasing toddlers, Megan is drawing or sewing or building, and generally trying to accumulate hobbies at a truly unsustainable rate. She has been published in *Translunar Traveler's Lounge* and *The Iowa Review*. You can find more of her various things at www.meganleebeals.com.

Bethany Browning

Bethany Browning's first novella, *Sasquatch, Baby!*, won the 2023 Best Independent Book Award for Fiction and an Indieverse Award. Her award-nominated short stories have been published in *Stories We Tell After Midnight Volume 3, Allegory, Bullshit Lit, Drabbledark II, Mudroom, The Drabble, Flash Flood, Filth, Reckon Review, Sage Cigarettes, Flash Fiction Magazine, The Hallowzine, Halloween Horrors,* and many more. Her story, "How I Cured My Depression," was an honorable mention in the *2024 Best American Mystery & Thriller* stories, edited by S.A. Cosby. You can find links to her published stories and her novels (including cozy mysteries!) at bethanybrowning.com.

Peter Damien

Peter Damien lives in the Seattle area with a million zillion books, a lot of tea, and a cat who probably won't do anything to save him if the books should ever avalanche. He's published short stories in an array of anthologies, magazines, and websites over the years, from *Fear and Fables,* to *Lit-*

erary Hatchet to *Something Wicked* to *European Monsters*, and lots of other places. His nonfiction has appeared on *BookRiot*, *QuirkBooks*, *SFSignal*, and *The Future Fire*. He plays more *Minecraft* than he cares to admit.

L. E. Daniels

A Shirley Jackson, Aurealis, Australasian Shadows, and Bram Stoker Award® finalist, L. E. Daniels, BA MFA, is an author/poet, editor of 140+ titles, and an American living in Australia. Lauren's novel, *Serpent's Wake: A Tale for the Bitten* (IP) is a Notable Work with the HWA's Mental Health Initiative where she now serves as co-chair with Mark Matthews. Recent short fiction publications include "Silk" in *Hush, Don't Wake the Monster*, "The Howling Places" in *Into the Dread Unknown* (Twisted Wing), "Darkness Repeats" (*Monsters in the Mills*, IP) and "Hangman's Coming" (*Where the Silent Ones Watch*, Hippocampus Press). Her non-fiction appears in *Out of Time: True Paranormal Encounters* (Timber Ghost) and 34 Orchard. Her poetry appears in the *Cozy Cosmic* series (Underland), *Under Her Eye* and *Mother Knows Best* (Black Spot Books), and Timber Ghost. Her poem "Speak" appears in *This Way Lies Madness* (Flame Tree Press). Lauren directs Brisbane Writers Workshop.

Brian U. Garrison

Brian U. Garrison (he/him) is President of the Science Fiction & Fantasy Poetry Association. Wall art featuring his words, combined with visual art from collaborators, is available on Etsy. His chapbooks include *Micropoetry for Microplanets* (Space Cowboy Books) and *New Yesterdays New Tomorrows* (self-published). He doesn't darkly dwell on death nearly as much as his poem might suggest. The tall tree in his Portland, Oregon backyard holds many fewer leaves during Krampustime. Find Brian online at www.bugthewriter.com.

Erik Grove

Erik Grove is a writer, writing teacher, editor, and dog wrangler living and doing things in Portland, OR. You can find his short fiction in places like *Nightmare Magazine, Escape Pod, The Cozy Cosmic* and *Even Cozier Cosmic*.

You can find links to stories, information on appearances, and more sundry shenanigans at www.erikgrove.com.

Elad Haber

Elad Haber is a husband, father to an adorable little girl, and IT guy by day, fiction writer by night. He has recent publications from the *Simultaneous Times Podcast, Silly Goose Press, Bulb Culture Collection*, and *Does It Have Pockets?* His debut short story collection, *The World Outside,* was recently published by Underland Press. Visit eladhaber.com for links and news.

Tobby Hagler

Tobby Hagler is a software engineering director with extensive experience in cutting-edge web content management system development and software development training. Having presented at local and international conferences, his career has involved breaking down complex systems for others, which has influenced his passion for writing accessible speculative fiction. His debut novel, *The Grove of Tau Ceti*, is scheduled for publication in late 2025.

He lives with his wife and their three dogs in the Carolina Midlands, where he enjoys the quiet inspiration of his pondside home nestled in a nearly unhaunted forest.

EB Helveg

EB Helveg is a science fiction author, poet, and artist living in the Pacific Northwest. To pay the bills he works as an anesthesia technologist, and he'd love to talk at length about diseases with anyone who will sit still long enough. His poetry can be found in magazines like *F&SF* and *Eye to the Telescope*, as well as the *Cozy Cosmic* series (Underland Press). His fiction can be found in the *Nonprofit Quarterly, SoulJar: 31 Fantastical Tales by Disabled Authors* (Forest Avenue Press), and *The Midnight Labyrinth* (Grendel Press). His art can be found in *The Future Fire* and at various night markets around the PNW.

Martha Hipley

Martha Hipley is a writer and filmmaker from Baltimore, Maryland who lives and works in Mexico City. Her stories have been published in *Maudlin House*, *The New Limestone Review*, and *surely magazine*, among others. When not writing, she trains as a triathlete and boxer and spends her weekends scouring flea markets.

Michael Huyck

Michael Huyck has published fiction and non-fiction in scores of anthologies and magazines since the mid-1990s. He edited fiction for *Carpe Noctem*, a gothic lifestyles magazine, and wrote non-fiction for *Speculations*, SFWA's *The Bulletin*, and the two-volume library compendium Supernatural Fiction Writers. A collection of Mike's short fiction, *Of Dark and Yesterday*, and his novel, *World's Fare*, were published by Crossroad Press.

He is a family man who, in the past, has worked on fighter planes and submarines, spent a summer as a bouncer, and ran screaming from being a businessman after four years of midnight proposal writing. Today he's a senior manager with a multinational non-profit research corporation by day and a scribbler by night. Michael lives in the Pacific Northwest.

Chris J. Karr

Chris J. Karr is a weird fiction enthusiast in Chicago, creator of *The Pnakotic Atlas*, and publishes *Weird Fiction Quarterly*, an ongoing weird flash fiction anthology series. You can find him online at notesfromthevoid.cc.

John Klima

Over the course of his career as editor of *Electric Velocipede,* John Klima received the Hugo Award as well as multiple nominations for the World Fantasy Award. He lives in Wisconsin with his family, where he does secret work for a large public library. Occasionally, he writes fiction.

Margo Pecha

Margo Pecha lives in southwest Washington state and writes about the things that fuel her anxieties. She studied creative writing at Eastern Washington University and completed graduate work in writing and publishing at Portland State University. When she's not reading and writing, she's wrangling chickens and working in her extensive gardens.

Nat Reiher

Nat Reiher's pronouns are he / him, and he currently lives with his wife and son in Brandon, Mississippi. He's previously been published in anthologies such as *Dead Letters: Tales of Epistolary Horror, You Took a Wrong Turn*, and *We're Vermin*. His work has also been featured on the *NoSleep Podcast*.

J. Rohr

J. Rohr is a Chicago native with a taste for history and wandering the city at odd hours. To deal with the more corrosive aspects of everyday life he makes music in the band Beerfinger. Currently, he writes film reviews and cinema articles for *Film Obsessive*.

Edward St. Boniface

Edward St. Boniface is Canadian by origin, permanently resident in London UK and writes across various genres from contemporary to fantasy and science fiction. He is interested in offbeat scenarios, characters and the outright deranged. Ed always looks for an interesting angle or approach for a story, writes and believes in the principle of Fun Fiction with meaning underlying. He honors the Great Old Ones and has always had the ambition to be one of the Spawn of Yog-Sothoth . . .

Em Starr

Em Starr is an Aussie horror writer. Her short stories have been produced by the *NoSleep Podcast*, and published by Kangas Kahn Publishing, Flame Tree Press, Eerie River Publishing, and IFWG Publishing, to name a few. Hailing from Melbourne, on Boon Wurrung land, she enjoys obsessing over beaches, blossom trees and bloody good coffee. Em is currently working on her debut novel, a coastal horror set in 1990s Australia. Get to know her more at www.emstarr.com.au

Jack Stein

Jack Stein is an emerging author out of Appalachia. Like many a rash and foolish youth, they left the mountains to seek their fortune, only to learn the hard way that the promises of wealth are but hollow lies. Having accumulated a solid 20 years of nightmare fuel working in the corporate world, they fear that nothing they write will ever be as horrific as reality, but they keep trying anyway.

Sydney Sylvester

Sydney Sylvester is a horror fanatic born and raised in NYC. She's written for the satirical women's publication *Reductress* and was a finalist in the 2023 NYC Midnight Screenplay Contest.

John Tures

John A. Tures started writing sports for an El Paso Texas newspaper, spun records for a radio station in college, worked at the Milwaukee Symphony Orchestra in graduate school, earned his doctorate at Florida State University, and analyzed data on foreign policy in Washington DC. He's a LaGrange College professor in Georgia who writes columns for newspapers and magazines and has published several short stories in various genres. His first book Branded will come out later this year. He thanks his family and friends for reading and listening to the tale and credits his wife Beth for coming up with the idea for the story.

Ryan Van Ells

Ryan Van Ells (he/him) is a queer author of dark fiction and lawyer based in Milwaukee, WI. His fiction has appeared in, among other publications, *State of Matter Magazine*, *Dark Harbor Magazine*, and *October Screams*. He is an alumnus of the University of Wisconsin-Madison and The University of Texas at Austin and a member of the Horror Writers Association. You can keep up to date with Ryan's publications at ryanvanellsauthor.wordpress. com.

Kevin Wetmore

Kevin Wetmore is a five-time Bram Stoker Award nominee, the author or editor of almost three dozen non-fiction books and many, many short stories, including his other Lovecraft mashups, "Tales of a Fourth Grade Shoggoth," "Are You There, Azathoth? It's Me, Margaret," and "The Statement of Eeyore Carter," as well as other Lovecraftian stories in such anthologies as *Fall of Cthulhu II*, *Whispers from the Abyss 2*, *Urban Temples of Cthulhu*, and *A Lonely and Curious Country*. Learn more at www.SomethingWetmore-ThisWayComes.com.

Sara Wilson

Sara Wilson is a graduate of Vancouver Island University, with a BA majoring in Creative Writing. Her poetry has appeared in various publications including *Dinosaur Porn*, *Sharkasaurus!*, *White Stag*, *Nod*, *Existere*, *Qwerty*, *Event*, and *The Fiddlehead*. She is a Red Seal Sheet Metal Journeyman, a terrible birdwatcher, and occasionally tunes her guitar.

KB Willson

KB Willson is a British author currently living beside the sea in Dorset with his miniature dachshund dog, who likes to sit on his lap while he is writing. He has had work published by NewCon Press, Little Red Writers, Timber Ghost Press, Quill & Crow Publishing House, The Slab Press, Other Worlds Ink, Gypsum Sound Tales, Wildside Press (Black Cat Weekly), and PS Publishing (Parsec magazine). For more information visit www.kbwillson.com

EDITORS

Frances Lu-Pai Ippolito

Frances Lu-Pai Ippolito (she/her) is a Chinese American judge, mom, and writer in Portland, Oregon. Her writing has appeared in *Nightmare Magazine*, Flame Tree's *Asian Ghost Stories, Chromophobia, Mother: Tales of Terror and Love, Death's Garden Revisited*, and *Unquiet Spirits*. She is the founder of game and book publisher Demagogue Press and the nonprofit, Qilin Press, which focuses on diverse, marginalized voices. Frances also co-chairs the Young Willamette Writers program that provides free writing classes for high school and middle school students.

You can find her on IG @francespaippolito, FB @ Frances Pai, and on the web at demagoguepress.com.

Mark Teppo

Mark Teppo is the publisher of Underland Press. He has written more than two dozen novels across a wide variety of genres, including historical fiction, eco-thriller, horror, western, mystery, science fiction, and dark fantasy. He lives in the Pacific Northwest, where he is busy making things.

His favorite Tarot card is the Moon.

For more information about Underland Press, please visit the website:

underlandpress.com

www.ingramcontent.com/pod-product-compliance
Lightning Source LLC
Chambersburg PA
CBHW020407110726
47899CB00006B/1888